REAL ESTATE, DATING, AND DEATH

A Vivianne Murphy Mystery

Ashley Addison

ISBN-13: 9798503915464
ISBN-10: 1477123456

Cover design by: Art Painter
Library of Congress Control Number: 2018675309
Printed in the United States of America

For Debbie

My friend who has saved me more than once.

Thank you

INTRODUCTION

In this, the second novel in the Vivianne Murphy Mystery series, a dead bride is discovered murdered at Vivianne and Venice's brokerage, a homeless family is found sleeping in a vacant house and Viv's mother, who is a force, is having open heart surgery.

On a personal level, Venice becomes romantically involved with Bryan, who is moving out of state and Vivianne becomes concerned Venice will follow him. That is, until Viv starts dating a former client who's handsome, amusing, and insanely rich.

In some of the many subplots, Viv's niece has a run in with a kidnapper, there's a wedding, another murder, and a tense final act.

CHAPTER ONE

My name is Vivianne Murphy and, with my best friend, and business partner, Venice Martino, we started our own brokerage, Rainbow Realty. We had our Grand Opening last summer. My sister Kat, with her daughter Nellie, as well as my Mom, Tess and stepdad, Wes, flew in from New York for our event. My cousin, Skylar and I were the only ones in the family who had left New York for greener pastures. Skylar moved to Washington, D.C. many years ago and still lives there with her husband, Jock. And he is quite the Jock. However, there are no pastures there, green or otherwise.

Venice and I live in Havenville, in the northwest part of Washington State. We met when I sold her the house across the street from mine. I live with Sassy, short for Sasquatch, a rescued terrier mix, and Venice is owned by Betty, a Border Collie, and Mr. Snigglebottom, who seems to be mostly Jack Russell, right down to his stubbornness. Venice and I complement each other, she with dark hair and olive skin, I, with red hair and fair skin. Italian and Irish, we incorporated the best of both ethnicities.

My Mom and Wes had gone home the day after the Grand Opening because, while she was here, she was diagnosed with a heart problem and she wasn't feeling well. She was going to have her mitral valve replaced next month. It should've been sooner but my Mom does what she wants on her own terms, in her own time. I also think she'd been in denial. The only reason she was having it done now was because she was tired of being tired. Mom was a force, usually to be reckoned with. We were all a little afraid of her. Except me, I was *very* afraid of her. Nellie, who would be thirteen this year. got along with Mom better than any of us ever did. Mom adored her. Maybe it was the first and only grandchild that did it but being a girl was a definite plus. She was the only human who seemed to be able to ignore my Mom's dulcet screeching, which was mostly directed at Wes.

Last year while still working for Morgan, Cromwell and Chase Realty, Venice and I sold an $8,000,000 house, or mansion would be more like it. The commission from that sale was what gave us the capital to open Rainbow Realty. What goes around comes around and, in this case, it was the mansion. John Berkman, the owner, gave us the listing. Since the debacle last year, which resulted in his divorce, he now loathed the place. He had been staying in a very nice rental which gave him time to decide where he wanted to live. He had other houses in other countries but he wanted something here, in the Pacific Northwest. He had grown to love this area.

The mansion's infamy, coupled with the price, made it more difficult to sell than usual, however, an offer had just come in. I would call John and run it by him after I had my coffee and became semi-human.

My phone chirped, I had a bird call for my ring except for my Mom and then it belted out, "The Bitch is Back."

I recognized the number; it was John Berkman. He must have read my mind.

"Hi John, I was just about to call you." I was lying, it was only 8 A.M. for God's sake."

"We received an offer on the mansion," I said.

"Excellent, and what would that offer be?"

We had it on the market for $9,000,000 because some updates had been made after the purchase, one of them being a brand-new kitchen. The old kitchen was pretty spectacular, I didn't see why it had to be renovated but it was none of my business.

"The offer is $8,500,000. I know it's not full asking price but it's been on the market for a while so they're hoping to get a deal. What do you think?"

"I think we should counter back at $8,750,000 just for the hell of it. Tell the agent I'm splitting the difference," said John.

I wish I could be so cavalier about that much money. Ah, what's $250,000 give or take? To John, a mere pittance, to me, a fortune.

"I was calling to see if you or Venice could show me that waterfront listing? The one on Sandy Point Road? I would love to get out of this rental and be in my own place again. If I don't find something here soon, I'm off to my house in Ireland."

"Let me take a look, hang on a minute…it's still active but the owners are currently living there and they require a twenty-four-hour notice to show. How about tomorrow morning at eleven?"

The Sandy Point home was $3,200,000, mainly because it was no bank waterfront. You could literally walk out the back slider and bury your toes in the sand. It was a magnificent house with 4200 square feet of living space on two acres. Why a single man needed all that room was beyond me but who was I to question his wants and needs as long as he could afford it. And he most definitely could. We'd get another hefty commission from this so I didn't care if he bought it and tore it down. Not only was "no bank" a rare find here, this house also came with a dock. The dock was a big deal because you could no longer get approval to build one. He wouldn't find another property like this. And I knew John had lots of boy toys, a speedboat being one of them. This would be perfect.

I called the listing agent who insisted on being there during the showing. This wasn't the protocol, but given the price and the fact that the owners still resided there, it was a precaution. They didn't want looky-loos traipsing through the house, and possibly stealing things. I didn't mind at all and an appointment was available at the specified time and date we wanted.

I'd ask Venice, if she'd like to show it with me. We shared all the commissions anyway. I had to make a duty call to my Mom but I wanted to talk to Venice first.

It was a little after 9 A.M. and I knew Venice would be up. She was an early riser, unlike myself. I walked over and knocked. Betty and Mr. Snigglebottom were out in the fenced yard. When they saw it was me, they smiled. And yes, dogs smile, but only if they like you. I could see homemade muffins on the counter. Venice was an excellent baker and last year had come up with the idea of baking cupcakes and decorating them to fit the businesses she was giving them to. For example, cupcakes that looked like dogs and cats for *Paws*. She had her realtor labels on the cupcake boxes and also handed out her business cards. Surprisingly, she got quite a few listings out of her unique marketing, as well as a few buyers. That was the catalyst that opened the door for her and now she was doing very well.

I saw her through the glass sliding doors, walking toward me. Acting like the adult I am I pressed my nose to the glass and puckered my lips. Venice was laughing when she let me in.

"Now look what you've done, there's lipstick on the glass. And how old are we today, twelve?"

Chuckling I said, "I've got good news or what could turn into good news." I told her about the impending showing with John. "I was wondering, if you'd like to go with me. It's a lovely house and I think you'd enjoy seeing it."

"I was going to tell you; I won't be in tomorrow. I'm taking the day off. I have a date."

"A date, like with a man and a woman date? I real date as in 'out to dinner?'"

"And why is that so surprising? Do I look like Godzilla or something?"

"No, no, it's just that…I don't know. I didn't think you were even looking. I guess I'm surprised."

"You know Viv, I wasn't looking, but I was thinking about it. I was so busy with house buying, renovating, selling my aunt's house, settling in, taking the real estate course, and getting my license. Don't forget all the time and work it took to start Rainbow Realty too. With all that behind me now, I feel like I can breathe. I was even considering joining a dating site."

"YOU JOINED A DATING SITE? WITHOUT ME?" I yelled.

"No, no, I didn't actually join yet. I was going to ask you to help me write my bio and answer the myriad of questions they ask. I figured you'd be better at getting me up and running since you've done it before. And there would have to be a good photo of me and the dogs. I looked at the site and it's very intimidating. But we can put that on hold for the time being."

"Oh? You met a man in the outside world then? A real man, not a digital one?"

"Yes indeedy. I was in the supermarket yesterday and dropped a can of crushed tomatoes and a very nice man picked it up for me. We got to talking and he asked me out to dinner."

"You're kidding me? Do you know how many times I've been in the market and have yet to meet anyone? I even read that food stores are very good places to find a man. I think some big supermarket chain made that up so more single people would shop there.

"I have this little game I play when shopping, it makes it less boring. If I see a nice-looking man alone, I glance in his cart. I can tell by what's in there if he's shopping for one. You know, single serving frozen dinners and nothing too fancy or nutritional. If there's a sporting magazine thrown in, I've hit the jackpot."

Venice said, "And how's that working for you? Here's a muffin, let's head to the office and I'll tell you more later."

"Just one more question. Is the date why you're taking off tomorrow? Not that you need permission, I'm just being my typical nosy self. All right, I have two questions. Why didn't you tell me you met someone? It's been weeks and I'm only hearing about it now?"

"I'm taking off because I don't have work to do tomorrow and I need a day to get beautiful for my date. And I *wasn't* asking permission, I was simply being considerate and letting you know. And, Ms. Drama Queen, it hasn't been weeks, I just met him yesterday."

I acquiesced, put Sassy in the car and off we went. Sassy now thought of the office as her second home. She got lots of attention and she was well behaved. My Sassy had manners, sometimes more so than humans. Everyone found her adorable, how could they not?

I had fenced in a small portion in the back so she could hang out and I wouldn't have to walk her all the time. Venice also brought her dogs to work if it was going to be a long day. We should have named the place, "Rainbow Realty *and Dogs*." My kitty Lola didn't like the car and she couldn't have cared less that we were leaving her. She usually slept most of the day anyway but insisted I put on saved episodes of Animal Planet. She especially loved the big cats and would caterwaul every time they made an appearance.

Venice came into my office and plopped her ass down but not before she handed me a coffee.

"Okay, I know you're dying to ask me a million questions, I won't make you wait until lunchtime," she said.

"Nope," I said, "I have not one question."

That deflated her. "What do you mean you have no questions? You're the nosiest...I mean the most curious person I know. Is that you Viv or have you been taken over by pods?"

"I said *I* have no questions but Sassy has many. She'd like to know his physical attributes, his financials, his marital status, widow, divorced? Oh, and his voice, does he have a deep timbre to his voice? Sassy loves a deep man-voice."

Laughing Venice said, "I only met him briefly in the market. And that sounds suspiciously like the list of attributes you'd like in a man. This one is mine, find your own. When we have dinner tomorrow night, it will give me plenty of time to interrogate him in the guise of conversation."

"But you just met him. Why the rush?" I asked.

"I believe that's what you do. You meet someone and then you spend a little time with them to see if you want to spend more time with them. That's called dating, Viv. And I *am* free tomorrow tonight."

"No Venice, you're certainly not *free* you're *available*. Must I teach you everything? I guess I don't have much time to prep you on the vagaries of dating so we'd better leave now for lunch."

"Viv it's only 10:30 A.M. It's too early for lunch. But we can go to lunch at the Hamburger Haven when it's a little closer to noon, what do you say?"

"I've got nothing on the docket so it's a date. Oh my, you have two dates in one day."

"I doubt very much," said Venice "if you're the same kind of date I'll be on tomorrow evening. You're a friend date, he's a man date. Oh, mandate. It's mandated I go on a man date." And she convulsed in laughter."

"Not only are you clever today, you seem downright effervescent. If you got any happier, I'd have to smack you. He must be quite the looker for this level of joy, or is it the fact that you haven't had a date in forever?"

"Now, now, don't be jealous. As your Mom would say, 'It doesn't become you.'"

We both went to our respective offices and worked until it was lunch time. I spoke to Annie, our spikey haired receptionist who we'd come to love and rely on for everything. She was our Gal

Friday. Today her hair was a vivid pink. Naturally, her attire matched her hair as it always did.

"Annie, what time are you taking lunch today? Venice and I are going to the Hamburger Haven but we'll work around your schedule."

"It doesn't matter to me. Just let me know what time. I have snacks if I'm starving."

"Do you want us to bring you back a hamburger?"

"Ugh, did you forget I'm Vegan?"

"No Annie, I just thought maybe you'd come to your senses and decided to eat some real food for a change. I don't know how you live on that stuff. I don't even want to tell you what those fake hotdogs look like but it's kind of similar to what comes out of Sassy's rear end."

"Gee, I thought you weren't going to tell me what they looked like. Thanks so much for sharing. I can't believe you eat animals given your love for them. And everything you own is leather or something made from animals. At least you don't wear fur."

"My Mom does. One time she was out in her mink coat and some animal rights people threw fake blood on her. I thought she was literally going to bludgeon them to death with her leather purse. Wes pulled her away just in time. And you know, minks are raised on farms for that sole purpose. Or should I say 'stole' purpose. Get it? Stole, like a mink stole?" Venice's puns were contagious.

Annie looked annoyed. "Yes Viv, I get it. You are such the comic."

"Not that farming the animals makes it better but as long as I don't have to know the process of a cow becoming a hamburger, I'm good. So, let's make a deal. I won't comment on your eating habits if you won't comment on mine."

Annie shook her head, "You do know you started this? But it's a deal. One I have a feeling you'll break, Ms. Boss Mouth."

"Now that's just impudent young lady. Have you never heard of 'respect your elders?' So, how about we bring you back a salad. However, that would be killing veggies."

Annie sneered at me.

Venice and I left for lunch a little before noon. We ordered our drinks and then I pummeled her with questions. Sassy's, not mine.

"Start at the beginning and tell me everything and don't leave out even the most inconsequential detail, it could be important."

"Important to what? Or whom? If you don't approve what are you going to do? Tell me to go to my room and ground me?"

"Now that's not a bad idea. Not only ground you but NO dinner, and NO video games."

"You're so silly. You know I don't play video games. Now let me tell you what happened.

"I went over to Park Hollow to go to the big pet store and while I was in the neighborhood, I thought I'd stop at the really nice upscale supermarket...what's it called again?"

"You mean 'Yummies?'"

"Yes, that's the one. I wanted to pick up some of that delicious ground sirloin and I was low on crushed tomatoes. They have the brand I used to buy in New York. So, in I went. I had my cart filled with more than I planned on buying but you know how that goes. I reached for the big can of tomatoes and dropped it. Missed my foot by an inch. The can ended up rolling halfway down the aisle. That's when Bryan, of course I didn't know he was Bryan yet, picked up the can and walked it over to me. I took in so much at that first glance and it was all good. Tall, muscular, blonde hair with a tiny bit of gray but abundant and wavy. With that hair I doubted he'd ever go bald. Oh, and no wedding ring."

"You noticed all that? At just a fleeting glance?"

"Yes, and when he started walking toward me, he had a good gait. Long legs, great posture, nice smile. Good teeth too."

"A good gait? What the hell does that even mean? And good teeth? Are you sure it wasn't a horse you were inspecting?"

"You're just a riot.. Now will you let me finish or maybe you would rather not hear any more about my horse date?"

"No, no, by all means continue. I'll try and keep my mouth shut. At least until you're done. I can't imagine there's too much more to this story unless he threw you down on the market floor and had his way with you."

"VIVIANNE! Really! You're so bad. When he handed me my errant can he said in a John Wayne accent, 'Thought this needed rescuing little lady.' I then swooned and he caught me in his big strong arms, threw me over his shoulder and had his way with me in the meat section. How apropos."

Now I was on the floor laughing. "Venice, you're killing me. That was hysterical."

"What makes you think I'm not telling the truth? That could have happened," she said with a straight face.

"Yes, you're right, it definitely could've happened...when hell freezes over." And that only started me laughing all over again.

"I guess you have a point. Okay, no swooning but I did return his smile, with one of my own. The biggest and best smile I could manage without splitting my face. He stuck out his hand and introduced himself as Bryan Davidson. Nice name too, I thought. I shook his hand back, telling him my name, and oh, his hand was big, with a firm grasp but not crushing and definitely manly hands. Honestly, I don't know what came over me. I was smitten to say the least. We chatted a bit and he asked me if I would have dinner with him. Smitten or not I wasn't going to be *that* easy. If he meant that very evening, I would have declined. After all I didn't want to appear desperate, or available at a moment's notice. We exchanged numbers and he said he'd call. And he did, last night."

"Here's what I gleaned from our phone conversation. Not married, not seeing anyone. Divorced. Oh, and he's moving to Arizona."

"He's moving to Arizona?" I asked. "So why are you going out with him? Please don't tell me you're thinking of moving to that inferno. You do know it reaches over a hundred degrees in the summer. Most of the people who live there go to cooler climes in the late spring and don't go back until October. Where in Arizona is he planning on living?"

"He told me Sunshine City which is not far from Phoenix. I've never been to the state so I don't know what that even means. Is that a good area?

"And I have no intentions of moving in with him. I haven't even gone on the first date yet. Don't you think you're overreacting?"

"You're right. As far as Sunshine City, I have no idea. Skylar and Jock would know. They got married in Tucson, at their friend's house, Linda and Mike. We all went, Mom, Wes, Kat and Nellie. It was lovely and since it was winter it was a perfect venue for their nuptials. At 80 degrees during the day, it sure beat winter here. I stayed for a week but never ventured far from Tucson so I can't tell you about any other area. I'll call her tonight and ask about that place."

CHAPTER TWO

I was feeling a little depressed. Was she going to fall head over heels for this guy and move away? I would be devastated to lose my best friend and real estate partner. It's not that I didn't want her to be happy, I just didn't want her to be happy at my expense. Now how selfish is that? Perhaps I was rushing to conclusions. After all it was just one date. Who knows, maybe she'd see a bad side of him over dinner. Disgusting eating habits? Picking teeth? Making her pay for her own dinner?

Oops, I forgot to call my Mom with all this dating crap going on. I picked up my phone and realized it was 8 P.M. which would make it three hours later on the east coast. Too late to call Mom but not Skylar, in Washington, D.C. They never went to bed early.

Skylar answered on the second ring. I heard her tell Jock to pause whatever it was they were viewing.

"Hey, what's up Viv? Is your Mom okay?"

"Yes, everything is good. I wanted to ask you about a place in Arizona, Sunshine City."

"Yes, we've been there. We visited Sunshine City the last time we were at Linda and Mikes, house. You remember them."

"Sure, I was telling Venice about them and their house. When I asked Linda how she dealt with the heat, she said, 'I don't feel comfortable unless it's at least 95 degrees.'"

"That's Linda," said Sky. "We rented a car and decided to drive around and tour some different areas. We're seriously thinking of buying a house there to winter in. It's so cold and snowy here in D.C.

"Why are you asking about that place? I hope you're not thinking of moving there because Sunshine City's population seems to be up there in the age bracket. And I do mean *up there*. Jock commented that it looked like one step away from a nursing home, although he exaggerates. But I would definitely say it's not for the younger crowd. And golf is God there. So many golf courses, so little time. Literally."

Laughing I said, "Jock golfs, doesn't he?"

"Yes," said Sky, "but not in the geriatric part of the country. His favorite spot for golfing is in Scotland. Remember a few years ago when a ball hit his head and he had to get ten stitches? He insisted on finishing his game before he went to the hospital. I hadn't realized golf was a blood sport. Why are you asking me about Sunshine City?"

"For Mom and Wes," I said.

"You're lying," said Sky, "Your mother would never live in a place like that because she wouldn't tolerate the heat, and furthermore, it isn't upscale enough for her taste."

Laughing I said, "You're absolutely right. I was testing you to see if you were paying attention. Venice met a man in the supermarket and is going on a date with him tomorrow evening. He's the one who's moving to Sunshine City. I want to be prepared, and knowledgeable. The more I know the more I can talk her off the ledge if need be."

"Don't you think you're jumping the gun? It *is* only one date."

"You have a valid point; I simply want to be ready with reasons why she shouldn't move, just in case. I'm wondering why she would go on a date with him at all, knowing he's moving away. Just a wee bit of concern."

I had sent her pictures of Rainbow Realty and she promised they would come for a visit soon. They're such a fun couple to hang out with so I was looking forward to seeing them. I could show them our brokerage and they'd get to meet Venice. They were in Prague when we had the Grand Opening.

I went to bed hoping sleep would come soon and it would be the day after tomorrow, so I could hear every detail of the dinner date. She'd probably get home too late to call me tomorrow evening. I tossed and turned and woke up feeling tired. Shit, I hated to be tired and I turned into a grumpy bitch when I was.

I had my showing with John. That perked me up some, that and my strong coffee that could put hair on your chest. No concerns there because *I* didn't have a date. Shaving my chest could wait.

It was May, buds sprouting everywhere and the air just starting to warm. Hopefully this meant spring weather would prevail. I wore my green suit which was professional but not too severe. I paired it with a lovely pale-yellow silk blouse, which softened the look. I grabbed my Gucci purse and off I went. I didn't get there too early because I couldn't go in without the listing agent. A few minutes after I arrived, she pulled up.

"Hi Angela, good to see you again. My client should be here any minute. Are the owners home?"

I knew Angela, she'd been in the real estate business forever, and I liked her. It was always a plus to work with a seasoned agent who got straight to the point and knew what she was doing.

"Hi Vivianne, no, I asked them to leave for the showing. They're a sweet older couple and have been very accommodating. I hope your buyer likes the house. My sellers are planning on moving to California where their children and grandchildren live."

John drove in at that very moment. Introductions made, we opened the door into a large foyer with a black veined white, marble floor. Looking straight ahead, you could see out to the beach, through the floor to ceiling wall of windows, offering an unobstructed expanse of water and mountains. It was breathtaking.

It was a smashing house, as the English would say, and everything was updated, including the kitchen which had quartz countertops and brushed stainless steel appliances. I'm not a fan of stainless steel but if you have to have it, the brushed finish is best for not showing dirt, and it's much easier to keep clean. But, let's face it, if you could afford this house you wouldn't be the one cleaning it.

There were five bedrooms, two of them master suites, all with full baths. One of the masters was on the main floor, which John had wanted, but this one came with a bonus. There were sliders in the master that led out to a lavish private patio where you could sit with your morning coffee, enjoying the sound of waves lapping against the shore, and the never-ending views, not only of the water but of the Blue Herons, eagles, ospreys, and let's not forget the sea lions and seals.

There was a finished basement and a three-car garage. But what he wanted to look at the most, was the beach and the dock. Doors led to the beach from the living room and kitchen where you could sink your feet into the sand and walk down to the water. We strolled the length of the dock which I could tell was his favorite part of this showing.

We were finally done and Angela locked up. When she was gone, I asked John what he thought.

"It's after noon, may I take you to lunch? We can discuss the house over a drink and a meal."

"You know, now that you mention it, I'm starving. How about the *Copper Bottom* in Kingsville? It's the closest and best restaurant in this area."

The *Copper Bottom* it was. Once seated with drinks, he took my hand and put a huge diamond on it and proposed. Okay, that's a little fib.

John was tall, my guess would be 6'2", a full head of grey, almost silver hair. His aquiline nose dominated a strong, handsome face, with eyes the color of blue agate. My guess has him in his sixties. Aside from his physical attributes, he was a nice person who went through a horrible ordeal last year but was recovering splendidly. I'm sure the monumental size of his worth helped the healing process. Anyone who says "Money can't buy happiness" probably has no money. John was beyond rich.

"I believe we've found my new home. I'd like to put in an offer. There are a few things I'd change but nothing major and the beach and dock are superb. I can have a boathouse built so I'll have a place to store my watercraft in the winter months. How about we put in an offer for an even $3,000,000, all cash, and see if they take it."

"That's a reasonable and if they don't think so, they can always counter."

"I'm willing to go up to full price if necessary, but considering there's no financing, the sellers may entertain a lower bid. It will also insure a fairly expeditious closing, even with an inspection, which is a must."

We finished lunch and, thanking John, I told him I'd be writing up the offer and sending it over for him to sign in about an hour.

A few hours later, Angela called. The owners had accepted John's offer and it would close in about three weeks. I had more good news for John. The couple who wanted the mansion came up to the $8,750.000 price and that was now going forward. This month was shaping up to be very lucrative one for Rainbow Realty.

My day was busy getting the inspection lined up for John and snipping away at loose ends. I was glad when my work was done. It was 4 P.M. and I was headed home, but first I made a stop at the market to buy a bottle of Pinot Grigio.

I was in the wine aisle looking over the selection when I thought, maybe I'll meet a nice man while I'm here and, it would be especially fortuitous if he too was picking out wine. I pictured the scene. Mr. Wine Connoisseur would be charming, good looking and tall. He would not only pick out the best wine for me, but pay for it too.

"Ma'am, hello?" My reverie broken, I looked into the face of a boy. A BOY. He was the clerk wanting to know if I needed help. I popped out of my stupor before my imagination could reach new heights, thanked him, paid for my wine, and left.

I no sooner opened my front door when my phone chirped. It was Venice.

"And how was your day? Did you go to a spa?" I asked.

"My day was great; I went shopping for a nice outfit for tonight. You know, I have a ton of professional clothes, and casual attire, but nothing for a date. I thought you might want to pop over before I leave and give me your opinion."

"I'll be right there. Do you have time for a glass of wine?"

"One glass won't hurt, yes, wine would be good."

I arrived at Venice's house with my newly bought Pinot. She answered the door looking fabulous.

"Wow, you look like a million dollars. I love the dress, and aren't those new shoes? And do I see *highlights* in your hair?"

"Yes, to all. I thought I would treat myself to a day of beautifying. Salon, shopping, I did it all. It would've been more fun if you were with me though. I could've used your slant on the clothes. Trying on clothes by myself was all work and no fun. I couldn't make a decision."

"Apparently, you did make a decision. The dress is perfect. If I was with you, one look at this dress and I would've insisted you buy it. So there. You didn't need me after all."

"Why thank you, but I will always need you. Let's have that glass of wine, I have to go soon."

Ven's dress was fire engine red with a little silver beading around the scoop neckline, and fell just above her knees. Her hair shone with rich auburn highlights that hadn't been there yesterday.

She looked gorgeous. I hope this Bryan guy was worthy of her.

"Where are you going for dinner?"

"I'm meeting him at the Copper Bottom," said Venice.

I opened the wine and had just enough time to tell her about the lucrative deals I had completed for John.

Smiling, I said, "Now you can actually pay for everything you bought today. Now go and have a wonderful time. And don't forget, curfew is 10 P.M. The dogs set that time, not me."

She air kissed me goodbye, leaving with a big smile on her face.

Once home, I drank and sulked. Wait, there was a knock at my door. Ah, Venice changed her mind and decided to have dinner at my house. I never thought I would be living vicariously through her. I flung open the door and my raccoons scattered. I had forgotten to put their kibble out and they were standing up, tapping their wrists, saying, "Hey LADY, where's the food? LADY! LADY!"

They were so demanding. I went out and filled their feeders which were in their little houses so the kibble would stay dry in the inclement weather. I asked them if they had any dating stories to tell me. I took their silence for a "No."

Sassy and I watched TV but not for long because I was tired. I gave up and went to bed early, at least early for me. I could hardly wait for tomorrow to be here so I could ply Ven with questions.

The next morning, I woke up feeling refreshed and optimistic. I took care of Sassy and put on my coffee. Taking my cup, I sat in my favorite chair and called Venice.

She picked up saying, "I knew you'd call. No, I can't come over. Bryan is here."

"WHAT? Ummm…okay then. Uh, see you later?"

"Ah HA, gotcha. You were actually at a loss for words which is an extreme rarity for you. I'm home and alone."

I can't tell you how relieved I was that she wasn't serious about *Him* being there. There was something about this whole thing I didn't like, but then I attributed that to my concern that Venice would fall crazy in love and leave. That's probably what was making me ambivalent, nothing more. Maybe I *was* jealous that she found someone. I didn't like my thoughts one bit. I had to stop and just be happy for her, even if it meant she'd move away.

"I know you want to hear all about my date but I have a doctor's appointment, just my annual check-up. How about I see you this evening? What can I bring?

"How about dinner," I said, laughing. "I jest. I have a surprise so don't bring a thing." I'd taken my turkey meatballs out to defrost and would make pasta. She loved my meatballs; it was one of her favorites. I even had frozen bread which, when put in the oven, came out as if it were freshly baked that very day. However, she wasn't getting food until she told me all about the date.

I got home early to get things ready. I even made my meringue shells which were beloved by everyone. Promptly at 6 P.M. she knocked, dogs in tow to play with Sassy in the backyard. I loved that Sass had playmates and they all got along so well. I'd set a place for two more at the table. Oh, wait, everyone knows dogs prefer *beef* meatballs.

Drinks in hand, cheese and crackers out, she started her dating tale. Or tail. No, no, I hoped no tail, at least not yet. Sometimes I even disgust myself.

"As you already know," said Venice, "I was meeting Bryan at the Copper Bottom. I didn't think he needed to know where I lived, in case he was a pervert. I picked that place for the path that goes around the water where the boats are moored. I thought, if dinner went well, I could suggest a stroll. It's so pretty at night with the lights shimmering on the water. And the moon was almost full, how romantic."

Romantic? Did she just say *romantic*? Why would she care about romance on the first rendezvous? I mentally slapped myself. I was thinking like a mother with a teenager who was out on her first date.

She was right about the path. It was part of the Kingsville community and had a gazebo where bands played in the summer months. It was well lit with lots of people about, especially in the nicer weather. Good choice.

"I'm really proud of you," I said. "Not too long ago you would have pooh-poohed me if I had suggested you be cautious. You did take your pepper spray, didn't you?"

"Yes, actually I did. Thanks to you, I no longer go anywhere without it. That, and you, probably saved my life last year.

"Bryan was a complete gentleman. He even pulled out my chair for me. He also complimented me on how I looked. We ordered drinks, a cosmopolitan for me and a martini for him. Once we settled in, I felt very comfortable with him. Conversation came easily.

"Before he retired, he was a manager of something to do with the food industry. He talked about pairing wines amongst other mundane things and frankly, it was a bit boring. I told him about our brokerage and blah, blah, blah. Nothing too personal. Then he started talking about his Harley. That's a motorcycle."

"Venice, I know what a Harley is for God's sake. I realize I'm older than you, but please, give me a little credit. I've even been on one. Several times."

"You have? When was that?"

"Oh no you don't. The Harley story is for another time. Now please, continue."

"Okay but some day I'd like to hear everything about your biker days."

"Biker days? Oh Ven, what am I to do with you? Now please, get on with this."

"Well, I told you yesterday that he's moving to Sunshine City. It seems he's purchased a condo for the ridiculous price of $65,000. Here, you couldn't get an outhouse for that. He's going to be driving down in his SUV which is huge. Much bigger than ours."

There was no need to tell her what Skylar had said about the place. At least for now.

"He and the ex-wife put their house on the market. They lived in a suburb of Seattle so they got a bundle for it. They split the profit from the sale and she moved to Oregon. He mentioned the divorce was acrimonious to say the least. Even though he gave her the choice to move with him, she hated the desert and wouldn't think of living there. They argued back and forth for a time. She was pissed he wouldn't stay here and he was annoyed she wouldn't go with him, to Arizona. He's retired and wants to make the money stretch and she wanted another big house. No meeting of the minds there. I realize I'm only hearing one side of this but really, does it matter? It doesn't seem like either one wanted to stay in the marriage."

"Since there seems to be no love lost between them, at least you'll never have to meet her," I said.

"He told me he's adopted. His adopted parents were wonderful and he said he never felt the need to know about his birth parents, even after his adopted parents passed away. He had no siblings. Talk about a small family.

"The evening went well, but I don't know, Viv. People always put their best foot forward in the beginning. Look at your Mom. She morphed into a completely different personality when she first met Wes, didn't she?"

"She most certainly did, so much so that we thought aliens had taken up residence in her body. Now the charade is gone, God help Wes, but he's still there so it must work for him.

"Oh shit, speaking of my mother I keep forgetting to call her. But she hasn't called me either. Which is not even a point. I'll still be in the shithouse."

Venice continued, "Better you than me, you know I'm terrified of her. I digress. In a few weeks Bryan will make the move to Arizona. Then that's that."

"What do you mean, 'That's that?' If he's going to be living far away why did you even go out with him? And why would he move in the hottest part of the year? He'll cook down there."

"I don't know, I never even thought of his timeline. As far as going out with him even though he's moving...Well, if I never see him again, at least I had a nice evening, enjoyable conversation and a free meal. It's all good. I won't miss him because I don't know him enough to miss him."

"Are you going to see him again before he leaves?"

"I will if he asks. He's staying at a friend's house not too far from here. If he calls, I'll have a few weeks to get to know him better."

"Okay Venice, I'm going to lay it all out. I don't want you to move. I don't want to lose my best friend and partner. I don't want you to get to know him better."

"Move? Whatever gave you that idea...Oh My God, you think I'm moving to Arizona? Now I get it. That's why you've been acting so weird." She started laughing.

"What's so damned funny? Stranger things have happened. Look at last year."

"I would never, in a million years throw all this away," and she made a sweeping gesture with her arm. "Are you on drugs? This dating is just a little adventure, something different for a change. I haven't been with a man in...forever. Not since my ex. I love you Viv, you're my best friend. You can stop worrying. I'm dating, not getting married. It's all good."

Boy, I felt a tide of relief swarm over me. I knew I was being an idiot. But, on the other hand, she kept saying, "It's all good." Nothing is *all* good.

The phone chirped. It was John Berkman.

"Ven, it's John, I have to take this. I hope nothing is wrong with our deals."

"Hi John, and to what do I owe this pleasure?" Oops, he's a client I shouldn't have said that. Now he thinks he's a pleasure.

"I wanted to know if you're free for dinner next Friday?"

"With you?" No tact at all. I was making this worse by the minute.

"No Vivian, I was asking for a friend. Yes, with me. Am I catching you at a bad time?"

"You just caught me by surprise, that's all. Dinner would be nice."

"If Friday at 7 P.M. is good for you, why don't I pick you up at your house? I'll make reservations for the New York City grill over in Seattle. Since you're a New Yorker I thought you might enjoy the place."

I gave him my address, my dog and my cat. Wow. A DATE! And with a hugely wealthy man. Oh my. Seven it was. I had Venice beat. Her date was moving into a cheap condo, mine was moving into a multi-million-dollar house. But then, this wasn't a contest. Or was it?

We hung up and when I turned around Venice was frowning.

"Viv, what's wrong? Is he pulling out of the deal? Is the mansion falling through?"

"No, he asked me out. A date. For dinner Friday, at the New York Grill."

"Oooohh how impressive, that's one expensive restaurant. And look at us. We're both dating now. At least you are, I haven't heard from Bryan."

"Bryan will call you. How could he not, given you were a knock-out when you went on the first date."

We had a nice dinner and I was happy she wouldn't be moving anytime soon, and, I was past my craziness and feeling quite good that I too had a date. This was going to be awesome. We could compare dating notes. I felt like we were teenagers giggling about our boyfriends. I was totally losing what little mind I had left. I was sure she'd be hearing from Bryan very soon.

CHAPTER THREE

T he next morning, I stopped at Venice's house for whatever she had baked. I now did extra miles on the treadmill just so I could partake of her decadent donuts, her scrumptious scones her mouthwatering muffins, and let's not forget the capricious cupcakes.

"Where's the muffins? Where's the cupcakes?" I asked. Not only did I not *see* anything, I also didn't *smell* anything.

"I didn't have time to bake so you'll just have to do without or stop at the market and pick up something."

"Are you kidding me? You expect me to eat market swill? After you've spoiled me with your sweet treats? I'm totally depressed. What could be so time consuming that you couldn't bake?"

"I was on the phone with Bryan for quite a while. Then it was too late for baking. And before you ask, yes, he asked me out again. I'm going to see him Wednesday night which is perfect so I'm hoping you can take care of the dogs, and Friday while you're out I'll have Sassy over here."

She was putting a conversation with Bryan ahead of baking? She's a woman, she can multitask. I was very disappointed in her. I was sure Bryan would turn out to be a serial killer.

The phone chirped at that very minute. I answered it, putting my depression on hold... I shouldn't have. I couldn't believe what I was hearing.

I'm sure Venice saw the look of horror on my face.

"There's a dead body," I said to Venice.

"Excuse me? I'm sorry, I didn't catch that. Funny, I thought you said there's a *dead body*. Maybe you meant a *hot toddy*?"

"Who would drink a hot toddy in May, and in the morning? If it had rum in it, I guess *I* would. That was Annie, we'd better get down to the brokerage now. She's already called the police. That's all I know."

"Are you telling me the dead body is ON THE PREMISES OF OUR BROKERAGE?"

"Yes, that's exactly what I'm telling you. Annie sounded like she was having a nervous breakdown. I thought it prudent to wait until we got there to ask questions. I do know the police are on their way."

Annie was our everything girl. She did all things office and then some. We adored her and were very lucky she was ours.

We both jumped in my car and headed out. My mind was whirling. The suspense was killing me. Oh, bad choice of words there. What if it was one of our agents, or maybe Sally, the cleaner? She was in there last night. Oh my God.

Arriving as quickly as possible, the first thing I saw was Annie, sitting on the curb outside. She got up when she saw us.

"Annie, what happened? Are you okay? Where's the body? Is it someone we know?"

Annie looked up, face ashen. "She's in the back. Oh, it's awful, just awful. I waited outside until the officers arrived. I'm okay and I have no idea who it is. I couldn't see her face."

Our brokerage used to be a bridal salon. The back was where the brides would try on wedding gowns. It was a big space, the changing rooms had been removed but the circular, raised dais, where the future bride would model the gowns, was still intact. We had decided to leave the space unused for the time being. If we eventually acquired more agents, we'd have the dais removed and put in more cubicles. Right now, it was being used as storage for the cleaning supplies, and some staging furniture.

A car pulled up just as we were heading over for coffee since we didn't dare go into the brokerage. Oh joy, it was Det. Traynor. She was both a detective and crime scene investigator. Venice and I, more I than Venice, had the misfortune of having met the detective at a few other crime scenes. Okay, I was the one who was involved in a few cases, Venice, only one, but that was a doozy.

"Well now, if it isn't Vivianne and Venice. I was wondering how long it would be before we met up again. Murder seems to seek you out."

"It's nice to see you too Det. Traynor. And, NO, we are NOT involved. At least I don't think we are. The policemen wouldn't let us back to see the body, so I was waiting for you to show up. Well, not necessarily you, but someone who would take over the crime scene and maybe let us have just one little peek?"

"You know better than to ask me that," said Det. Traynor. "Who called 911?"

"That would be me," said Annie. "The policeman who's in the back took my statement. I didn't touch anything; I didn't even know if it was a dead person or just a prank. Once I saw it, I ran out the front door and that's where I stayed."

"You did the right thing. I'm glad it wasn't Vivianne who found her. I'm sure she would have messed up my crime scene."

I couldn't argue with that, but I'd be damned if I was going to admit it.

"We'll have someone at the front door so nobody can enter. You might want to call your agents and explain the situation. Tell them there's been an incident and you'll let them know when the brokerage is open for business. That's all they need to know right now."

"I asked, "Do you think we'll be able to go in sometime today?"

Det. Traynor said, "Yes, I think we'll be finished here in a few hours. Once the medical examiner removes the body it will probably take us another hour. Meantime, you can all go home, I'll get the list of everyone who works here from the officer."

Annie gave the policeman the contact info for us and all the agents. "Before you go, when was your cleaning person here last? I was told the cleaning supplies were stored back there."

"Her name is Sally," I said. "She was here last night; she always comes in on Sunday evenings because there usually isn't anyone working at that time. My guess would be around 7 P.M. Sally has the key to the place and after we leased it, we had all the locks changed so one key fit all the doors, except mine and Venice's office. She's got separate keys for them." I wrote down

Sally's name and phone number and gave it to the detective.

Det. Traynor told Annie not to go too far as she'd like to question her further after she was done with the scene.

Annie said, "I'm going with Viv and Venice. I can go with you guys, can't I?"

"Sure," said Venice, "if it's okay with the Detective." It was.

"I bet you're sorry now that you didn't bake," I said to Venice.

"I'm not sorry, I've got scones in the freezer. I'll put them in the microwave so you won't starve to death. Really Vivianne!"

Coffee made, scones eaten, Annie whispered, "I've got something to show you."

I asked, "Why are you whispering, the dogs won't tell, whatever it is. There's nobody else here. You can speak up."

She whipped out her cell phone and scrolled down, showing us the pictures on her screen. It was the scene of the crime.

"Are you kidding me Annie? You took pictures? I love you, let's blow them up."

Venice looked like she wanted to kill me, and Annie. "Annie, are you crazy? What if the murderer had still been there? I suppose, if you went to the trouble, the least I can do is look at them," said Venice.

Annie answered, "I figured, if it was a dead person, the murderer wouldn't still be there, not when he knew the broker-age would probably be opening any minute. I was betting he was long gone. Or, maybe he was watching from a distance. Maybe he got off on all the commotion. When I was sitting outside, I was looking around, I had sunglasses on so if he *was* watching he wouldn't see me looking. I'm sorry about the pictures, but I thought it might be important."

We huddled around looking at the photos. Annie had taken the pictures from the doorway of the crime scene so; she didn't mess up anything. I saw no harm, and was glad she even though of it.

It appeared the deceased was posed in the middle of the dais, where, if alive, she'd be smiling and twirling around showing off her gown. Now, she was in a sitting position on the floor, the full skirt of the dress arranged so it puffed out all around her in a perfect circle. We could make out a rhinestone tiara that held the veil in place. Her head was slumped down, resting in the folds of the garment. That, and the veil, obscured her face. The only thing I could see was one of her hands, and her hair, the color of burnished copper. Looking closely, I saw what appeared to be a ring on her left finger. Hmmmm.

"Annie, can you please send the pictures to me? I'll want to transfer them to my laptop; the screen is bigger."

"VIVIANNE," said Venice. "You are *not* getting involved in this. Didn't we go through enough last year?"

"Just curious Ven. Don't get all bent out of shape, how in hell can I get involved? Unless we know her."

"Even if we do, this remains a police matter," said Venice. Annie agreed but she sent me the photos anyway.

I asked Annie if she could go over what she told the officer.

"Sure, I'm feeling okay now. It was just the shock, you know? I got there around 7:30 A.M. which is my usual time. I opened up, turning on lights and when I got to the conference room, I noticed the door to the back was slightly open, and there were lights on. I know that's where Sally has the vacuum and her supplies so I thought maybe she'd forgotten to turn off the lights. That's when I saw her. I ran back to my desk and got my phone to call the cops and then went back and quickly snapped as many pictures as I could without going in the room. And I definitely did NOT want to go near that thing. I didn't know she was a dead woman at the time, I couldn't see her but it didn't look good to me.

"Anyway, I told the officer my movements from the time I entered. He wanted to know if I saw anything suspicious when I pulled up to the building but I wasn't looking for anything so that was a negative. He also asked about the room where the woman was and I told him about Sally and the cleaning supplies. He asked if Sally ever left the lights on accidentally and again, I said no. He was very pleased that I hadn't entered the room which would mean the crime scene wasn't compromised. I like that, 'compromised,' I think I got that off of NCIS."

"Good thinking Annie girl." Annie was tiny and looked ten years younger than she was so I always thought of her as a girl, not a woman. She didn't seem to mind.

Annie asked if she could go out and play with the dogs. They knew her well given they were at the brokerage with us and she walked them occasionally.

"They would love that, throw the balls until you get tired. When fetching is involved, they can go at it all day long."

Venice and I chatted about our dates coming up. Over an hour had passed when my phone chirped.

"It's Det. Traynor, I have her in my contact list now. How

depraved is that?

"Hi Detective, what can I help you with?"

"The medical examiner is here and I'd like you all to come down to take a look at the body before he takes her."

"We'll be right there. Give us about twenty minutes."

I told Annie and Venice we were going to view the body, which sounded more like we were going to a wake.

Venice looked at me aghast. "I don't want to look at a dead body."

"I'm sure it will only be her face; you don't need to see all of her for an ID. What about you Annie, are you okay with this? If either of you would rather look at a photo, I'm sure that would suffice."

"I'm in," said Annie. "I'll feel better if I don't recognize her, c'mon Venice, don't be a wuss."

With a sigh Venice gave in.

We went into the reception area that led to a hallway, which was out of view from the public. There were gawkers outside, straining to see what the commotion was all about.

Once we were all there, the medical examiner unzipped the bag so that only her face was visible. She was so young, and the word *dainty* came to mind. Her hair was a chestnut color, thick and loose around her head. She had delicate features, a face like porcelain. Full lips painted a soft pearl pink. I didn't have a clue as to how she died but was glad her face remained intact. Who would do something so awful? And why?

We all breathed a sigh of relief that it wasn't someone we knew. The ME left and Det. Traynor said we could go back and make coffee, which was in a room at the other end of the building, Aside from the coffee room we were only allowed access to the reception area and our personal offices at this time.

Annie made a pot of strong brew and came out with a tray of cups, coffee, cream, and sugar. We really had to give her a raise. I was so impressed that she took pictures of the scene. Maybe we could sell them to the tabloids. Maybe not.

CHAPTER FOUR

We were all in our respective homes, reeling from the day's events. I was given the green light to tell my agents what had happened. I didn't know much, just that the victim was yet to be identified. She was murdered but I still didn't know how. Not much solace but at least they didn't think she'd been murdered on the premises. We still had to wait for time of death.

All our agents would be questioned and shown the picture to see if anyone knew the victim. I would've asked Det. Traynor to let me know how that went but I knew she wouldn't tell me.

I called Sally. Maybe I'd find out something good.

"Hello?" "Hi Sally. Did you talk to Det. Traynor today?"

"Yes, I did. This is all very disturbing. I'll tell you what I told her. I did NOT leave any lights on and the doors were closed. I don't know if the back door, the one leading outside, not the one going into the brokerage, was locked. I never use that door so it's possible it wasn't. To tell the truth, I'm now afraid to go and clean. I was going to call you about that."

"We'll probably get a security system but for now, one of us will be there until you're done. Do you think you could start at 6 instead of 7 P.M., just for the time being?"

She agreed and was thankful she wouldn't be alone. I'd run this by Ven and Annie. Between the three of us we'd have her back.

And it was only two nights a week.

I called my Mom. Sigh. Really, I had to. If she found out about this mess before I told her, I would be sent to my room and grounded for a week. And NO television. Wait, I forgot, I'm now an adult and I don't live with her anymore. Ah, but the long reach of my Mom's wrath is not to be trifled with.

"Hi Mom, I've got some news."

"News? Like in John Berkman news? Has he proposed yet?"

I knew I shouldn't have told her about my upcoming date.

"MOM! I haven't even gone out with him yet. Even you took longer than that to get engaged, for the THIRD time I might add."

"You might add that Vivianne, but I warn you, I haven't had my wine yet. If you remembered correctly, you'd realize there was no engagement with Wes. We went from dating to marriage and skipped that part. However, no engagement most certainly did not mean no ring, thus the beautiful diamond I wear every day, along with the matching wedding band.

"WES? WES! Get me my glass of wine, will you?" I heard him breathing hard as he ran to the kitchen and back with wine in hand. I think he may have had a minute to tip the bottle up and swig a good amount first. He had long ago mastered running with a full glass of wine with nary a drop spilled. The man was a saint.

"Okay Vivianne, I've got my sustenance, now you can tell me the news. For some reason I always feel like drinking when you call."

"How special that makes me feel, Mom. Funny, but I too feel the need to imbibe."

"Vivianne, do you not know humor when you hear it? You're always in the middle of something, and it's usually not good. You, on the other hand, have no reason to feel the same about me. That must have been your failed attempt at humor, and of course, YOU'RE OUT OF THE WILL."

Laughing I said, "Yes, yes, I was only kidding. I always look forward to our calls." God would strike me dead for that big fat lie.

I told her about the *Bridal Murder* which is the moniker I had given it. I left nothing out, except the negative comments that Det. Traynor fabricated about me.

"Now you see, Vivianne. This is exactly why I need my wine. This is most disturbing. Did you call the station to see if they have any news? You had better think about security and make sure it includes cameras, both inside and out. Didn't I tell you that when you first opened? Nobody ever listens to me and I'm *always* right. Why does it take you so long to learn these things?"

Oh boy. Nobody listened to her? Is she a lunatic? It was impossible NOT to listen to her. She spoke, we obeyed. However, only Wes ran, we merely walked quickly to get her what she wanted. Sigh.

"Mom, relax, I called the security company when I got home. They'll install a security system in a few days." I was lying through my teeth. I hate to admit it, but she did have a valid point and I would follow up on that. "You see, I do listen to you." My fingers were crossed.

"No, only after the fact. Let's talk about my surgery. You are coming home." That wasn't a question. If I didn't show up, I really would be out of the will.

"Yes, Mom, I wouldn't miss it for the world." I almost asked, 'What kind of daughter do you think I am?' I've learned never to ask a question you don't want the answer to and that was one loaded question that would not bode well for me. Also, I didn't know why she kept referring to her house as my home. My home is here, with Sassy, in *The Little House in the Woods*.

"I would like you here a few days before I go into the hospital. We'll have time to go out for a nice dinner at that Chinese/Polynesian place. Uncle something. Your sister and Nellie love that place. Kat is so considerate; she's taking a week off from work. Nellie will be here too. The best granddaughter I could ever have hoped for. After all, it's too late for you to give me a grandchild. You're probably in the middle of menopause by now."

Bitch, I thought. You didn't actually think I said that? "Yes Mom, you are lucky. Nellie is a gem. And I am absolutely NOT in menopause."

"It can't be far off. Just prepare yourself, that's all I'm saying Vivianne."

Pleasantries over, okay there were no pleasantries, but my duty as her daughter, the lesser one, was done. Kat was still number one or maybe Nellie had moved up to that spot. I was coming in at a distant third. Wait, maybe Venice was now third. Wes didn't count.

I picked up the phone and dialed, well, nobody dials anymore, I pressed a button and Kat answered. I greeted her, saying, "Hi Sister and most honorable favorite daughter of Dragon woman."

"Ah, you just got off the phone with Mom."

"Gee, you must be telepathic. I'm flying in next month for the big day. I'm planning on staying a week, do you think that will be long enough?"

"No," said Kat. "The doctor seems to think she'll be in the hospital for a week so you better plan on staying for at least ten days. If you left while she was still in there, you'd probably be OUT OF THE WILL!"

We both started laughing. This was my Mom's favorite four words to say every time we did something she didn't like. Which was often. It was a running joke and she never meant it. My mother wasn't devoid of humor, but she didn't hold a candle to her offspring. My sister and I were hilarious together. Sometimes I thought we should change careers and become a stand-up comedy team.

"It won't be that bad. I took the week off and counting the weekend Nellie and I will be there for nine days."

"Wait, wait, wait. What do you mean you'll only be there for nine days? If I'm there for ten days and you're only there for nine that means I'll be in the house with her alone, day and night. I can't breathe, I'm feeling faint."

"Sister, I want you to slap yourself, hard. Get a grip. You won't be there alone; Wes will be there. And it's only one day. God, you're so dramatic."

"Oh joy, I forgot about Wes. That's such a comforting thought. Wes my ass. First of all, he'll be running around like a chicken without a head, attending to her every need. Now that I think of it, it won't be any different than it usually is. But there'll probably be more running with her recuperating. And you know how he goes on, and on, and on when he tells a story and it will be excruciatingly painful given I've heard them all a hundred times."

"Oh, I don't think you've heard the latest. Sanddabs."

"Sand dabs? What the fu…I mean, hell, are sand dabs." I was trying to clean up my foul language. The "F" word was out but would probably be back when I had to stay with my mother.

I could tell my sister was trying not to laugh. "I don't think I'll tell you, I'll let Wes do that. If I tell you, it won't be new and interesting. I don't want to ruin it."

"Thanks, you're so considerate. I appreciate that. NOW TELL ME WHAT IN THE HELL SANDDABS ARE?"

"No need to yell. It seems sanddabs are flatfish that live in the Pacific Ocean. Wes thinks this could be a good business. Fishing for sanddabs and selling them to local restaurants."

"Please tell me you're kidding. That brings to mind the Meyer lemon fiasco." Wes was certain they were under appreciated and told us the story of their origin, where they came from, how many centuries back they went, and blah, blah, blah. I thought that was the end of it. Shortly thereafter, I arrived home to find a Meyer lemon tree had been delivered and was on my front porch."

Kat asked, "What ever happened to that thing? Did you even get lemons?"

"I managed to keep it alive, but it was getting too big for me to continue moving it inside when it was cold, and it was taking up all the space in my living room. When Venice bought the house across the street, I begged her to take the damned thing. I considered giving it to her as a house warming gift but I didn't want to start off with her hating me right off the bat.

The tree is now happy. She has a lot more room than I. It's thriving at her place. I take pictures of it and send them to Wes. He's very pleased and believes we'll be in the lemon business momentarily. I have to say, it does make great lemonade because Meyers are sweeter than regular lemons. Venice is thinking of leaving the brokerage and opening her very own lemonade stand."

"That's not a bad idea. Not the stand but maybe she could bottle it and give it away with her cupcakes. A new marketing plan."

"Let me get off the phone and run right over there with that idea. I'm sure it'll go over well. After all, she just sits around eating bonbons all day. I'm hanging up now, you idiot."

My sister said, "Love you too, talk soon."

I had told her about the *Bridal Murder* and she too said I shouldn't get involved. Why did everyone say that? I didn't seek murder out, it sought me out. And there was only that one time. There were other unpleasant circumstances I seemed to be involved in but again, I didn't go looking for them. And I'm still alive and doing very well, thank you.

Crap, it was only Monday, I had to wait all the way until Friday for my date.

CHAPTER FIVE

I did call the security company but they couldn't come out until next week and then they'd install cameras and an alarm system at the brokerage. Meanwhile, I asked Annie not to go into the office alone. I'd meet her there at 7:45 A.M., which, given the early hour, would probably kill me. I also put out a memo telling my agents not to be on the premises alone until we were sure it was safe. When that would be was anyone's guess. It was probably okay now but I didn't want to take any chances.

The phone chirped.

"Hi Ven, what's up?"

Just wanted to remind you that I'm going on my date Wednesday. I was wondering if you'd take the dogs for the night."

"You mean you're going to be gone ALL NIGHT? Until the NEXT MORNING?"

"Jeez Viv, no, I'm not going to be gone overnight. We're going out to eat and then to see a play. It will be late by the time I get home so I thought you would do me the favor of dog sitting. I don't need a lecture. He's going to pick me up around 6 P.M."

"I see, but if he picks you up, he'll know where you live and he'll also be dropping you off. Maybe it *will* be an overnighter."

"Are you going to take the dogs, or not?"

"Yes, of course I will. You don't have to get snippy."

"I'll see you tomorrow. Goodnight." And with a click the conversation was over.

Now who was being a child? Me, obviously, but she didn't have to get crabby. I get it, it's none of my business but it really was. Now I felt we were at odds and that never happened before with us. I better get a handle on this before she expels me from her life forever, I thought. I didn't think she'd do that but, love makes people do strange things. I truly believed Venice was falling for this guy. I told my mind to SHUT UP and plopped down in the chair to watch television while I had a good sulk going. That would take my mind off things. For an hour maybe.

The next morning there was a knock on my door. I opened it and there stood Venice with a basket full of raspberry scones.

"Good Morning Viv, I come bearing gifts. And an Olive Branch, although it looked suspiciously like the stick she threw for her dogs. It had a cute pink bow tied around it and a label that said "Peace?"

Laughing I said, "Why thank you, Venice. How sweet of you. Do come in."

Venice looked at me warily saying, "What's with all the good manners? That is so not you. Stop being weird and get the coffee and I'll take out the scones. I'll tell you all about my conversation with Bryan."

Now that's what I wanted to hear. With the murder, I forgot all about the "Bryan" conversation. Scones in place, coffee poured, I was all ears.

"When we talked the other night, I did ask him why he was leaving for Arizona at the height of the inferno season. He said it just worked out that way and once settled he might come back up here for a while. He's staying with a friend, Pete. Pete's wife was in Florida taking care of her sick mother but she's due back in a few weeks and Bryan said he won't be able to stay there once she's home."

"I wonder why Pete's wife won't let him stay there? Maybe she doesn't like him."

"Funny you should say that, I don't think you like him either and you've never even met him. Possibly, they don't have the extra room for Bryan to stay."

Venice continued, "The rest of our conversation were stupid things, like movies we both like, our favorite foods, and getting to know one another talk."

Once Venice wrapped up her exciting phone call (boring), and I was just about to doze off, she broke my reverie asking if I'd called the police station for any news yet. I hadn't so I made a call to ask if there were any updates. I was told we could take down the crime scene tape and open our doors. Hooray. They wouldn't tell me anything else. I asked if they would leave a message for Det. Traynor to call me when she got a chance. Maybe I'd get a crumb or two from her. Or maybe I was being overly optimistic. Or maybe she wouldn't call at all.

I then called Annie and told her we were open for business and I'd meet her at the brokerage. Venice put her dogs in her car and my Sassy went in mine and we headed to Rainbow Realty.
Once the babies were in the backyard, I walked around to the door that led into the room where the body was found. Venice

followed asking, "What are you doing back here?"

"I'm checking the door to see if it was jimmied and I'm looking for footprints. Also, anything the killer might have dropped."

"A footprint? How would you even know if it belonged to the killer? You're wasting your time Viv; don't you think the detective would have found it all by now? That's her job, yours is to sell real estate so how about we go into the office and work on that."

I was taking Cammie out to look at houses today. She was a nice person but nuts if you ask me. She said she was very sensitive to smells and wouldn't buy anything that had pressboard, glue, and the list went on. When I had an appointment with her, I didn't dare wear any scent or hair products that had a smell. She was also a germaphobe on top of everything else.

She turned to me and said, "I so appreciate you not using those dryer sheets, I can smell them a mile away and I don't smell them on you. They cause cancer you know."

"Thanks Cammy and you're so right, I would never use those cancerous things in my dryer."

Ha. I most definitely did use dryer sheets. Who doesn't? What a liar I was and a damned good one at that. Wasn't that an indication that she really couldn't smell every little thing?

I showed her a custom-built house that only had the highest quality materials. She liked it which was a shock. It was the first one she didn't have anything negative to say about. That was it for the day. The past month I must have showed her 30 houses. There weren't any that fit her smell criteria. Maybe she'd buy this one and I'd finally be rid of her. She was exhausting.

When I got back to the office, I got a call from the listing agent of the house I had shown Cammie. I assumed she wanted feedback and to know if my client was interested in purchasing it. Surprisingly, I was wrong.

"Hi Viv, it's Helen, the listing agent for the Deerpoint Road house you showed today."

"Hi Helen, my client said she would take it under consideration. I'll speak to her later or tomorrow and let you know."

"That's not why I'm calling. It seems the neighbors on either side of that house got a visit from your client. They both have wood burning fireplaces and she asked them, if she bought the house, would they please refrain from burning wood. The smell was offensive to her."

"Oh God, I'm so sorry. I had no idea she would do that. Please apologize to the neighbors and tell them it won't happen again." Unless she buys it, I thought. "I'll talk to her and let her know that was inappropriate. I can't believe she did that."

"It's not your fault. Is she some kind of fruitcake or what?"

Aahh, the confidentiality clause reared its ugly head. Instead of saying I thought she was certifiable I said, "She has allergies and some odors seem to trigger them."
We said our goodbyes. If Cammie wanted the house, I think both of us were professional enough to work a deal. The owners had moved on to another house in another state, they didn't care who bought it as long as they got their money. The bottom line is, a deal is a deal.

If the wood burning bothered her, maybe she'd be willing to have another heat source installed for the neighbors at her expense. Yeah, right.

At least the sellers had move out. I had a young couple last year who desperately wanted a cute two-story house I had shown them, but there were multiple offers coming in so they wrote quite a long letter and enclosed pictures of their children saying they wanted to raise their family there. That one letter made all the difference and even though my clients weren't the highest bidders the couple loved what they had to say and sold them the house.

When my couple moved in, they started a meth lab. No, they really did want to raise their family there. No meth labs.

I was through for the day and headed home with all three dogs in tow. Venice had a late showing so I took the kids home, and fed them. Then I put Betty and Mr. Snigglebottom to bed, tucking them in and, started reading them their bedtime story, "Big Dog, Little Dog." It was their favorite. They fell asleep before I got halfway into it.

CHAPTER SIX

The phone chirped and Det. Traynor's name appeared. I was still trying to find a distinct ring so I would know it was her but there were no ringtones that sounded like gunshots.

"Hi Detective, do you have news for me?"

"Now Ms. Murphy, you know it's an ongoing investigation, however, what are you doing right now?"

What's with the Ms. Murphy shit, I thought. She never called me anything but Viv or Vivianne. I'm sure there were other names she called me when I was out of earshot but sometimes ignorance is bliss.

"In answer to your question, I'm trying to decide whether to have the macaroni and cheese I made with chunks of lobster or a frozen pizza."

"I thought I'd drop by, I wanted to talk to you about something. In case you'd like to invite me for dinner I'd go with the mac and cheese."

"Sure, what time did you have in mind?"

"Now would be good, I'm in your driveway."

Springing into action I took out my casserole of macaroni with three different cheeses and chunks of lobster. If I do say so myself, it's delish. I threw it in the microwave. It was frozen solid.

Knocking at the door. Wow, she really was in the driveway.

"Hang on, I'm coming."

Bread, I forgot the bread. That too was frozen like an ice flow and it went in the oven. Everything frozen, I felt like Trader Joe's.

Why was Detective inviting herself to dinner? She was alarming me. Was I in trouble? Was there another murder? Was adding lobster to Mac and Cheese a crime?

"Before I open the door, are you here to arrest me for something?" I asked.

"Vivianne!" I heard her sigh through the door. "Have you done something you think I should arrest you for? You sound awfully guilty to me." And then she laughed.

I almost passed out. She actually *laughed.* I'd never even seen her crack a smile much less laugh.

I cracked the door open, trying, unsuccessfully, to keep Sassy behind me. She was jumping and barking madly. My cute little savage sentry.

"Are you going to ask me in or just stand there with your mouth open. And maybe you could shut that thing up."

Okay, cop or no cop, she wasn't going to talk that way to my Sassy.

"That *thing* is my beloved baby, Sassy and she's barking her greeting at you. If you pet her, she'll stop, if you have food, she'll be your BFF."

Gesturing for her to enter, she got the message, loud and clear. She squatted on the floor and gave Sassy tickles and rubs, capturing her heart completely by pulling a side of beef out of her pocket. Actually, a side of beef wouldn't fit in a pocket. I surreptitiously slipped Detective a treat for Sassy and they were now besties, or maybe beasties.

It appeared Detective also had some modicum of social grace, having brought a bottle of wine. Of course, that was also quite presumptive. What if I were busy, or not home? I got out cheese and crackers, opened the wine tilting it up to my lips and drank the entire bottle in one gulp. No, I didn't, but I wanted to. She could probably arrest me for CWI. That would be "Cooking While Intoxicated."

I handed her a glass of wine, it was nicely chilled, which I hoped she was also.

Det. Traynor looked around. I could see her police eyes going everywhere. Thankfully I'd had just enough time to hide the machine gun and the assault rifles. Let's not forget the Smith and Wesson with silencer attached. Those are all out in the shed. The Uzi was under the bed.

"I'm off duty, you can call me Gloria. And do not refer to me as Gloria when I'm on the job. If you do, I'll have to shoot you."

"No need for threats, I already knew that." What I hadn't known was that her name was Gloria.

"So, what do you want to discuss, Gloria? Since it's not official, I'm guessing it's not about the murder."

"No, it's not, and if I thought you were involved in any

way, I wouldn't be here. Just the same, I'd like to keep this as low key as possible. You can fill Venice in but nobody else at this time. We have to come to that agreement before we go on."

"I won't say a thing, except to Venice. Please, torture me no further, I can't stand the suspense."

"I'm interested in using your realtor services. I'm getting married soon, and it's time for a house. I live in an apartment right now."

"Congratulations Gloria, (I felt very uncomfortable calling her by her first name) who's the lucky guy? And when is the big day?"

"The lucky guy is a woman and we're getting married sometime in August. It's not going to be a huge affair, just immediate friends and family."

"I'm very happy for you. What are you and... what's your fiancé's name?"

"Erika,"

"I'd be happy to help, what are you and Erika looking for? What areas are you interested in? I'll also need to know your criteria, time frame and most importantly, price range."

"I've talked this over with Erika and we've decided on approximately 2000 sq. ft., she wants a large yard so we can get a dog, I guess the normal stuff. Three bedrooms, at least 2 bathrooms and a nice kitchen. Erika is the cook in the family, and a very good one at that. If you can gather up some listings, we're both free this weekend. That's if you're not going to throw anymore murders my way."

I saw she was still the smartass which made me feel better. I didn't know her at all unless she was investigating a crime. I was trying to wrap my mind around the Gloria thing.

"Very funny, Gloria." That was still not rolling off my tongue. Maybe the more I called her Gloria the less weird it would get.

"Vivianne, are you going to call me Gloria in every sentence you utter? You seem to be enthralled by my first name, stop saying it all the time, it's annoying. Now let's get down to business. We both live in Blainton and work in Silverhill. Erika is the dispatcher at the station. That's how we met. I thought maybe Park Hollow, that's not too far from work and maybe Silverhill. We've always liked those areas. We don't want to exceed $450K. And the sooner the better. Is this doable?"

"Sure is Gloria, Gloria, Gloria," I said laughing my fool head off. Gloria wasn't laughing.

"Does the station know you're getting married?"

"If you're asking if they know I'm gay, yes, they know. It would have been a little difficult to hide being as Erika works there too. Being Black and female was harder for them to accept. Being gay is a piece of cake. Given I'm now Detective/Investigator, they wouldn't dare fuck with me."

"Okay then. I'll get some homes ready and email them to you. Take a look and let me know what piques your interest. I may have to make appointments ahead of time if any of them are currently occupied." I was going to end that sentence with "Gloria," but I didn't think she'd find that amusing. I was hoping Erika had a better sense of humor. Gloria evidently did not. Unless she was hiding it and if so, she was doing a damned good job.

I was checking on the doneness of the food when my phone chirped. It was Venice. Hmmmm, my evil mind kicked in.

"Hey Ven, I was just going to call and see if you'd like to come over for a drink and my lobster macaroni and cheese. There's someone here I think you'd enjoy meeting."

"May I ask who? It's not a potential date, is it?"

"No, no, nothing like that, but it may be a potential client."

"Really? I guess that's all you're going to tell me. I'll be right there."

Even though we were the best of friends and were over each other's house frequently, we never opened the door and walked in. That was probably a New York habit. She knocked and I yelled, "It's open, come in."

She entered, gaze going straight to Gloria who was sitting on the couch, having her wine and eating cheese and crackers. Gloria was dressed in a bright blue blouse paired with black pants. The blue brought out her lovely brown complexion. She was a stunning woman. At least in civilian clothes. She was intimidating in her cop persona.

I could see Venice was a little confused. "Venice, I want to introduce you to Gloria, I believe you've already met?"

Venice took a second and then blurted out, "Gloria? Oh my God, is that you, Det. Traynor? I didn't even recognize you. I'm sorry, it's just that I've never seen you dressed like a person, I mean..."

Gloria laughed, "I do clean up nicely, don't I? And I'll tell you what I told Vivianne, you can call me Gloria outside of business but you will refer to me as Det. Traynor when I'm in a professional capacity."

"Of course, of course." Poor Venice was actually stammering, and turning redder by the second. This was so comical. Venice didn't know how to act, or what to do. That's how I felt too at first, but I was getting used to the Gloria side. Venice still needed a little time.

Handing Ven a glass of wine, I said, "Drink this, you look like you need it. And please, sit down and we'll explain everything." I could see the detective was enjoying showing off her other side and watching us squirm. She was an imposing figure but now, she seemed softer, nicer. Ah, the wolf dressed up in sheep's clothing, but I had no doubt the wolf was just below the surface.

I explained that Gloria would be house hunting for her upcoming marriage.

"Detective...I mean Gloria, that's wonderful news. Would you excuse me for five minutes, I just have to run across the street and get something. I'll be right back."

Gloria said, "Jesus, the both of you are very strange. Is this *strange* trait indigenous to all New Yorkers or is it mostly unique to you and Venice?"

"No," I said. "I think we'd probably be strange no matter where we came from. Maybe not. I don't know. Why do you think we're strange anyway?"

"Forget I said anything. How's dinner coming along?"

Excusing myself, I walked the five feet to the microwave and oven. It was starting to smell delicious. At that moment Venice poked her head in, a bottle of champagne in one hand and cupcakes in the other.

"I thought we might give a toast to Gloria, and I wasn't sure if you had dessert. If you do, no problem, I can leave the cupcakes here, they surely won't go to waste."

Champagne popped and poured we raised our glasses. Venice said, "To Gloria and her wedding."

I interrupted and whispered to Ven, "It's Erika, the bride is Erika."

"As I was saying, to Gloria and Erika and their new home."

We all clinked glasses and I put dinner on the table. Gloria ate with gusto so I imagine she liked it.

Gloria said, "This is really good, you'll have to give me the recipe for Erika. And Venice, thanks for the champagne toast, and cupcakes. I'm looking forward to having them for dessert, unless Viv, you have something else in mind?"

"The cupcakes will be fine. I forgot all about dessert so I'm glad Venice thought to bring them along with the bubbly."

I promised to send Gloria and Erika houses to view online. We'd meet up on Saturday for a day of showings. Before she left, I gave her some of the leftover mac, cheese, and lobster, and the rest of the cupcakes so she could share with Erika. We both waved goodbye as she backed up the driveway.

Venice turned to me, "Well that was a quite the shock, you

could have given me some warning, I didn't see that coming."

"I had a feeling she was gay," I said.

"I wasn't surprised she's gay, more that she looked human. Like one of us. With nice clothes on."

"Yeah, that was a surprise for me too. And she wants *us* to be her realtors. I'm excited to meet Erika. I bet she compliments Gloria in that she's a little more feminine. I'm so used to the hardass detective, you know?"

"I thought she looked lovely this evening," said Venice. "We got so caught up in the wedding, and the house hunting, we forgot to ask about the murder."

"I'm glad we didn't bring that up. I get the feeling she wants to keep them separate, the professional versus the personal. I think we should honor that. And God help us if we slip and call her Gloria when she's on a case. Our ass will be grass."

CHAPTER SEVEN

It was Wednesday, Venice's big night out. She left work early to get ready for Bryan who would be picking her up at 6 P.M. She asked him to arrive a little early as I had invited them \over for a drink. It would give me a chance to meet him and put my worries to bed. I hoped that was all that would be put to bed. STOP IT!!

I got home at 4 P.M., tidied up a little and put Sassy in the back yard while I quickly ran the vacuum over the place. I had the sliding glass doors open and just the screen partway closed so Sass could come back in when she wanted to. She didn't like the vacuum so I knew she would stay out until I finished.

I went out the front to do some leaf blowing which only took a few minutes. When I went back in the house, much to my surprise, there stood Birdie, the raccoon, in the middle of my living room.

Smiling I said, "Oh Birdie, have you decided to move in? I don't think Sassy will be very happy about this." I opened the back door and shooed her out.

When I first got Sassy, I let her know, once she came home with me, there were raccoons about. I trained her not to bark or bother with them unless they were actually IN the backyard. Rarely did they venture into Sassy's territory and I think, and don't tell Sassy this, it was Venice's dogs who kept them out. I was surprised that Birdie walked within a foot of my little dog and Sassy never even blinked an eye.

Venice and Bryan arrived at 5 P.M. She introduced us and I have to say, I kind of liked him, at least the way he looked, especially his height. They made a cute couple. Were they a couple now? This was only the second date after all.

Drinks in hand I said, "So Bryan, when are you planning on leaving for Arizona?" Daggers shot from Venice's eyes. Oops.

"I'm planning on going in about two weeks. I know it's going to be up there in temperature, but there is air conditioning. It'll be too hot for golf so I probably won't be playing until the fall. I don't know if Venice mentioned, my condo overlooks the golf course."

"Yes, I believe she did. Are you a good golfer?"

"I like to think I am. Even if I were a bad golfer I'd play. I enjoy the game and its good exercise. I still have to buy a golf cart; I'll probably get a used one." He did have a nice smile and, as Venice noticed, good teeth.

"Are you there for the whole summer then, or do you plan on coming back here to cool off."

Venice spoke up then and said, "Question and answer time is over Viv, we really have to get going to make the ferry."

I stood up and gave both a big hug. I thought a hug would make up for giving Bryan the third degree. I only asked a few questions and they barely had time to finish their wine. I looked at the table and realized they had left half of it. Uh oh, I think I was in trouble.

It was just 6 P.M. when the phone chirped. "Good Evening, it's Det. Traynor." Oh boy, she now had the cop hat on. "I have some news about the case."

"Yay, do you want to stop by then?"

"No, Vivianne, this is business, meet me at the *Copper Bottom*."

"Sure, just let me feed Sassy and Lola, but first I have to find Lola. She's the kitty and hides whenever anyone comes over. My friends all think she's my imaginary cat. Sort of like Harvey, the rabbit. Did you ever see that movie with James Stewart? Of course, I wasn't even born yet, but it's a classic."

"VIVIANNE, focus. The *Copper Bottom* at 7 P.M." And with that she hung up. Well, that was rude. I hope Erika talks more than Gloria does or it's going to be a long Saturday showing them houses.

Arriving at the *Copper Bottom*, right on time, I walked into the back where the mahogany bar spanned the length of the room. It was dark and subdued; I expected fog to roll in at any moment. The bartender was making conversation with a middle-aged man who was nursing a beer. It was Wednesday so it probably wouldn't get too crowded later on.

Det. Traynor was sitting in the corner, back to the room, facing the door. She too had a beer. I slid into the booth, said hello and signaled the barkeep for a white wine. The restaurant section was in the back so, aside from the man at the bar, we were alone.

"Have you solved the murder already?"

"Don't you think if I'd solved the crime, you'd know about it by now?

"There was a missing person report filed in Oregon and it turns out it's our girl."

"And?" Was I going to have to pry information out of Det. Traynor? She's the one who called me.

"Her name was Lauren Dinkel. She lived alone in a small apartment just outside of Portland, Oregon. Tyler Jenkins, her fiancé, drove up and made a positive ID."

"Dinkel," I said. "What a funny name. Sorry, I shouldn't be rude, after all the poor woman is dead. And now, she'll forever be a Dinkel."

Det. Traynor ignored me. She had a gift for that. She continued as if I had not spoken.

"I'm going to tell you the facts, most of them will go public any minute if they haven't already. I think journalists must have a sixth sense. They seem to know more than we do."

"Vivianne, this *has* to stay between us. Most of what I have to tell you will be in the news, but there are things the reporters don't know. I don't want them leaked, is that clear?

"Even if I wanted to leak something," I said, "I don't know any reporters. And if you didn't trust me, we wouldn't be sitting here now would we?"

"For once, you're right. For some unknown reason I do trust you and Venice too. You best not make me regret it. We're withholding certain information that only the murderer could know."

"Can I tell my mother?"

The Detective looked at me as if I'd lost my mind. Ah, but then she remembered meeting her briefly last year.

"Tell her what's already on the news. That's all. I'm glad I don't have to make that phone call. She's...formidable."

I laughed at that. I was glad to know everyone else was of the same mind. And they hadn't even lived with her.

"We got the autopsy report. There was Midazolam, which is a benzodiazepine, in her system, as well as Isoflurane. The theory is, a rag was saturated with the Isoflurane and put over her mouth so she inhaled it. When she was unconscious, he injected her with the Midazolam."

"Boy, I never heard of any of those things. I'm thinking she was already dead when he posed her at the brokerage, at least I hope so."

"Vivianne, I'm going to ask you not to interrupt me again. I want to lay out the facts. Then, you can talk, as I'm sure you will."

It was such a delight to hang out with Det. Traynor. I especially loved it when I thought she was asking a question and in truth, she was giving a command. She was reminding me of my mother. I best call Mom before she found out about this on the news.

"In answer to your question, Isoflurane is used as part of the anesthesia that's commonly used by veterinarians. Lauren was most likely dead before she was placed at Rainbow Realty. He either killed her on purpose or he accidentally overdosed her. We have no way of knowing."

Det. Traynor continued, "Last Saturday she was at the bridal salon at around 3:15 P.M. They all knew her; she'd been in, not just to buy the dress but for many fittings. The dress had to be altered to fit her small frame. She tried it on for the last time on Saturday. The staff said it was a perfect fit. They described Lauren as exuberant. While the saleswoman was carefully boxing the dress, Lauren told them her bachelorette party was that night at 7 P.M. She was very excited about it. The saleswoman also remembered her saying, 'This time next week I'll be Mrs. Tyler Jenkins.'"

"How sad," I said. Christ, now I was getting depressed. So many people affected. The groom, the parents, friends. The months of planning for their big day, all for nothing. All the love and excitement for a future that had crumbled in moment.

"Did I not just tell you to shut up until I finish? I can't afford emotions. I've got to concentrate and stay unbiased if I'm to find the murderer. When Lauren didn't show up for her bachelorette party, or answer her phone, her sister, Lorna, and her friend, Gail, went to her apartment. They knocked and when there was no answer, Lorna opened the door with the spare key Lauren had given her. The apartment is very small; one bedroom, one bathroom. Everything was as it should be but no Lauren. They were just about to leave when Gail went back to the bedroom and opened the only closet. No bridal gown.

"At that point they probably should have alerted the authorities but they waited, hoping Lauren would show up. They finally called Tyler and he told them he hadn't heard from her. He tried calling her too.

"They waited another hour and Tyler called the police. Lorna and Tyler went down to the station to file a missing person report. In real life, you don't have to wait 24 hours.

"Mostly everyone's whereabouts were accounted for. They were either at the bachelor or bachelorette party.

"We questioned Tyler, not as a suspect but for any information that might help us in the investigation."

He told us the following and she handed over a typed transcript. I gathered this was only what she was willing to share. It wasn't the original transcript, rather a condensed one.

Tyler Jenkins:

"About a year ago, when we were just dating, Lauren mentioned she thought someone was watching her. She didn't want to make it a big deal because she couldn't be sure. Lauren was very level-headed. She wasn't prone to dramatics or paranoia. I wanted to call the police but she said it wasn't necessary. She had no proof, and it was just a feeling, maybe even imagining it.

"After we were engaged, she never mentioned it again. When I asked her she said that feeling was gone. We put the whole thing behind us, you know, busy with the wedding and all.

Det. Traynor:

"What do you think Tyler? Do you think she was imagining a stalker?

Tyler Jenkins:

"I didn't know what to think. I told you, Lauren wasn't like that, where she'd make something up. I was even going to hire a private detective but then it stopped, so I didn't do anything. I guess I should have."

Det. Traynor:

"What happened when you reported her missing?"

Tyler Jenkins:

"The police took all the information down but I don't

think they were too concerned. I mean, she wasn't gone even a day yet. We gave them a picture of her and left. We had already called the hospital, there's only the one in the area. No Lauren. I have a copy of the police report if you need it."

"We cancelled the parties but told the guests to stay. It was all paid for anyway. Me, Lorna, Gail, my brother, Chris, and my best friend, Paulie, all drove around looking for her car. We went everywhere. Lauren's parents and mine were at my house waiting to hear if we found her. As the minutes turned into hours, we were out of ideas. We went home to wait. I kept thinking she'd call, that there would be a reason for all of this. It would be silly, and we'd laugh about it.

"By morning I was out of my mind. I called the police station again. Maybe now that it was the next day, they'd take it more seriously and do something."

Det. Traynor:
        "I spoke to the officer on duty, the one at the station who took down all your information. He sent a BOLO out to all of Oregon and the surrounding states. They also tried to track the GPS in her phone but got no signal. It was either off or destroyed. I wanted you to know that the police did act on your missing report immediately."

That was about the gist of it all, or at least what was in the transcripts Detective allowed me to see. There were more, interviews with family and friends. All the people who were invited to the parties were questioned. The area where she disappeared was canvased but nobody saw or heard anything. Very frustrating.

"I appreciate you telling me this Det. Traynor? And what's a BOLO?"

"BOLO is an acronym for 'Be On The Lookout.' As for why I'm telling you Vivianne, I thought you and Venice might give me a civilian's perspective on this case. So far, we're getting nowhere. By the way, where is Venice?"

I had forgotten Venice was on her date but thanks to the detective it slammed back home. "She's out for the evening with a gentleman friend."

"You couldn't just say she's on a date? God Vivianne, sometimes you're just...weird. I want you to think about what I've told you and maybe you can come up with something new. It's highly unlikely, but maybe we missed something."

"Will you be having a bachelorette party, Detective?"

"ME?! I will kill the first person who even thinks of doing that. So, the answer is unequivocally, NO.

"Here are some more things to think about. The wedding gown she was found in was the one she had picked up at the bridal salon. It was her gown. We believe she was abducted in the parking lot of the salon. The salon is the last place anyone saw her alive. It would have been easy for the perp to knock her out and throw her in the car. One thing that isn't known is that a button from her gown was missing, and the ring on her finger wasn't' the engagement ring Tyler had given her.

"I received a call from the Oregon police, and they found Lauren's car, parked in a vacant lot that was not visible from the road. He could have transferred her into his car and then taken her car, parked it and walked back to his own vehicle. The police investigated, but since some time had passed and it had rained, they found no footprints or anything else."

"Thanks for trusting me with this Det. Traynor. I'll run this by Venice and we'll brainstorm. Who knows, you may be right and we'll think of something, it's worth a try.

"Maybe the perp, I love saying that word, had his car parked in the vacant lot. When he put Lauren in her car, he drove it to the lot where he transferred her to his car. Maybe he gave her a shot of those drugs then because the ride from there to here would have been about three hours and he wouldn't have wanted her to wake up midway."

"That's the vein we were thinking in. You've got a good mind for this Vivianne."

After I mentally congratulated myself, I looked at the clock over the bar and it was 8 P.M. already. People were starting to wander in.

Time flies when you're having fun. We wrapped things up and I left to get home to the children.

The sun, streaming through my bedroom window, woke me up. I had forgotten the blackout shade. I hate light in the morning. Grudgingly I got out of bed, slipped my feet into my pink bunny slippers, and hopped to the kitchen to put coffee on. My brain was slowly awakening. Ah HA, Venice! I wondered if she was home alone. I would absolutely not call her.

Coffee in hand, I let the dogs out and walked up to the road in my robe and pajamas and peeked down Venice's driveway to see if Bryan's car was there. I couldn't see around the bushes, so I crept down just enough to see there was no car. A sigh of relief. "Casing the joint, lady?" Christ, I just about wet my penguin jammies.

"Jesus, Venice, you scared the shit out of me. Why did you do that?"

"I might ask you why you're in your nightclothes, in my driveway?"

"Um…I was making sure you were home so I could bring you Betty and Mr. Snigglebottom."

"I see," said Venice. "Did you ever hear of calling? I would think that easier than running around in your pajamas. That sounds like a pretty flimsy excuse for spying."

"I was not spying, I was looking for baked goods," I lied.

Venice started laughing. "No Vivianne, there are not, nor have there ever been, baked goods at the top of my driveway. Bryan isn't here, Ms. Nosey body. Really! What would you have done if his car was here?"

"I would have slunk back to my house and pouted for an hour. Then I would have called you. Then I would have asked for baked goods. Speaking of which, do you have any? Baked goods, that is? And what the hell are you doing on the road. And I'm not nosey, I simply have an inquiring mind."

"I just walked down to get my mail. I saw you sneaking around and thought I'd quietly come up behind you and I got just the reaction I was hoping for. You jumped a foot," and she started laughing all over again. "Why don't you get the dogs and come down, I have frozen scones I'll throw in the microwave. I suppose you want a blow-by-blow description of everything we did last night?"

"I'll be right over with the children. I'm sure they've

missed you."

Once we got the animals settled down and coffee with scones in hand, I said, "Your date story can wait, I have to tell you about *my* date first."

"Your date? What are you talking about? You didn't have a date last night. You're not seeing John until Friday. Are you cheating on him already?"

"Nah, I was with...*Drum Roll*, are you ready...DET. TRAYNOR!"

"What happened to 'Gloria?'

"She was a cop last night so I guess I can't really call it a date. It was strictly professional. But I found out a lot more about the *Bridal Murder*. And, get this, she trusts us. You and me. She wanted to get a new slant the case, from *us*."

"Oh. But she doesn't want you actively involved, does she?"

"No, no, she wanted to pick our brains, that's all. See if we could come up with something they've missed." I bit into my second scone. Yumalicious.

"Crap, I forgot to call my mother."

"Why don't you do that now while I clean up and then we can have more coffee and you can fill me in. This must be good, you never even asked about my date last night."

"Don't you worry about that. I have NOT forgotten. Don't even think you're going to skate by."

My phone played "The Bitch is Back." Venice glanced over

her shoulder at me and said, "Now you're in for it. Should've called her first."

"Hi Mom, I was just about to call you."

"Don't give me that shit, Vivianne, you always say that when I call first, which is most of the time."

I looked at Venice and rolled my eyes. So much so that they fell out of my head and bounced all over the floor like little rubber balls. The dogs went to fetch. Ugh.

"I swear, I was calling almost at the very minute you called me. Here, ask Venice." I held the phone out signaling that she should say something on my behalf.

"Hi Tess, for once Vivianne is telling the truth. You know *I* wouldn't lie to you."

"The two of you are thicker than thieves. Let's get to it, Vivianne. What the hell is going on there? Must you always be in the middle of murders? I hope you've called that Detective, whatever her name is. And did you have the alarms installed? I was also calling to get an update and talk about times and flights for your arrival."

"I've spoken to Kat, and she's going to pick me up at JFK, on June 1st at 10 P.M. You're not having surgery until the 4th so it'll give us plenty of time to do whatever you want."

"I could have picked you up you know."

"Yes, I know that, but given it's at night you would have had to forgo your wine time."

That shut her up fast.

"Since you made plans for Kat to get you, I don't want to

interfere."

I had to take deep breaths after that statement. She didn't want to interfere? Sometimes I didn't know if she was delusional or what.

She continued talking, "But the next time run it by me first.

"I'm sure you know more about the murder than you're telling me. It did happen at your place of business after all."

"I quickly told her a little of what the detective told me last night, but that was already in the news. "Detective Traynor told me she'd let me know if there are any updates. And yes, I called the security company and they're installing cameras and alarms next week. That's the earliest appointment they have and they come highly recommended."

That seemed to appease her and thankfully there were no more orders in the guise of requests. We hung up. I always breathed a sigh of relief when I was done with her. I wasn't even lying about the alarm people. Venice and I didn't think it necessary to alarm our homes, but Mom didn't need to know that. She never asked about our houses so I didn't even have to lie. Besides, how could that murder be connected to us in any way?

"Now," I said to Venice. "About your date."

"I must say, I regret agreeing to drinks at your house with Bryan. First of all, I wanted to put duct tape over your mouth with all your questions. I was mortified. You sounded like an overly protective father, minus the shotgun."

"Well, that's just not true. I certainly do not look like a man, and I'm way too young to be your parent."

"Then stop acting like one."

"Let's not bicker. I'm sorry, okay? Now tell me all."

"Bryan actually found you endearing and funny. And my dogs liked him too so that's saying something. Did I forget to mention I'm also fond of him?"

I choked back a long sigh.

"I heard that," said Venice. "We went to dinner at a lovely place by Pike's Place market, a little hole in the wall that had a ton of ambiance and delicious food. Then we took a cab to the theater. It was a pleasant surprise to find out it wasn't a play we were seeing; it was the ballet. He held my hand the whole time."

I gagged.

"When the ballet was over, we caught the ferry back because the last ferry leaves at 1 A.M. Did you know that?"

"Yes Venice, I know the ferry schedule. So, what else do you have for me?"

She continued, "We talked about our marriages. When he first married Cynthia, they lived in Oregon and then they moved up here for his business. That's why she went back to Oregon after the divorce. She had kids by a previous marriage. Bryan was younger then, weren't we all, and he said he decided he wanted a family. And she came with one. Sounds kind of odd to me. What kind of man wants to settle down with a bunch of children who aren't his?"

"I agree. It seems a bit convenient, like he went to Walmart and purchased a ready-made family. So, none of the kids are his?"

"Seems not. And the father of the kids was a deadbeat and has been in and out of rehab. Never contributed one cent for the kids but once Bryan was in the picture, he supported them all. The father never did show up to claim them or see them and they were young enough not to care. As time passed, they probably just thought their Dad was Bryan, never having any contact with their real father."

I asked, "So where are you headed in this relationship now? He's moving, what comes next?"

"I honestly don't know. And you do *not* have to worry, moving for me isn't in the picture but I may go down to visit him on occasion. Let's wait and see. I'll probably see him one last time before he leaves."

CHAPTER EIGHT

It was Friday and I was looking forward to my tine with John tonight. He called last night and, since he'd been in New York and hadn't heard, I filled him in on the *Bridal Murder*.

It was time to start preparing for my date, it was already 10 A.M. John would be picking me up in just nine hours. I stood in my closet for a long time. This was especially difficult, given I didn't have a walk-in closet.

I finally decided on a red wrap dress which would be paired with my black rhinestone heels and my black Gucci purse. It was the perfect outfit for an upscale restaurant. He had asked me if I wanted to go to the theatre after dinner or if that would be too much? The theatre it was. I didn't even care what we were seeing.

He picked me up right on time. I liked that. He brought flowers, I liked that too. I can't tell you how long it's been since a man brought me flowers. No, really, I have no idea when that would have been. Maybe 1873? I invited him in because Sassy was going out of her mind by now. I let him coo at her, while I put the flowers in a vase. I asked if he'd like a drink but he said no, we could have one in the car. Uh oh, Red flag. Drinking while driving is a no-no and something I would not tolerate. After all, he was responsible for me while in the vehicle, and for the duration of our date too.

Walking out, the first thing I noticed was a big, beautiful hunk of machinery. John told me it was a 2014 Bentley Mulsanne. I guess that was ritzy, I didn't know that much about cars, all I knew was that it was impressive.

Behind the wheel was a black clad chauffeur, complete with hat. It was Bitterman from the movie, Arthur. We got in the back and I literally sank into the cushions. Was I really in an automobile? This was pure decadence. The upholstery was filled with duck down, there was a full bar, tables that folded down and a privacy curtain. Wow, even if I never had another date again, I would remember this forever. And we could both drink while driving. The red flag flew away.

We sipped champagne while eating delicate little canapés. I asked him if I could see his financial statement. Never mind, I wouldn't have time to read it, it was probably 1,000 pages long. Hmmm, was he up there with Bill Gates? Did he know Bill Gates? Would it be crass to ask? I decided it would, but I bet he knew Warren Buffet.

Over filet mignon paired with lobster tails, (at the restaurant, not in the car) he told me he descended from the Astor family, one of the first aristocrats in the country. His mother married down, to Jonathon Berkman who was very wealthy but not old money. I never could understand Old versus New money. I'd take either one. Money is, after all, money.

"My name full name is John Astor Berkman. Frankly, the family was rather stuffy and staid. I started my own business after college, and went into finance. Enough about me, let's talk about you."

I told him how I met Venice and all about the start-up of Rainbow Realty.

After dinner we headed for the theatre and I was pleasantly surprised that we had the best seats to the play, *Hamilton*.

By the time we headed home, I was tired, it was well past my bedtime. The car was so comfy, I almost fell asleep. Not good to fall asleep on the first date. Maybe the third.

John declined an after-dinner drink that was offered when he dropped me off. I think he knew I was done in. I thanked him for a most wonderful evening and, with a peck on the cheek he was gone. Sassy was at Ven's house and it was too late to pick her up, so I'd see her in the morning.

I slept like the dead. I knew Venice would be eager to hear all about my night but, it was Saturday and I was off to meet Gloria and her fiancé Erika at the first house they wanted to see. And, Venice had a listing interview so my dating extravaganza would have to wait.

Erika arrived, and extended her hand, "Hi, I'm Erika, so good to meet you. Glo has told me so much about you."

Glo??? Where are the smelling salts when you need them?

"I can only imagine what she's told you. I just want to say, it's not true. And, I hear congratulations are in order."

"Thank you. And if Glo had said anything bad I wouldn't tell you, but she didn't, I promise."

Gloria said, "As you can see, Erika is the nice one."

Erika was the cute one too. A head full of blond curls and an effervescent personality and she was only around 5'5" while Gloria was at least 5'10". They looked good together.

I was thrilled with Erika. I was so hoping she was the opposite of Gloria in that there would be a little levity to her, and there was. Gloria was too serious but then I usually met up with her at a crime scene. Not exactly the venue to showcase a sense of humor. I liked Erika immediately, she was delightful and "Glo" was a lucky woman.

We were in Kingsville, the only house I was showing there. It was too good to pass up even though I knew they were hoping for Port Hollow, which would be closer to work.

I held the door open for them and in we went. "I'm glad you decided to see this place. I know it's a little further out but it just came on the market and it's an estate sale."

Erika asked, "What's an estate sale? Is that a good thing?"

"In my experience it's usually very good. The heirs aren't as emotional about the place, they want to sell it as fast as they can to reap the proceeds, and they don't want to get stuck paying taxes, upkeep, etc. The listing agent told me they live out of town so that makes it even better. And the price is excellent. I wouldn't be surprised if there's more than one offer on it by end of day."

Gloria said, "It is a bit far, but I like the house. What do you think, Sweetie?"

Boy oh boy, I don't know how much more of this I could stand. Glo and now Sweetie? I was having a hard time separating the Detective from the Gloria. I'd only known Gloria as Det. Traynor for so long and didn't know anything about her outside of the job. I liked this new person. She was actually nice and you could see how much she loved Erika.

I tried very hard to eradicate the Detective from my brain and just let the Gloria persona take over. I succeeded, mostly. "Let me show you the rest of it before you make any decisions."

It had 3 bedrooms, and 3.75 bathrooms. The .75 meant it had everything but a bathtub. The bonus was the finished basement with a propane stove for heat. The floor down there was tile, upstairs it was all hardwood, except for the bedrooms which had brand new carpeting. The house wasn't that old, it was built in 2010 and it had been well taken care of. It was a two story with one bedroom on the main floor and the other two upstairs.

When we were done seeing the inside, Erika said, "I think this is a real possibility. Yes, it's a bit of a trek to work but it's so private and not a thing would have to be done with it. I especially love the kitchen. Lots of room and counter space."

"Wait until you see the outside," I said. I opened the sliders and we stepped onto a covered patio with a grill. It was on almost an acre of land and it was fairly level. You could just make out the mountains, it had what we call a "peek-a-view." Tiny but there.

Gloria's eyes lit up. "I love this. We could grill out here most of the year. Does the grill come with the house?"

"Yes, it does. It was too big and heavy to bother with so they said to leave it here."

"Erika, can you see us here? There's no fence but we could certainly have one put up, and then you can have your dog. What's the price on this piece of heaven?"

"You're not going to believe this but it's only $375,000."

Gloria said, "Can you give us a minute please?"

I walked out to my car so they could talk privately. This house really was a gem. The kitchen was a nice size for Erika and I could see her happily cooking away. It had grey appliances; I forget what color they call that. They looked fairly new. The refrigerator was the size of my bathroom. The cabinets were good but not my taste and the countertops were granite which also isn't my favorite. At this price they could always make some changes. Oh, and there was a pantry off to the side.

Gloria signaled me to come back in. "We've decided we'd like to put an offer in at $395,000. Do you think that's a good idea, or should we go higher?"

I think we should give it a try. We're the first ones to see it and the offer is a good one so it's very possible they'll take it. Are you sure you don't want to look at more houses? This is only the first one you've seen."

Erika said, "Actually, we've seen plenty. We've been going to open houses for about six months now. We weren't ready to buy then and Glo wanted to use you and Venice when we did. This is the nicest house we've viewed that ticks off all our boxes and then some. Yes, we're sure. Erika gave me a big hug. Gloria wasn't quite as effusive but I could tell she was pleased.

They came back to the office with me and waited until I wrote up the offer. I emailed it to the listing agent and then called her to make sure she received it. She said she'd get back to me, she had to call the heirs, there were three, and present it to them.

It was still early, only 10 A.M. I called and cancelled the other viewings we had scheduled. "Why don't we go to breakfast? My treat," I offered.

Gloria said, "Sure, it'll be a diversion while we wait, you hungry, Erika?"

"I could go for breakfast, we only had toast this morning," said Erika. "And, Vivianne *is* paying," she said with a big grin. "After all, we're almost home owners, we have to watch every penny."

We were almost finished eating when my phone chirped. It was the listing agent. I held up my crossed fingers. We all stopped breathing. I listened for about two minutes that seemed to stretch out to two hours. I said goodbye and clicked off. Remember when we used to say "I hung up?" I'm old.

I put on my solemn face and said, "There is one thing you have to know about the house. It seems the old lady who lived there wrote in her will that whoever bought it had to be warned not to put any holes in the walls because the angels would get out. The angels watch over the house you see. Other than that, IT'S YOURS."

Erika was deliriously happy. Gloria tried to be more stoic but failed miserably and they were both grinning like Cheshire cats. I was too. It sure was a *feel-good* moment and moments like that don't happen often enough in this business. They promised they would be careful of holes in the walls.

I paid the bill and they gave me their earnest money check for $5,000. I told them I'd call later with the time and date for the inspection. I was headed to the title company with their check, which would be held in an escrow account and would go towards their costs at closing. Oh, wait, it was Saturday, the title company was closed until Monday.

I decided to go into Silverhill anyway and called to see if our accountant was available. I could stop in and catch up with *Rainbow's* finances.

I called Venice to bring her up to date. "Hi, where are you?" I asked.

"I just finished up the listing presentation here in Silverhill. Why?"

"I'm here in Silverhill too, why don't we meet for lunch at Goldens." Goldens was a brewery/sports bar. I drank a good IPA every now and then but given it made me burp, pee, and full, I'd rather bourbon or wine. I don't particularly like sports either. But the place was always lively with the constant hum of conversation, laughter, and a few HOORAYS when a team did something good. A lot of GOBs frequented the place. *Good Ole Boys.*

I walked in and Venice was already seated. She had snagged a coveted booth in the bar. The bar was preferable because you could seat yourself, whereas the other areas you had to wait for a table. She was waving frantically; I thought her arm was going airborne any minute.

Venice said, "Hey, I'm glad you called. What brings you to Silverhill?"

"I dropped in on Morris to see where we are financially, and it seems we're doing very well. I'll fill you in later.

"I have exciting news. Gloria and Erika had an offer accepted this morning on a house in Kingsville. It's perfect for them and they were lucky to get it even though they offered $20,000 over asking. I'm thrilled for them."

"That was fast, did you only show them that one house?"

"It was love at first sight. They've been going to open houses for months so it's not like they don't know what's out there."

My phone chimed. Chimes signaled a text. I had sent the offer in immediately, when we were in the restaurant. Gloria and Erika electronically signed the contract and I just got it back with the seller's signatures. It was official and I sent it on to them.

"So, what's Gloria like when she's exuberant? I don't know if I've ever even heard her laugh."

"It was funny because Erika was jumping all over the place, she was so happy, and I could see Gloria kind of bursting at the seams but she wasn't about to lose her big bad cop façade. I could see it cracking though. Just a little bit, and that's saying a lot since she doesn't do 'Exuberant.' They're so cute together, or rather Erika is cute. I think she brings the light heartedness to the relationship, and that balances Gloria. You can't be a tight ass every minute or you'll get cramps in your butt.

"How was your listing appointment?" I asked.

"Let's order drinks and I'll tell you. It was...interesting," said Venice.

While enjoying our wine and coconut shrimp Venice told me her listing story.

"My interview was with Mr. Novak, a nice old man. He said his wife had died and the house was too big for just him and he couldn't keep it up the way the missus had. His words, not mine. He thought he might want a condo, it's much less work and the association is responsible for the grounds and upkeep.

"I got there at 10A.M. and rang the bell. I could hear quite a commotion on the other side of the door and hoped, if he had dogs, they were friendly. Finally, the door opened, and there stood two little multi colored piggies."

"Pigs, like in oink, oink?"

"Yeah, the little pot-bellied ones. They're so sweet, but by the time I left I told myself I would never have them as pets. They never shut up. Snort, snort, snort, the entire time. That would drive me crazy. I explained that it would be best if the animals were gone for showings."

He said, "No problem, they go everywhere with me. We'll take a ride to the park. I have leashes for them and they enjoy a good walk. We sure do get a lot of attention. That's my social time too. I get lonely now that my dear Ethel is gone. We were married almost fifty years."

"I felt sad for him. Maybe, after his house sells, we can have him over for dinner. How do you think the dogs would do with the pigs?" asked Venice.

"I read somewhere that many dog breeds don't get along well with pigs but we could try it with supervision. I think Betty would definitely get along, she's a border collie, she may think she's supposed to herd them. I don't know about Sassy or Mr. Snigglebottom."

"Just a thought," she said. "He showed me their crates in their very own room, complete with children's furniture for the little oinkers. They even had their own beds. And they were housebroken.

"I left him with my listing package and told him to get

back to me if he wanted to list it with Rainbow Realty, the BEST realty in the whole world. I also broke the news that condos wouldn't allow pigs. Now he's thinking of buying a smaller house. He told me he'd only need two bedrooms, one for the pigs and one for himself and the money he'd save by living in a smaller space would allow him to hire a housekeeper and gardener. Problem solved.

"After that I went over to the mall to shop which is a good thing, otherwise I wouldn't be here having lunch with you. Oh, I put Sassy back in your house too."

Venice asked, "Are you ready for your New York visit? I know you don't want to go but you have to so you may as well make the best of the situation. Maybe you, Kat and Nellie could do something in the city since that's where the hospital is. You could even ask Wes to join you."

"Have you lost your mind? Visiting hours are ALL DAY LONG, and I'm sure Mom will want us there ALL DAY LONG. I'm hoping she'll let us go out for lunch. Wes can take us, his treat. There's a great place on the corner that's been there almost a hundred years and they make the most delicious Bloody Mary and the food is superb. Pub food, hamburgers, fries and they have daily specials. Nellie will love eating, we'll love the Bloody Mary's', even Kat who doesn't drink much. This ordeal may make an alcoholic out of her yet."

My last real estate duty was Gloria and Erika's house inspection. Gloria would be meeting me, Erika was working. Gloria was probably the best of the two to be there for the inspection. After all, she was a detective. They inspect all the time.

We met Joe, the inspector, at the house at 11 A.M. that Monday. It took a few hours but the prognosis was pretty good. He'd have the report to us by tomorrow. I wanted to put this to bed before my New York trip.

The next day I received the report as did Gloria and Erika. Erika called to tell me they were going to discuss it tonight and would give me a call.

I was almost out the office door when my phone chirped. It was Gloria, so I went back into my office to bring up the report. I figured that's what she was calling about.

"Hi Vivianne, it's Gloria. Erika is on speaker with me. We've looked the report over and there are some things that are a concern to us. There are no smoke or carbon monoxide detectors. The main bathroom has a small leak under the sink and there seems to be a small amount of mold in the attic. The inspector has suggested we get in a mold expert to evaluate it. He said it may be nothing and an easy fix, but it has to be done. That's about it. The other stuff is minor and we can deal with it. What do you think?"

"I think you're absolutely right. With all the rain and damp weather we have here, it's a breeding ground for mold growth. That's why I have a mold remediation team I use. I can call them and they'll let us know what has to be done, not only to remove it, but to prevent it from happening again."

I was lucky to get my mold experts over the next day. Thankfully, it wasn't black mold. The roof was fairly new and they think it may have had a small leak in that part of the attic before it was replaced. They would remove the mold and coat the area for prevention.

The sellers didn't have a problem with any of our concerns and they would be taken care of before closing. Joe would reinspect and sign off on the repairs. Hooray.

Maybe Gloria liked me better now. Maybe not.

CHAPTER NINE

The dire day dawned. Venice was picking me up momentarily to take me to the Airporter which would deliver me to the airport two hours before boarding. If you didn't catch the earlier bus you ran the risk of being late so it was worth the wait at the airport.

I was treating myself to first class, round trip. If I had to go, and I did, at least I could do so in comfort. I hated coach; it was like squeezing into a cattle car. I always had an aisle seat so when people were boarding, getting hit with backpacks was unavoidable. In first class I didn't have to worry about that.

I hugged Venice goodbye. I sure was going to miss being home and I hadn't even left yet.

I arrived at the airport with plenty of time to spare. When it was time to board, first class was the first to be seated. Once seated, I was asked what I would like to drink. And the coach passengers were still boarding. Champagne seemed appropriate. Hmmm, maybe the seat next to me would remain vacant and I'd have the row all to myself.

Just when I thought I was home free, here came my seatmate. A woman, in her thirties, attractive, slim, and light brown hair streaked with golden highlights. When she came to my row, she extended her hand saying, "Hi, I'm Georgia, I'll be sharing the flight with you." Why was she introducing herself? I shook and said, "I'm Vivianne, and I'm not going to be sharing anything with you." Okay, I just told her my name.

I opened my magazine hoping she'd see I was busy and leave me alone. Not happening. She had a newspaper that she must have bought at the kiosk. She pointed at the small article on the bottom of the front page. I looked. It was about the bridal murder.

"Could I see that a minute?" I asked.

"Sure," she said, handing it over to me. "I'm following the murder because I knew her." She said this with a look of importance. Why do people do that, feel they're part of something when they're not. However, my ears perked up.

"Really?" "Did you know her well?'

"No," she said. "I mean, I knew her from work. We'd sometimes all go out to the bar on Friday nights but that was about it."

I leaned over and whispered, "You know, she was found at my brokerage."
"NO! How awful, are you the one who found her?"

"My office manager found her. What do you think happened? Do you have any ideas?" I asked her.

Now I was talking in a conspiratorial tone. I'd become best friends with Georgia if need be.

"Just between us, she was seeing a married man."

Just then more champagne came along with menus for dinner. This first class was new to Georgia. She was impressed with everything. Her company was flying her to New York for a convention. As soon as the flight attendant left, I continued.

"Why do you say she was seeing a married man? When was this?"

"It was over a year ago; I forget exactly when. We went out for drinks one night and she got a little hammered. That's when she opened up about Mr. Married. She never told me his name. She said they'd meet out of town so he wouldn't run the risk of anyone seeing them. She would pay for the room and wait for him. She always asked for a room in the back so nobody would see their cars. They were very careful.

"She said he promised to leave his wife, he was waiting for the right time. Huh, that's what they all say and it rarely happens, you know what I mean?"

"She fell for the oldest line in the world," I said. "Men never leave their wives, even if they want to. Divorce is expensive. Did she confide anything else?"

"After that night she never went out with the gang from work again until much later. I don't even know if she remembered what she told me. Then, about three months later she did join us for our Friday fun night. That's what we used to call it. I could tell she was upset over something so we got a table away from the crowd. Again, she was drinking a few more than she should. Me, I don't like to be drunk so I watch it when I'm out. She asked me if she could trust me. I told her sure, and reminded her about what she had already told me and that I never said a word to anyone. And, I didn't. I'm not a gossip. Now that she's gone, I'm assuming it's not gossip."

"No, it's only gossip if the person is alive." I was lying. Gossip is gossip whether the gossipee is alive or dead. "Did you tell anyone this? The police maybe?"

"Hell no. I switched jobs and we lost touch. I hadn't seen her for over a year when she was killed. I still can't believe it. I never knew someone who was murdered.

"That Friday when we went out, she said Mr. Married told her he was now free to be with her. She had just met her guy; I'm guessing he's the onewho she eventually got engaged to and she told the married one good-bye."

Taking a sip of my drink and trying to appear nonchalant I asked, "How did that go? Mr. Married must have been pissed." Oh God, she had me referring to him as Mr. Married too.

"She told me that after she told him, he was really upset and she ran out of the motel, got in her car and left. She said she felt awful but it was too late for them. She did end up engaged to the new guy so I'm pretty sure she was telling me the truth. I don't know anything more than that. She called it a night so I couldn't question her anymore. And, as I said, I left for greener pastures and I never saw her again.

Shit, just when I was getting close. Close to what, I had no idea but this was big. He could be the murderer. I asked, "Are you still living in Oregon?"

"No, I got promoted at the pharmaceutical company I work for and moved to Washington."

We spent the next hour eating, drinking and chatting. I got her name, email and even her cell number. I gave her my business card, who knows, she might want to buy a house. I wanted her to think of me as her new friend, just in case she remembered something about Lauren's murder. I didn't see how something that happened so long ago would be relevant, but it was more information than we had. I would tell the detective and leave it up to her to figure out.

We arrived in New York and I gave Georgia a list of places she might enjoy seeing while she was there and said goodbye.

My sister and Nells were waiting for me in the terminal. I was so glad to see them I practically hugged them to death.

"Mom took a nap," said Kat, "so she'd be awake when you arrived. Lucky you. Actually, you are lucky, she seems to be in a good mood."

"Give it five minutes after I get there. Then let's see if she's still in a good mood."

"Oh, Auntie V, she's not that bad."

"Auntie V?" Is this my new name? I think I like it, Niecy Nell."

"And I like your new name for me. I love alliterations."

"Have you started college you little smarty?"

"Auntie V, you're so funny. I've known what alliterations are for years. At school they call me Nacho Nellie because I always bring a bag of nachos with me for lunch, so I have an alliterative nickname too."

We were now at my mother's house. Kat and Nellie walked up to the door. Kat looked back and I was on the sidewalk, just standing there.

"You do know Mom can probably see you?"

I ran up the walkway. Wes opened the door and I was forced to enter the den of the devil. The queen was ensconced on her jewel studded throne. Okay, she was in her recliner. I bent down to give her a peck on the cheek.

"What's that smell?" she asked, wrinkling her nose.

Hmmm, that didn't even take thirty seconds. I was hoping for that five minutes.

"Sorry Mom, I put my Green Tea scent on this morning. I didn't think you'd still be able to smell it all this time later. It's not overpowering, is it?"

Hadn't I warned myself, never ask a question of my mother unless it had something to do with her? I guess not.

"It isn't now but if I can still smell it then I'm sure it was overpowering when you put it on. How was your flight?"

Leaving out my conversation with Georgia, I told her the flight was excellent and since I was in first class, I even had a decent steak dinner.

"I hope you haven't ruined your appetite. I have a surprise."

Wes had made a pitcher of Pisco sours and Mom had set out a huge plate of homemade hors d'oeuvres They were my favorites, soft taco shells wrapped around cream cheese mixed with her secret ingredients. I could taste chives, everything else in it was a mystery, and this was paired with her homemade salsa. Yum. There were lots of other goodies. We weren't going to bed hungry. It was close to 11 P.M. but I was still on Pacific Standard Time which would make my body clock 8 P.M. I guess I'd just have to drink the sours until I was tired.

Mom had given Kat and I her and Wes's room because it had two single beds, the smaller guest room was for Nellie and her and Wes slept in the other guest room in the queen bed. Ha ha, a queen for a queen.

Nellie joined Kat and I in the big bedroom after Mom and Wes had retied. "Do you think Grammy is going to be okay?" she asked.

"Grammy is too ornery to die, she'll live to torment us all. Really, she's strong and I'm sure she'll pull through brilliantly."

Of course, I wasn't sure of anything but I really did think my Mom would do fine. It would be a grueling recovery though. After all, it *was* open heart surgery.

The next day we were all on our best behavior. We went to Uncle Li's restaurant which was a fun place to eat. The theme was Polynesian but the owners were Chinese. The food was a mix of both cultures and excellent. We ordered a pupu platter which consists of at least six appetizers on a Lazy Susan so you could spin it around and pick out what you wanted. I could have just had that as a meal. That is, if I didn't have to share.

We all got drinks with umbrellas in them, even Nellie's coke had one. We made a toast to my Mom for luck with her surgery. Clink, clink, clink.

Over the next few days, we went shopping, had lunch out, and just had a good time. Mom and I got along fairly well, which was a miracle in itself. Tomorrow it was surgery time.

The plan was that Wes would take Mom to the hospital since they had to arrive in Manhattan at 5 A.M. for her 7 A.M. surgery. The whole thing would take three to five hours and then she'd be in the recovery room and then on to the ICU for a day, which was the norm for heart surgery patients. Wes would come back, take a short nap, and we'd go in later when we could see her. Given she'd be in ICU we could each go in for no longer than five minutes every hour.

When we got to the hospital, Mom was still in surgery. We waited around for about an hour and Dr. Sheckal came out looking somber. I felt my breath catch.

He said to Wes, "Your wife's heart stopped…"

This is where we all gasped, hands reaching for hands, clasping tightly.

"She's okay, it stopped, but for no more than about ten seconds. Other than that, the surgery was a success. She's in the recovery room now. In about an hour, she'll be moved to ICU and you can each have your five minutes visiting. You may want to wait though; she'll be sleeping for another few hours."

Kat still had hold of my hand, the hand that wanted to slap the doctor's stupid face off.

I hissed at her, barely keeping my voice down. "What kind of idiot leads with 'Her heart stopped?' Why did that insensitive fool even tell us her heart stopped? Why did we have to know that? It didn't kill her. It's beating now. Moron."

Kat, the good sister smiled at the doctor and said, "Thank you so much, Dr. Shitel."

Thankfully my sister had let go of my hand because I needed it to clamp over my mouth to suppress the laughter that was bubbling up and would spew out any minute.

The doctor gave my sister a sidelong glance and said, "It's Dr. Sheckal. And you're very welcome. She'll be as good as new, even better than new."

He said he'd be by later to check on her and he turned and walked away. I'm sure the "Dr. Shitel" wasn't lost on him.

My hand still clamped over my mouth, I ran outside. I could hear Wes asking Kat if I was going to be sick.

That did it for Kat and Nellie, and they joined me outside, all of us laughing like hyenas. People were staring. Wes was clueless, as usual.

Mom was still in recovery so we decided to go for lunch, we were all starving. Wes asked if we could bring something back, he wanted to stay and Nellie had to use the lady's room and said she'd meet us there. The restaurant was just down the block from the hospital so we agreed and left.

Once seated, Wanda, the waitress said, "Tess and Wes are in here at least a few times a month. There certainly isn't any mistaking you Vivianne, you're a double for your Mom. And this must be the other daughter, Kat. Is your daughter, Nellie here too? How's Tess doing?"

Jesus, she knew the entire family. I'm surprised she didn't ask after our dogs.

I answered, "My mom is doing well, thanks for asking. She's in ICU and we can only see her briefly every hour. Wes wants us to bring him something back but I'm sure he'll be in tomorrow. Nellie is on her way; she should be here momentarily."

Wanda said, "I'm glad to hear the good news. We all love

Tess, she's so funny."

Hmmm, did Wanda have the right Tess? They thought she was funny? That wasn't an adjective I would use in conjunction with my mother. And they LOVED her?

I ordered a Bloody Mary and Kat had a seltzer with a wedge of lime.

"Where is Nellie? She should have been here by now," said Kat. "I'll call her and see what's going on."

The phone was picked up on the second ring by Wes. Kat looked at the number and sure enough, she had dialed Nellie's cell. Why was Wes answering it?

"Hi Wes, where's Nellie?"

"She left to meet you and she accidentally left her phone here. She should have been there by now."

My sister got off the phone with a look of panic on her face.

"Where's Nellie? Wes said she left and should've been here by now."

At that moment Wanda came with our drinks. I asked her to put them on hold but took a long pull on the straw before she took them away. I opened my cell and started typing.

"What are you doing Viv, we have to find Nellie. Maybe she's in trouble. Why are you still sitting there? Get the hell up and let's GO."

"Wait Kat, I'm tracking her GPS signal. She appears to be around the corner."

"What? What are you talking about? Nellie doesn't have a GPS signal, remember, she left her phone at the hospital."

"Shut up and trust me on this. She's around the corner. I bought her a tracker for her birthday last year," I said as we were running toward the signal.

"Why didn't you guys tell me? Nellie never said a word about it."

I was getting winded, and talking while almost running wasn't making it any easier. My uncomfortable, but stylish, shoes were also a hindrance. I held up my hand and said, "Can't breathe and talk. She's straight ahead."

We rounded the corner and sure enough, we spotted her. She was at the end of a deserted alley, struggling with a man who was trying to force her into a van. As he pushed her into the vehicle she turned around quickly and said, "Fuck you asshole," and doused his face with pepper spray. As he fell, writhing and screaming, he had a handful of Nellie's shirt and she went tumbling out of the van, landing on top of Mr. Asshole.

A surge of adrenalin sent me into a sprint and I got there just before Kat. I thrust my taser into the man, making him flop like a fish out of water, rendering him temporarily incapacitated. The doors of the van were still wide open, the driver got out and ran. Thank God he didn't back out because he would have run us all over.

Breathing hard I said, "Nells, are you okay?"

"Yeah, Auntie V. I'm fine. What an asshole."

"Yes, we get it. I think we can all agree, he's an asshole," I said.

Kat was just about catatonic by now. She hugged Nellie so tightly I thought she'd break her in half. She was sobbing uncontrollably.

"It's okay Sister, Nellie is safe. It's okay."

A few more shudders and she stopped crying. Uh oh, now she looked...either confused or angry. I was hoping for confusion.

"What is the matter with you two? 'You,'" and she pointed at Nellie. "Why didn't you tell me your crazy aunt gave you a tracker? And, OH MY GOD, what language. You sounded like Grammy."

"And you," she said, her finger indicating me. I leaned back as she came closer. She was scaring me. Her arms shot out and all of a sudden, the breath was being hugged out of me. And she was crying again. Can one die by hug?

"Uh, Sister? What's going on?" At least she wasn't mad at me, unless she was trying to crush me to death.

Kat yelled, "ARE YOU INSANE? Never you mind. *Of course* you're insane. I'm insane for even asking if you're insane. Insane though you may be, you've saved my baby." Then she released me and suffocated Nellie in kisses.

Yes, I would take all the credit. After all, I bought the tracker. Even if I didn't tell Kat. Frankly, most of the credit went to Nells who seemed pretty good at taking care of herself. I love that girl.

The asshole was trying to get up, so I leaned over and tased him again. Flip, flop, and immobilized. "Kat, call 911, I can't keep tasing him."

The police were there almost before Kat finished dialing. Ah, the New York minute. We explained it all to them, Nellie's arm was turning black and blue where Asshole grabbed her. The very nice and good-looking policeman said, "The van was reported stolen but thanks to you we've got his partner in crime. He'll talk, we've got our ways."

He wasn't referring to torture although that would be my preference, he was talking about cutting a deal if he ratted out the driver. Attempted kidnapping carried a hefty jail sentence.

The cops arrested Mr. Asshole whose name turned out to be Igor. It really was something innocuous...Gus Lathorpe. Yes, that was it. Never heard of him. And I doubted this would make the news, it was business as usual in New York City. Nobody was kidnapped or hurt, the perp was on his way to jail, and I'm sure the van driver wouldn't be far behind.

We gave our statements and our contact info to the police. By now an hour had passed. Shit, Wes would be wondering where we were. I guess we weren't eating out after all. We did go back to McGee's, but it was so late we just ordered take-out. We'd have to make up some story for Wes. While waiting for it to be ready I gulped down the Bloody Mary I had started before this whole horrible mess.

When we were walking back to the hospital Kat asked Nellie, "Why didn't you want me to know you had a tracker? I thought you told me everything. We're close, aren't we?"

"Oh Mom, don't get all mushy on me. We're close, we'll always be close, except maybe in my teenage years when I will grow to hate you, we'll have lots of fights, and then I'll get married and love you again.

"I didn't want you to know because, one...you would have freaked out just from the mere thought I might need a tracker and two...when I'm a teenager I don't want you watching me all the time. Come to think of it, I don't want you watching me now."

"What makes you trust Aunt Viv then? She could watch you. Why is it okay if she watches you and I don't?"

"Will you two stop it. Kat, you're her mother, you wouldn't be able to help yourself, you'd be tracking her every movement. I'm her aunt and I live clear across the country and even if I wanted to track her, I wouldn't know where the hell she was. I'm not that familiar with Westchester."

"Okay," said Kat. "You two win but Viv, you have to swear on your favorite pizza place that if anything at all is out of whack, you'll track her and tell me. If you don't promise, that pizza shop will go up in a plume of fire."

"I promise, I promise. Sheesh. It's pretty bad when you stoop to pizza terrorism."

CHAPTER TEN

We met Wes in the waiting room and took the food to the cafeteria to eat. Wes did ask why we didn't eat at McGee's. I lied and told him Nellie had gone out the wrong exit and got lost and it took us a while to find her.

It was partly true. Nells *had* gone out the wrong door but we know what happened then, and there was no need for Wes to know and leak it to Mom who would pop her new valve if she got wind of this.

Wes had seen Mom already and he went for a walk. He'd been sitting for quite a while and needed to stretch his legs. He said she was sleeping and didn't even know he was there.

We were just about to take our turn visiting when Dr. Shitty Sheckal stopped to talk to us as he was making his rounds. I asked when my Mom would be awake and he said we all might as well go home and come back tomorrow, she'd be sleeping most of the day and night and wouldn't even know we were there. What a ray of sunshine and optimism he was. However, he also said she'd be in her own private room by tomorrow.

We stopped at the nurse's station and asked them to tell her we'd been here, and we'd see her tomorrow. The nurses were all so wonderful. Better by far than the doctor. Nurses are underrated, and probably underpaid too.

Back to the house we went. It felt oddly empty and devoid of loud noises, like my Mom screeching at Wes. Poor Wes. I don't think he knew what to do with himself.

I felt sorry for him so I screamed, at the top of my lungs, "Don't just sit there, make us our drinks."

Kat was appalled and Nells was speechless that I would talk to him that way. That is, until they realized he had run into the kitchen to make drinks.

"I'm doing him a favor," I hissed. "I'll be nice to him when he comes back with our libations. I promise. Now he won't miss Mom so much, he's back on familiar territory."

We all went out for pizza and got to bed early because we'd be at the hospital first thing in the morning. I sure hoped Mom would be awake.

When Kat and I were alone she said, "I just wanted to thank you for thinking of Nellie with that tracker thing. I should have thought of it. And even though we found her I'm starting to believe she really didn't need us."

"Yes, she did. If she were alone, she would have run after pepper spraying him but she was a little lost since she went out the wrong door so we saved her from wandering around. And I tased the Asshole and the police arrested him. I'd say we were all needed and we all did an excellent job. The bottom line is, Nells is okay and she doesn't even seem traumatized. She's got our tough genes in her. That kid will do fine in life. And who do you suppose made her like that? YOU DID. Certainly not Hector, her father." Ahhh, I thought, it does take a village. A village of strong women.

Kat felt better and we all got a good night's sleep, even with the walls vibrating from Wes's snoring.

The next morning, Mom was still in the ICU and Wes was the first in to see her. She told him to let us know we could see her in her own room, she didn't want us in the ICU.

It was now nearing noon and we told Wes to go have lunch, we'd be here in case she was moved. After he was gone, a nurse came out to the waiting room and told us Mom had been taken to her own room and gave me the room number.

We didn't want to all go in at once so I went first. Shit, she was still sleeping and she had tubes everywhere. The beeping was enough to drive anyone crazy. I couldn't even look at her, all of this was scaring me.

I warned Kat and Nellie it wasn't a pretty sight and she was *still* sleeping. They both entered the room and when Kat came out, she said, "I think we were in the wrong room, that's not Mom." Nells looked at me and said, "Auntie V, you gave us the wrong room number."

They were in denial. Wes came walking over and asked, "What are you girls doing here?"

"What do you think? We're visiting Mom."

"That's very nice but you're not visiting her here. I just stopped at the nurse's station and they gave me her room number. It's down the hall"

"Oh, for Christ's sake," I said. We all started to laugh. "Does this count as a visit?" And we started laughing again.

Unfortunately, the merriment didn't last long. We may have been in the wrong room but Mom was still hooked up to everything. But, hey, she just had open heart surgery. Somehow, I expected her to be…alive. No, no, she wasn't dead but she sure looked dead. The only thing that convinced me she was still kicking was the unrelenting heart monitor beep, beep, beeping. Every beep signified a breath and breathing is always a good sign.

It was a wonder anyone in here could sleep. I was aghast at the sight of it all, and Mom, lying there looking so frail and helpless. At that moment two things happened. My frail Mom opened her eyes and smiled. Kat and Nellie had just come in. Ah, and I thought she was smiling at me.

She was very weak and her dulcet tones were gone, replaced by a raspy whisper. We were told that was from the tube that had been down her throat. Oh God, did they have to tell us that? I wanted to be sick. I wasn't meant to be in the medical field, that's for sure.

Each day she was getting stronger and she got her voice back, but still, no yelling. When we walked in on day three, she was sitting up WITH HER MAKE-UP ON. Wow. And her hair had been done by the hospital hair stylist. She looked terrific.

She was back to being the Mom I knew and sometimes loved. She started ordering Wes around and gave him the task of going to the liquor store and buying a good white and red wine. And some cheese and crackers.

"Mom, you're not drinking wine already, are you?"

"Don't be ridiculous Vivianne, the wine and appetizers are for my guests. Just because I'm stuck here doesn't mean I can't entertain properly. And Wes will be here to serve them."

Wes had bought her the most beautiful, arrangement of flowers. He was back to being to serving her and was very happy. Now, every day he'd be running out to bring her food as the hospital swill was gross. That is, once she was past the jello and broth stage. I assumed that would be any minute now.

Mom continued to get better. I knew a full recovery wasn't far off when she asked for a glass of red wine. It made my heart flutter with pride. You can't keep a good woman down, even if she's a bitch on wheels.

I did plan on staying a few extra days so I'd be there when she was home. Kat had to get back to work but Nells stayed with me. Have I mentioned how much I love that kid? She was planning on staying for the rest of the week. Kat would pick her up over the weekend, when she came to visit Mom but I'd be home by then.

My Mom tolerated me but, she doted on Nellie so it was a good balance. It didn't matter to me. I was used to being last, at least where Mom was involved, and I was always the happiest when her attention was focused elsewhere.

Mom came home and was settled in. She had a daybed in her sewing room on the first floor which she would temporarily use until she felt strong enough to climb the stairs. She was doing everything the doctor told her to do. She was exercising which was really just walking as much as she could. Wes would walk with her up to the park where she'd sketch and take pictures for future paintings.

The day before I was leaving Sky and Jock came to visit. They had sent Mom flowers, and not just flowers, I think they cleaned the florist shop out. They'd been in Hong Kong when Mom was in for her surgery, but they were here now.

"How was China? You two look good as usual." And they certainly did.

Sky said, "We found it overcrowded and a little too hectic. We won't be going back again. The next trip will be to London. Jock is taking me for our wedding anniversary."

They visited for a while and then they were off to their apartment in New York. They'd be back to visit Mom tomorrow but I'd be on my way back to normal life. I was glad I got to see them though.

The night before I was leaving, even though it was still June and Nellie's birthday wasn't until July 13th, I decided to present her with her gift early. It was purely selfish on my part. I wanted to be there, in person, when she opened her present. Most of her birthdays were celebrated long distance so this would be a treat for me.

Mom had gone to bed downstairs. I still had her room and instead of Kat, Nellie was sleeping in the twin bed next to me.

We were in our jammies and I said, "I've got a little something for you. You know I won't be here for your birthday so I thought I'd give it to you early."

I gave her the box and, seeing what it was, she sucked in her breath. "Oh, Auntie V, these are so cool. I love them."

She was referring to the small ruby stud earrings, not too big but a beautiful brilliant color, called Pigeon's blood. Not a particularly nice name for a color, I could picture the poor pigeon being bled to death but Nellie didn't have to know that. They were stellar and just right for a new teenager. Ruby was her birthstone.

I also gave her a gift from Venice which was a red rhinestone cell phone case. Kat had bought her a small ruby ring but she'd have to wait for her actual birthday to get that. And I knew she'd treasure it.

This was a very special birthday, hence the jewelry. She was going to turn 13, a teenager. Where did the time go and how did she get this old?

My Mom would probably give her a trip to London. Who knows, but when it comes to Nellie anything is possible. Maybe I could go as her chaperone. Maybe she could meet Sky and Jock there. Maybe my Mom wouldn't really give her a trip to London. I can see Mom waiting until her 16th birthday to give her that.

My plane wasn't leaving until 1 P.M. When I went downstairs my Mom was making pancakes. "Are you sure you should be cooking?" I asked her. I shouldn't have.

"You're leaving shortly so please, try to refrain from getting on my nerves before you go. Nellie sweetheart, do you want chocolate chips in your pancakes?"

I don't know about Nellie but I would have loved blueberries in mine. However, I was not asked, I would get whatever Nellie decided on. I think I liked the hospital Mom when she was unable to talk. Okay, that was mean. I didn't want her to be in the hospital, I just wanted her to become mute until I left.

I was so happy to be going home. It felt like I'd been here for months. I'd miss Nellie and Kat though. Maybe even Mom for about two minutes. Two minutes would be a stretch, maybe two seconds. Goodbyes and hugs had, I left.

I got off the Airporter bus in Port Hollow and there was Sassy on a leash with Venice. She went insane with joy when she saw me. Aaahhh, someone loves me. Unconditionally. I will concede, Venice loves me too, even if I do drive her crazy. I was home. Home, home, home.

I kissed and hugged both Venice and Sassy, then asked Ven what was new. I had spoken to her while in New York and told her all about the almost kidnapping. "Anything on the murder?"

"I have no idea since Det. Traynor never tells us anything."

"She told us who the victim was," I said. Oh my God, I completely forgot about Georgia, the woman on the plane. She knew Lauren."

"Are you kidding? Why didn't you tell me? Never mind, did she tell the police? What does she know?"

"One question at a time, please. She didn't talk to the police because this happened over a year ago but it seems Lauren was involved with a married man. He actually left his wife for her but Lauren had just met Tyler, and told Mr. Married goodbye. Georgia didn't know anything else. Maybe his wife forgave him and he continued his life as it was before Lauren."

Venice said, "Maybe he killed Lauren. Or maybe the wife killed Lauren. We have to Google him."

"Can't do that, Lauren never mentioned his name. Georgia also told me they were extremely careful. This was in Oregon, where Lauren lived. She told Georgia that they'd go to different towns and always got a room in back of the motel so the cars couldn't be seen. Also, it seems Lauren was the one who secured the room. I hope he at least reimbursed her.

"I wonder, if we went down to Oregon and showed Lauren's picture at motels, if someone would recognize her? No, it wouldn't matter if they did. We know she was there, what we don't know is what her lover looked like, and it seems he was way too careful to be identified."

"Listen Viv, you promised you wouldn't get involved. I think you should call the Detective and tell her all of this. I mean it. They have more avenues and manpower to follow this up than we do."

"Yeah, yeah, yeah. Another thing," I said. "While I was at my Mom's house, I studied those pictures that Annie took and sent to me. I enlarged every inch of those photos and I found something. It could be nothing."

"What did you find? Maybe it isn't nothing. Maybe it's something."

"Let's wait until we get home and I get settled in, then I'll show you."

Though my flight left at 1 P.M. and was six hours long, and the Airporter bus added another few hours, it was now only 6 P.M. in Washington. I was on New York time and my body was telling me it was really 9 P.M. I was starving.

We headed home to eat. Venice had food, I didn't even care what food, as long as it was edible, which would be a given if she made it. No doubt there would be some fabulous dessert too.

"Last night Sky and Jock showed up with more flowers than an entire funeral home and we all got to visit. I hope she's serious when she said they'd make it out here. Let's face it, this isn't exactly Fiji. But Seattle has lots to offer.

"I would love to meet them; they sound like very fun people and I bet they could tell stories of their travels that are much better than Wes's stories, or as your Mom would say, his *pontifications*."

We arrived at Venice's house. I'd go to mine after I ate. We still had more to talk about.

Venice asked, "So what something, or nothing, did you find in the pictures?"

"Come over here and see." I enlarged the photo as much as I could before it wouldn't be compromised. Damn those pixels. "Here," I pointed. "Does that look like something?"

I was pointing to the back bottom of the dress. It was tiny but it looked like a very small piece of the gown had ripped away.

"What do you think? Is it something or nothing?"

Venice leaned forward, her forehead almost touching my iPad screen, eyes all squinty. "You know, it's really hard to make out. It could be a tear or it could be a shadow from the folds in the dress. We're back to square one. It could be something, it could be nothing."

"That was a big help."

"Again, why don't you bring this to Det. Traynor?"

"And get Annie in trouble? Don't forget, the Detective doesn't know we have these pictures, and I'm sure she's got a million photos of the dress, and better ones at that. The dress! I wonder if she'll let me see the dress?"

Venice said, "Maybe they don't even have the dress anymore. I wonder what happens to it when they're done. It's part of Lauren's belongings but I doubt if anyone wants it or would ever wear it. It's now bad luck, very bad luck."

"So, how's it going with Bryan? He must have left for Arizona by now."

"Yes, he left last week. I'm surprised to say this but, I really miss him. We talk on Facetime every other night. I feel like I've known him for years, isn't that crazy?"

Yes, it was crazy, and disturbing. Smiling, I said, "That's... encouraging."

"Encouraging? Is that the best you could do Viv, *encouraging*?"

"You know what I mean. I'm not good at this shit. Okay, it's breathtakingly wonderful. It's stupendous, thrilling..."

"Enough already, I get the point. You don't have to think it's anything. The week after next I'll be flying down to Sunshine City to visit Bryan and see his condo. And I know it's going to be breathtakingly wonderful, stupendous, and thrilling. So there."

"You forgot to add sweltering, blistering, scorching and torrid, so there."

"Yes, like a torrid love affair."

"Oh please, spare me," I said.

That's the fun of us. We can act like petulant children. But not for long. Then the boring adult side reappears. I really don't have an adult side, I just pretend.

"We're planning on taking a motorcycle trip to Sedona. It's a bit cooler up there and there's so much to see. Plus, the wind will be on me the entire way."

"That does sound nice. And I'll take care of the dogs and drive you to and from the Airporter bus. That goes without saying, but I hope it's not going to be at the crack of dawn or the dark of night. You know I can't see that well at night."

I felt like I'd redeemed myself. I didn't know what was the matter with me when it came to Bryan. Was it him, or would I be like this with any man who Venice was dating? Or maybe it was that Bryan lived far away. Even though Ven kept saying she wasn't going anywhere, she could always change her mind. I guess I'd just have to learn to be happy for her and keep a civil tongue in my mouth. Maybe not. Civil tongues are only for clients. And my mother, sometimes.

We were almost home when my phone beeped a text message. It was John Berkman.

"Who's that?" asked Venice.

"It's John. He wants to know if I'm home yet. I'll send a quick text back telling him I'm on my way at this very moment."

Beep, beep. "Crap, John wants to take me out tomorrow night. I'm going to be jet lagged so I think I'll pass."

Venice asked me, "Do you like him, Viv? I mean, in the boyfriend way?"

"I sense that you sense that I'm a little ambivalent about him. He's a very nice man but I think he's a little old for me and then there's all that money. Money is good but that much is too much. I know, you probably think I'm crazy but it's not my kind of lifestyle. And I like my men a bit more edgy. He's very laid back. He does have a sense of humor and you know humor is key with me, so I'm not throwing him away just yet. He has possibilities."

Ven said, "I wish I had just recorded that. If your mother ever heard you say his money was *too much,* she really and truly would disown you. I could've held that over your head for years. Damn."

CHAPTER ELEVEN

J et lag or no, I was headed for the office. I was glad to be back into my routine. Now I'd have to call Mom every day. At least until she was totally recovered which, knowing her, would be tomorrow.

The alarm system had been installed so I felt it was now safe for Annie to open the brokerage alone. There was a keypad and she'd enter the four-digit number to disarm the alarm. The office was now closed at 6 P.M. because Annie would set the alarm and, besides her, the only other people who knew the code were Venice and I. However, and this was the cool part, if an agent wanted to bring clients there in the evening, all they had to do was call Annie, Venice, or myself, and we could disarm it from our phone, iPad, or computer.

The surveillance cameras worked so you could have a split screen showing what all the cameras were seeing, or you could pick just the one you wanted to view. What I thought was the best was the ability to manipulate the cameras remotely to make them point in different directions. We also had the capacity to record a video clip or just take a picture. All this remotely, from our devices. I always say, technology is great, until it's not. When something breaks our lives stop. When it's going well, it's miraculous.

I didn't stay long at Rainbow Realty; I really was tired. Venice had some work to do so I said good-bye and left for home and a nap.

That night, Odette, one of our agents, wanted to meet with her client later that evening at the brokerage. Annie told her to call when she got there and she'd remotely enter the code so Odette could get in. Odette would let Annie know when she left so she could arm the system from home.

Odette got to the brokerage around 7 P.M. and phoned Annie to let her in.

About an hour went by with no call from Odette, so Annie brought up the camera screens to see if she was still there or left and forgot to call.

My phone chirped. "Hi Annie, what's up? Everything okay?"

"No, I think you need to see this. Bring up *Rainbow*'s security system on your iPad. Make sure you're looking at the camera in the area where the agent's cubicles are."

"Is it a break-in? Should we call 911?"

"No, just look at the screen. And make sure you zoom in. I'm recording a video clip as we speak. You can decide what you want to do with it."

Oh, sweet Jesus. I sure hope it wasn't another murder. I hooked up to the security camera in the area that Annie told me to look. It took me a second to comprehend what I was seeing.

"Oh my God, is that Odette?"

"Yes indeedy, it sure is. Do you see what she's doing?"

"I do and I wish I didn't." Seems like Odette was having a

little tête-à-tête on her desk. And looking closely I could see, it most definitely wasn't her husband, whom I had met last year at the Christmas get-together.

I called Venice and told her to get her ass over to my house, pronto. I wouldn't tell her why so she was at my door in seconds. I think I scared her.

I showed her my iPad screen.

"Vivianne! *Porn*?! This is what I ran all the way here for? What...

"Venice, shut up and look. Does this not look vaguely familiar? The person? The surroundings?"

"Oh shit, that's Odette. On the desk. In the office? Oh, my oh my."

Venice didn't often use profanity, I used plenty for both of us and my mother used enough for the entire state of New York. Annie had the phone on speaker. I started to laugh which was contagious because all of us were now howling. Tears were running down my face. I couldn't catch my breath.

"Yes," I said. "And from this vantage point, we're not seeing her best asset." That started the hilarity all over again.

When I came up for air, I told Annie to stop recording it and we all turned our devices off.

Annie choked out, "What are you going to do?"

"I could tell her to find another brokerage but she's a decent realtor and I don't want to cut my nose off to spite my face. No, I think I'll tell her that having sex in the office is frowned upon and if it happens again, she'll have to look for a new agency."

"I still have to arm the place once she leaves," said Annie. "Should I wait and take a peek to see if she's still there?"

"That gives me an idea. Give me a minute, Venice will call you right back."

If Venice called Annie back, they could put that call on speaker and I was going to put my phone on speaker and call Odette. We took bets if she would pick up or not.

I won, she picked up on the second ring. Yippee, I just made $2.00. "Hi Odette, I'm just checking to see if you're still at the office. It's getting late and we'd like to put the alarm on for the night."

"Thanks, I'm just finishing up here."

I had to mute the phone because that started a lot more giggling.

"Give me ten minutes," said Odette. "I'll call the second I'm out the door."

She did call about ten minutes later, we set the alarm, and I asked Annie not to mention this to anyone. I would handle it tomorrow. I wanted to talk to Odette in person.

I knew Venice wouldn't say anything and I trusted Annie not to either.

"How is your Mom doing?" asked Venice. "I sent her flowers today. I didn't want to send them to the hospital where she probably wouldn't get to appreciate them so I waited until she was home."

"That was very thoughtful of you, I'm sure she'll call to thank you tomorrow. She's doing pretty good. I think she'll be back to her old self sooner than we'd like," I said, smiling.

"Oh, I spoke to Bryan and I've got my itinerary for Arizona. I won't be leaving at the crack of dawn and will be landing before dark so you don't have to worry."

"How long will you be gone? This will be your first trip away; I'm sure going to miss you."

"Bryan wanted me to stay for ten days but that's way too long for the first trip. I told him I'd be there next Monday and would leave on Friday. That leaves three days for Sedona and anything else we want to do. I'm not counting the day I arrive or the day I leave."

"Sounds reasonable to me. I hope you're planning on baking and freezing before you go," I said.

"Maybe you could diet while I'm away."

"Diet? Why, do I look fat? I look fat, don't I?"

"No, Vivianne, you most certainly don't look fat. I'll see if I have time to bake."

We said goodnight and I let Sassy out in the fenced backyard. I didn't walk her after dark. I had to do that when I first got her, before I had the fence put up, and it was scary. I imagined all sorts of horrors lurking in the bushes. And, on occasion I could hear the coyotes howling away. I was very glad I had the fence now.

Since I stayed at my Mom's a little longer than I thought, it was now past the middle of June. I was just heading in to Rainbow Realty when Annie called and said Odette was in. I wasn't looking forward to confronting her, but my brokerage wasn't going to be used as her love nest. No way. And she had better sanitize her desk. Oh, gross.

When I arrived, I buzzed Odette and asked her to come into my office. "Good morning Odette, have a seat."

"Have I done something wrong?" she asked. "I called when I left, I didn't forget."

"Well Odette, it seems you were spotted on the security camera here last night. We both know what was going on so let this be a warning. If this ever happens again, I will not hold your license at this brokerage, is that understood?"

Her face was the color of a ripe tomato. I hated having to do this.

"I'm so embarrassed," she said. "I swear, I won't do that again. Does everybody know?"

"No, I thought we would just keep it between us. It's nobody else's business, not even mine as long as you don't use this as your motel again. Now go out there and sell some real estate."

I wanted to leave it on a positive note. She was mortified but it had to be addressed. I didn't tell her to clean her desk, however. That might have been overkill. And, she definitely didn't need to know the three of us saw her.

I called Mom. "How're are you doing today Mom?"

"Why don't we skip asking me how I'm doing. Everyone is asking me that and believe me, they will know if I'm not doing well, which is improbable since I *am* doing well. I'll call Venice when we're done to thank her for the beautiful flowers. That was so thoughtful of her. I like that girl."

Now I was no longer third on the chain, I had just been bumped down to fourth, Kat, Nellie and now Venice pulling ahead. Honestly, I didn't care. Mom would never appreciate me even if I kowtowed to her every minute of the day so it was a useless endeavor to even waste my energy trying. It also gave my sister and I fodder for laughs. I would much rather laugh with my sister than be in my mother's good graces. Which was excellent since I wasn't. In her good graces that is. Ever. And that made me laugh. I'd have to call Kat when I was done.

"Since I'm now banned from asking about your health, what have you been up to? Any new paintings or are you too busy planning a sit-down dinner for 50?"

That made her laugh, a tiny bit. "I must say Vivianne, if nothing else, you're funny."

Ah, there it was, give with one hand and take away with the other.

"You're our Eveready bunny you know," I said. "I'm sure Wes is yelling at you to get in that kitchen and cook."

"That will be the day. The day I castrate him. Speaking of your father, he bought me the nicest diamond and sapphire teardrop pendant necklace for my get-well present. That man can be so thoughtful."

Christ, I hated when she referred to him as *my father,* even though both Kat and I were legally adopted by him. That was my mother's doing. We were both adults when this occurred and my Mom had nagged him into it. Wes had no other family except those in Bolivia and my Mom wanted us to get his money should he die first. My mother was way too stubborn to go before he did. I absolutely never called him Dad. Nor would I, and neither would my sister. Nellie did refer to him as Grampy. She'd probably be the one to inherit it all but Nells would most definitely share. She loves her mother and her Auntie V. And Grammy and Grampy too. But Kat and I more. I'm sure. And Wes was very much alive, not kicking, but alive.

Looking at the time I realized Kat would still be at work. My Mom and I had wrapped up our short conversation. She probably had to go and stand in front of the mirror, and stare at her new pendant which I was positive was around her neck this very minute. I will not say my fingers should be around her neck. That would be wrong.

CHAPTER TWELVE

I decided to give Det. Traynor a call to ask about the dress and if she was any closer to solving the Bridal Murder.

Det. Traynor was in for once and I was transferred right to her. "Hi Detective, it's Vivianne."

"I know, and no, there's nothing new."

"I was calling to ask if you still have the bridal dress, and if you do, could I come down and have a look at it?"

"As a matter of fact, that was released back to the family last week. Why do you ask?"

"I just wanted to take a look. Just in case you may have missed something."

"Really." Detective didn't seem happy. "And just what is it that you think we *may* have missed?"

"Nothing. I think you probably did a thorough job, I just wanted to have a looksee. Is that a crime?"

"With you Vivianne, everything is a crime or seems to become one. And you say *Probably*? We *probably* did a thorough job? Vivianne, we're professionals. How would you like it if I wanted to stick my nose into your real estate?"

"Honestly? I wouldn't mind. Maybe you could steer some clients my way."

She hung up.

I called her back, and she answered, "Now what?"

"I completely forgot what with my Mom's surgery and all, (I didn't forget) but *I* have news for *you*."

I told her about my conversation with Georgia. I mean, what the hell? I couldn't do anything with the information, maybe she could, and she thanked me. That was a first.

I had an idea. I would contact the Dinkels and ask to see the wedding gown. Then we could see if there really was a tear. But she just lost her daughter, maybe I shouldn't bother her. Then again, if I found something it could help solve the murder. But then I'd have to drive down to Oregon.

I called Mrs. Dinkel. She answered on the first ringy dingy.

Hi Mrs. Dinkel, this is Vivianne Murphy..."

"If you're a reporter we aren't interested. This is difficult enough without you bloodsuckers calling all the time."

"I'm not a reporter, please don't hang up. As I was saying my name is Vivianne Murphy and your daughter was found at my brokerage. I'm so sorry for you and your family, this must be very hard."

"Very hard doesn't even begin to cover it. What do you want?"

"I'd like to come down to Oregon and take a look at the wedding gown if you still have it. Even though the police are working hard to solve this, it doesn't hurt to have a fresh pair of eyes. Maybe I can help in some way. I've worked with Det. Traynor before."

"I do have the dress. It was sent to us last week with the rest of Lauren's belongings. It's still in the box it came in from the salon. I couldn't even look at it. Come down. Take the damned thing. God knows Lauren won't be wearing it."

Now she was sobbing. Patiently I waited, not saying anything. There was nothing I could say to comfort her. I could just be there, a stranger on the other end of the phone, and all I could offer were meaningless platitudes.

When she got control of her emotions, she asked, "When do you want to come?"

"Whenever it's convenient for you, Mrs. Dinkel."

While I was in New York, Gloria and Erika closed on their house with Venice's help. This coming weekend would be their house warming, so maybe she'd consent to tomorrow.

"How about tomorrow, if that's not too soon? It would be around 1 P.M."

I heard her talking to someone and then she came back and said, "Tomorrow is fine, Lorna, my other daughter, will be here then too."

"Thank you so much. And again, I'm so sorry for all you're going through."

I didn't know what else to say. Anything short of bringing her daughter back wasn't going to ease her suffering.

I gave her my contact information and told her she could call Det. Traynor if she wanted to check me out. I'd see her tomorrow. We hung up. That was a very depressing call, I can't imagine what tomorrow would be like. I truly hoped she didn't call the Detective because my ass would be in a sling.

Venice had left for the day and I called her immediately. It went straight to voicemail. Damn, she was probably on the phone with Bryan. Bryan, Bryan, Bryan, I chanted in a whiney voice, accompanied by a smirk. I slapped myself. Then I left a message for her to call me as soon as she could.

Half an hour later, yes, that would be thirty whole minutes, she *finally* called.

"Hey Viv, what's up, I was on the phone with Bryan."

Ah HA, I *knew* it.

"Oh, I hope I didn't make you hang up."

I didn't make her hang up; she didn't call me back for an eternity.

"I wanted to know if you could do me a huge favor."

"Huge, huh? Before I commit, I think I need to know how huge."

"Now don't be judgmental. I spoke to Mrs. Dinkel and she said I could meet with her tomorrow at 1 P.M. and I wanted you to go with me because it's a long ass drive and you drive better."

"Who? I don't know a Mrs. Dinkel. Where is she that it's such a long drive and who is... Oh no. No, no, no. That's the bride's mother. I remember that name now. NO, the answer is unequivocally NO."

"We have to be there by 1 P.M., I think you should pick me up at 9:30 A.M."

"Didn't you just hear me? NO, means NO. 'No' is a complete sentence."

"And by NO, do you mean you won't go with me? Do you trust your best and most loyal friend and business partner to be on *highways*? You know I don't do highways. I need you Ven. Really and truly. I promise I'll be in your debt forever, or at least for the next month. Maybe a week."

Venice said, "A month. You owe me for a whole month. And the week I'm away doesn't count. And I want it in writing. And I want it signed in blood."

"A deal" I said. "I'll type it up right this minute and we can both sign it. In blood."

"You want to come over for dinner?" I asked. "That's the least I can do and I'll explain why we're going to Mrs. Dinkel's house. With all your vehement 'NO's' you didn't even ask the why of it."

"What are you making?" she asked.

"Domino's pizza?"

"God Vivianne, I don't know why I put up with you. I'll bring dinner." This was followed by a very long, drawn out sigh.

"You love me, that's why you put up with me and let's face it, with me in your life it's never boring. What's for dinner?" I asked.

Shocking as it may seem, she disconnected the call. Fifteen minutes later she appeared on my doorstep with Betty, Mr. Snigglebottom, and dinner. I think it was her lasagna. Oh joy.

Lola immediately slithered under the bed. I was hoping she'd attack some dust bunnies and make herself useful.

Over dinner, which *was* her lasagna, she finally asked me, "Why are we going to visit Mrs. Dinkel? Wait, let me take a deep breath to prepare for this."

While she exhaled, I told her about the wedding gown.

"I cannot believe you called that poor grief-stricken woman to ask for her murdered daughter's wedding dress, the one she was killed in no less."

"Well, if you put it that way, I guess I suck. But wouldn't it be helpful if I solved the murder so she could have some justice for Lauren? Also, I don't believe she was killed while actually wearing the gown."

"I'm sure that will give Mrs. Dinkel some solace. And, you seem to get yourself in lots of trouble in the name of justice, don't you? Why do you always have to drag me into it?"

"I disagree, I get myself in trouble because I have a curious mind. Also, there has been no dragging here. I even signed our agreement, in blood. Here it is, you can sign it too."

"I see. Hmmm, I didn't think blood had sparkles in it. You used your red sparkle pen, didn't you?"

"Since I'm such a bling girl," I said, "My blood most certainly does have sparkles in it."

The next morning dawned bright and clear. At least we'd have good weather although, I always say "The sun is overrated." I find it blinding when I'm driving and when it's summer and I'm walking Sassy; it burns right into my skin. Okay, maybe I exaggerate a tad. However, I much prefer a good overcast day.

Venice drove down my driveway. I was waiting for her and opened her car door, sniffing like a bloodhound on a scent.

"What on earth are you doing Viv, get in."

"I do not detect the lovely smell of scones, or any baked goods for that matter."

"Don't look a gift horse in the mouth. You invited me for dinner which I had to bring and now you think I have breakfast too? You better learn how to bake your own scones."

"I'll bake them if you'll eat them. It won't be pretty," I said.

"We'll stop at McDonald's on the way. I could go for a sausage McMuffin," said Venice.

My stomach made grumbling sounds. It was yelling, FOOD, I WANT FOOD. McDonald's it was.

With Venice behind the wheel, we took the highway and zipped right along. I thought this great fun, being able to relax and gaze out the window.

"Oh, look, cows. When I was a kid, I wanted to live on a farm. Can you picture my Mom on a farm, hanging around nature and cow manure?"

Venice glanced at me and said, "Only if there was an upscale mall nearby."

We were nearing Mrs. Dinkel's, and I was wishing I had poured bourbon into my insulated coffee cup.

"Okay," said Venice. She had parked the car in front of the house saying, "I'll see you when you come out."

"What? No! You have to go in with me."

"Did you tell her I'd be coming along?"

"Well, no, but I'm sure it will be okay. At least let's give it a try. If she has any objections you can go sit in the car. C'mon. Be a sport."

"You're infuriating. What is most annoying is that no matter how much I try to say no, you don't seem to comprehend."

At that moment I saw Mrs. Dinkel part the curtains and look out. I guess now that she saw us, we'd better go in. We didn't even have to knock; the door was opened by a woman I imagined was in her forties but had aged over the past months. Without her grief she would've been very pretty. Lauren had looked a lot like her.

"Hi Mrs. Dinkel, I'm Vivianne and this is Venice, my business partner. Thank you so much for letting us come today."

"It's Doris, come on in. And this is Lorna, my daughter. Would you like a cup of coffee, or maybe some tea?"

"Thank you," I said. "That's very kind of you. I don't want to put you to any bother."

"No bother, I just put on a pot anyway. You had a long

drive down, sit."

We sat.

She put out cream and sugar and, are you ready? SCONES! However, they were store bought. What a scone snob I'd become.

I wanted to ask questions but didn't know how to start. Now that we were here, I was tongue tied. This was so awkward. It was a little bit different than asking a client about their home criteria.

Doris helped me out by saying, "I know you must have some questions. We'll answer what we can, but the police already interviewed us. I can't imagine there's anything more we can tell you."

I sipped at my coffee, it was dark and delicious.

"You're probably right. Do you know if Lauren seeing someone before she met Tyler?

"I don't know. Now that you ask, I remember thinking she was seeing someone. When I asked her, she said she wasn't, she'd just been distracted with work lately. I didn't pry but she was definitely on edge the last few months before she met Tyler. I thought it was her job that was troubling her.

"Everything changed once Tyler was in the picture. She seemed to glow. She was happy and she told me she thought she'd met her soulmate.

"I remember when she got engaged. She didn't call me, instead she said she wanted to come over for dinner and she called Lorna and asked her to be here too. When she arrived, she had a sparkle in her eyes. She was talking to us, waving her hand around dramatically. It was her father who finally noticed her ring.

"I'm sorry, I need a minute. This is so hard."

"Take your time Doris, why don't we take a break and enjoy these lovely scones."

Lorna spoke up, "About a year before Lauren met Tyler, she was very secretive. We always told each other everything and, I don't know, I sensed things weren't right with her. When I asked her about it, she said I was imagining things. Maybe I was. Why do you ask, do you know something?"

"No," I lied. "Just wondering if there might be a jealous boyfriend in her past."

Doris gathered herself and said, "Lorna and Lauren shared a bond, one that was between sisters. If Lauren told anyone anything, it would've been Lorna, not me. We were close but some things you don't discuss with your mother."

Venice asked, "Did you tell the police this Lorna?"

"Yes, I did but there really wasn't anything to tell. Whatever was going on, she didn't confide in me. I'm sorry I can't be more help."

I said, "You're helping more than you know. Do you remember when Lauren stopped acting differently, secretive?"

Lorna said, "Yeah, it was right after she met Tyler. I think she fell in love with Ty at first sight. Once they started dating, they were inseparable."

Lorna started crying. "I'm sorry, it's just that I miss her so much and Tyler is as devastated as we all are. I can't imagine anyone who would do this to her. She was genuinely a nice person."

"I know this won't bring Lauren back but Det. Traynor is the best. No matter how long it takes, she won't ever give up and forget her. I promise you that."

We stood up then and I said, "Thank you both so much, I realize this hasn't been easy for you. I'll be in touch."

"Wait," said Doris. "I don't know if the police told you but they sent her belongings back, that's why we have that cursed dress. The engagement ring we received wasn't hers, the one we got back was a cheap knock off. It didn't even resemble the lovely ring Tyler had given her. Your detective said that's what was on her finger when she was found."

"Yes, we already know that. Tyler told the detective."

Doris disappeared upstairs and came down with a large box.

"Here's the dress. Nobody has opened this since it was returned to us. Take it. I don't care what you do with it. Burn it. Just don't return it."

"Thank you, and I understand. Here's my card. If you think of anything, anything at all, just call me."

Venice got up and hugged both women. "We very much appreciate you talking to us. Thank you both, how is Mr. Dinkel doing?"

"As good as can be expected. This has been a very hard time for him also. He always doted on both his girls. I don't think he can add anything to what we've already told you but if he remembers something, we'll call you. He's back at work now."

I gently took the box from her and again, thanked her and Lorna.

Once in the car I turned to Venice and said, "That was one of the hardest things I've ever done."

"It wasn't a piece of cake for me either," said Venice. "I have to admit, it didn't take long and I think Lorna just confirmed the affair Lauren was having. Lauren must have known her sister wouldn't have approved, and that's why she kept it secret."

"Yes, I agree. Unless Lorna knew him."

"It seems likely that's who may have killed her. But why wait so long? Why didn't he kill her after she broke up with him? She had been seeing Tyler for months before the wedding date. So why, that's the big question."

I said, "The ring, what do you make of the bogus ring?"

Venice said," I have no idea what to make of the ring but sometimes murderers keep souvenirs. Why don't you bring the dress over to my house? There's more room to spread it out and we can both examine it. Oh God, did I just say that? Little by little you're sucking me into this."

"Hey, I didn't suggest we do this at your house, or that you help at all."

Venice rolled her eyes. "Oh please, it's like reading a mystery and never finding out the end. Now that you've managed to get me involved, I need to see it through. If this leads us to the killer, you're going to have to take this to Det. Traynor. We are not going to apprehend him, or her, on our own. Got that?"

"Yes, Ma'am."

CHAPTER THIRTEEN

I t was good to get home and stretch our legs. We took the dogs for a long walk up to the tree farm. We needed it as much as they did.

When we got back Sassy and I went with Venice to her house. The dress was in her car. We let the dogs out in the yard and I brought the gown in.

"Where should we spread this out?"

"Just a minute," said Venice. She went into the laundry room and came out with her cordless vacuum. "I want to make sure we don't get dog hair on it."

"I have an idea; do you have a sheet? We can spread that on the floor after you vacuum just to be safe."

"Good idea."

Finally, we took the dress out and laid it on the sheet. Venice started at one end, me at the other. The dress had multiple layers, so it took us quite a while to inspect it all.

"I think I may have found something," said Venice. She opened a kitchen drawer and came out with a magnifying glass with a light in it. Both of us took a look.

"Oh my God, look at that," I said. "It's tiny and on the

under layer so that's probably why Det. Traynor missed it. Or maybe she didn't, maybe she just didn't want us to know."

There was a tiny ragged piece of the dress missing. Venice didn't really see it at first, she felt it when her fingers were roaming over the fabric.

"What're your thoughts Venice? I don't think it would've been like that when she picked it up. Let's think about this. Got wine?"

"Need you ask?"

Venice poured us each a glass but we sipped it and left it in the kitchen. It would not do to spill red wine all over the dress. I don't know why we were being so careful. Nobody wanted the damned thing.

Venice said, "I'm thinking…Lauren wasn't wearing her gown when she was abducted. It was in a box so I'm guessing the tear happened later."

"Yes, yes, you're right. It probably happened when he was at our brokerage putting the gown on her. Det. Traynor said there were no signs of forced entry, so how did he even get into Rainbow Realty?"

I took a close-up picture of the place where the missing piece had been. I don't know why but I thought it important.

"Ven, I know we all have new keys but is the old key accounted for? Do you still have it?"

"Yes, my key was on my keychain and I had to remove it to put the new one on, how about you?"

"Mine was there too. We know Annie's key was with her because she opened that morning. Who knows, he could have taken it from one of the agents, copied it and put it back. I'll send out an email to everyone and ask if they remember losing the office key."

"Let's drop it for now. Maybe something will come to us later. I'm tired. But, just one more thing occurred to me. If the tear happened at the brokerage, what happened to the missing piece?"

Ven said, "Maybe he took it with him, or maybe Detective found it but didn't tell us. Why don't you ask her when you talk to her?"

"Good idea, I'll do that." I got Sassy and went home to settle in for the night. Maybe I'd dream the answers to our puzzles.

The next morning, I checked in with my Mom. Wes answered and said she was feeling tired so she was taking a nap.

"I'm glad I got you on the phone. I'm sure you'll tell me how she's really doing. With Mom, it's always 'I'm fine.' Is she really fine, Wes?"

"Well, Vivianne, she's been through a lot and she's still a bit weak, but every day she's improving. You know your Mom; she won't let this keep her down for long."

"I heard that Wes," said Mom. "And you're right about that. Let me talk to Vivianne."

Oh boy, just when I figured I had gotten out of a duty call. Damn.

"Hi Mom. You talk, I'm not going to ask you anything, especially how you're feeling."

"You're so dramatic. Wes, is delusional, I am NOT weak. He doesn't know what he's talking about. Do I sound weak to you?"

"Hell no. You sound perfectly okay to me. Wes is just imagining things, I'm sure. But he does take good care of you."

"Excuse me? Who takes good care of whom? It's me who plans meals, cooks, has parties, bakes, makes sure he's well fed and I could go on and on. But I'm sure you get the gist."

Oh yeah, I got the gist all right.

"Yes, Mom but he did buy you that beautiful necklace."

That seemed to mollify her. We said our good-byes. Now that I called her every day, the conversations weren't too long. And she didn't ask about John or the murder so I knew she wasn't fully herself yet. Just a matter of time but I was going to enjoy this Mom while it lasted. The old Mom was already leaking through.

It was Saturday and Gloria and Erika were having their house warming party this afternoon. Venice and I had bought them some very good wine, and plants for their yard. Gloria enjoyed gardening even though it was hard for me to picture her on her knees, gently patting soil around flowers, with the same hands that could probably knock me senseless.

I had invited John to go with me and we were meeting at my house. I'd be driving and Venice would also come with us. My ride wasn't as plush as his vehicle but it would have to do. He had met Det. Traynor before, but not Erika. I was hoping this would count as a date. I wasn't ready for a another one-on-one yet. Sigh, my Mom would be livid if I screwed this up.

John, being the perfect gentleman as usual, opened the front passenger door for Venice, he sat in the back.

"It's good to see you John, how's the new house working out?" asked Venice.

"I'm enjoying it very much. I was going to wait until later but while I have you two lovely ladies to myself, I'd like to invite you both for a day out on the boat. Venice, you can bring someone if you'd like."

"I'm leaving to see my guy on Monday, why don't we make plans when I get back. I'll only be gone for five days. Who knows, I may be able to talk Bryan into joining us. I was just telling Viv yesterday that we moved up the date for my visit because the week after he won't have the Harley, it'll be in for its annual maintenance."

John said, "Vivianne, why don't we go down to my Tucson house and visit Venice and Bryan? That would be fun."

"I'd love to but I'm the dog sitter. And, it's roasting there at this time of year, ask me again when it's cold and rainy here, I'll be on the next plane out." I wondered how many other houses he had and where they were?

We arrived a bit late which was fashionable. I broke my "Be Early" rule for parties. It's 'Vogue' to show up a bit tardy.

Gloria looked fabulous, I hardly recognized her, and Erika looked equally alluring. We all air kissed and went in.

They took our gifts with many thanks and Erika pulled us out back where the most adorable puppy came bounding up to greet us. "Oh," I said. "Who do we have here?"

"I wanted to introduce you guys to Sheba, our golden retriever puppy. Isn't she wonderful? I may have to bring her to work with me. And, we got her at a shelter. Her Mom recently gave birth there and Momma was adopted out and this was the last puppy they had. As you can imagine, they went very quickly. Good thing too or we might have had to adopt the others also."

Venice bent down to cuddle with her. "Erika, I'm so happy you two got a dog. You can take it from both of us, it's a sure investment for many years of happiness. I don't think either one of us could live without our dogs."

"Or cat," I reminded her. "Don't forget my Lola."

Erika said, "We'd have a cat too but Glo is allergic to them."

"So was I. I adopted sister kitties and soon after, found out I was very allergic to them. I went through four years of allergy shots and now I'm cured. I no longer have two kitties though. Lola's sister passed away a few years back. Lulu was the smaller kitty but boy, was she a bully," I said.

Erika asked, "Will you get more kitties in the future?"

"No, I'm happy with Sassy. Both my kitties were finicky eaters and they both had hyperthyroidism. It got to be very expensive. Lola has had that fixed to the tune of $3,000 which I didn't mind paying, but after she came home, she wouldn't eat and almost died. Lulu couldn't have it done because she wasn't in good enough shape.

"Sassy likes to be the only princess in the house. She tolerates Lola but I think, if Sassy wasn't so determined to ignore her, they could be friends."

"We better get back to the party. We haven't even mingled yet," said Venice.

The party was fun. There were many faces I recognized and John was talking away. I met Glo's and Erika's families who were very nice. I felt like I was just a little more a part of their lives. Especially Gloria. We'd have to have them over for dinner soon. I say 'we' because Venice always has more room and a bigger kitchen. I could do a lot of the cooking; she could do the baking. But first, we'd have to wait for Ven to get back from her romp in the cacti. Ouch.

I looked at the clock and it was later than I thought. Time flies. We said our goodbyes and I dropped Venice off and asked John if he'd like to come in for a drink. He said yes. Crap, I thought he'd decline.

He stayed for about half an hour. "This was fun Viv; I had a nice time, thanks for including me." I walked him to the door and he pulled me close and kissed me. "That was nice too," I said. He smiled and left. Whew, dodged that bullet.

Ringy ding, ding. "Hello," said Venice. "That was quick. Now what could you be calling me about? What has happened in the last half hour that I warrant a call?"

"We had sex."

"You're such a liar Viv. You barely had time to sit down much less have sex. There wasn't even enough time for a quickie."

"VENICE!"

"You do know I was married, right? You do know we consummated that union, right? Why are you always shocked when I say things like that? I'm not exactly chaste."

"Because you hardly ever say things like that. Oh, never mind, Miss Priss, HE KISSED ME."

"And?"

"And, what?"

"Did you like it? Did you kiss him back or did you throw him out on his ear?"

"I threw him out on his ass." We started laughing. "I did kiss him back; it was too late not to. He caught me off guard. It was a 'Pretty Good' sneaky kiss. I may have to rethink this whole thing."

The next day was Sunday and I called Det. Traynor. I wanted to ask her about the tear on the wedding gown. Maybe she did catch that but if not, I'd love to gloat.

"Hi Det. Traynor. Before I begin, I want you to know it was a great party and we enjoyed it immensely, especially meeting Sheba."

"I'm at work now, what do you want?"

Boy, she really needed Erika. The Gloria was missing, Detective had taken over. "I have the wedding gown and I wanted to know if anyone found a tiny tear in it?"

"You have the dress? Don't tell me you went down to Oregon?"

"Okay, I won't tell you. But we did, Venice and I."

"Sometimes you amaze me, and not in a good way. I can't believe you did that. Hold on."

I held on. She did say she wanted a fresh perspective. How was I going to give that without all the information, including the dress? I'm sure she withheld plenty.

"I'm back. I just spoke to forensics and they took pictures and documented everything that had to do with the dress. They found no fluids or fingerprints on the dress except those of the victim, the sales people, and the woman who does the fittings and alterations. There were no unidentified prints. There were many little buttons down the back of the dress and there was one missing. That's it. There was no tear documented. So, you're saying *you* found a tear?"

"Yes, we did. I took pictures of a tiny piece of fabric missing on the underside of the gown. I can send them to you if you'd like or, bring the dress back in."

"Send the photos. You can bring the dress back too. Since the chain of custody is now broken, we won't be able to use the gown but we can use the missing piece if it shows up and matches the tear on the dress. Just one more thing. How do I know you or Venice didn't tear it accidentally when you picked it up?"

"It was still in the box that was sent back to the Dinkel's from you, or forensics, or whoever sends back belongings. The Dinkel's hadn't even opened it, and we didn't remove it until we got to Venice's house. and then we spread out a clean sheet on the floor before we went to work inspecting it. So, the answer is, we absolutely didn't tear it, even by accident."

"Okay Vivianne, I'll concede. And, good catch."

Wow, she told me it was a good catch. And she didn't yell at me. I should have recorded her.

"Since I now live in Kingsville, why don't I stop by on the way home and pick it up." That wasn't a question, she would be stopping by.

"Okay, I've managed to squish the dress back into the box. I'm glad to give it to you and believe me, Lauren's Mom doesn't ever want to see it again. I attached a safety pin to the spot where we found the tear."

"I'm going to have someone's ass for missing this. Maybe we should employ you."

"Oh yes, can I be a consultant? Venice too? Or Venice can be the assistant consultant."

"Goodbye Vivianne."

At least this time she said goodbye. Hmmm, I wonder if she was serious about me being a consultant. She wouldn't even have to pay me.

When Det. Traynor came by, I didn't know whether she was Gloria or Detective. I just said hello and, didn't call her anything. I asked if I could take a button since one was missing anyway. If I found the errant one, I would have something to compare it against. She said yes so I snipped one off and gladly handed the boxed gown over to her. I asked if she'd like a glass of wine but she declined and left.

Tomorrow was Venice's departure. In the morning I'd be driving her to the Airporter and bidding her farewell for five whole days.

I didn't know if I was going to survive this.

At the bus I asked, "Will you be calling me every day?"

"No, I most certainly will not. And do not call me unless it's an emergency. I'll call if I get a chance though. But not every day." Kiss, kiss and off she went, happy as can be. Maybe a little too happy. I felt lonely already.

CHAPTER FOURTEEN

VENICE

I got on the bus and waved goodbye to Vivi. I knew she was going to miss me but it was only five days. I think I'd miss her too if I didn't have other things on my mind, namely Bryan. I was so excited about seeing him again, and taking this to another level. I felt butterflies just thinking about that next level.

But I was worried about Viv. If this relationship with Bryan really took off, I didn't know what I'd do. I would never leave Viv and the business. And, I loved my house too. I wanted Viv to like Bryan and not see him as a threat. Sigh, I'm going to put that all aside for now. No use worrying before I even know if there's anything to worry about.

The flight was only three hours but it felt like an eternity. I could hardly sit still. Finally, finally, we were landing. He'd be there to greet me. Maybe with flowers. Ohhhh, wouldn't that be nice.

I flew off the plane and through security. I looked left, then right, straight ahead, behind me. No Bryan. I felt a little deflated. Hmmmm. He couldn't have forgotten. Where was he? I texted Viv first to let her know I arrived safely and then called Bryan.

"Hi Venice Sweetie, where are you?" I looked up and said, "I'm at gate five, where are you?"

"I'm outside, just keep walking until you see Gate one,

that's where I'm parked."

He was outside? I was inside, why was he outside? He stayed on the phone while I trudged through the airport, passing gate four, three and then nine. Where was gate two and one? I asked at the desk and Gate one was all the way on the other side of the airport. I wanted to cry.

"Bryan, I just asked the information lady and she said I'm on the wrong side of the airport. Gate one is on the other side. Can you please come in and get me?"

By now I was becoming more and more irate. He should have been there to greet me when I got off the plane. My suitcase with my purse bungeed to it, rolling behind me, carry-on over my shoulder, was getting heavier and heavier the longer I walked. Now I was pissed and mumbling under my breath, looking down when I almost bumped into someone. It was Bryan.

"There you are," I said. If I were Vivi, I would have said a lot more. "What happened, did you have the gate wrong, did you get lost?" I was giving him an out but he didn't take it.

"No, nothing like that. Parking is $10.00 so I thought I'd meet you outside."

Through clenched teeth I managed, "I see." But I didn't see. Here I was, flying for three hours and paying my own fare, and he couldn't even spend ten bucks to be there when I got off the plane? Uh oh, red flag, red flag. I wasn't even here ten minutes yet. It seemed like hours. I let it go. I didn't want this trip to start off badly even though, obviously, he wasn't concerned about that. Or maybe he was just clueless. And, NO flowers. Okay, okay, I still have five days ahead of me, I didn't want to start it off angry, but I was angry.

We went outside and the heat hit me like a blast furnace. My God, it was beyond hot. It was a solid wall of suffocating heat. Yikes. Thankfully, we made it to his car quickly and he was gentleman enough to carry my bags. I think if he hadn't, that would have been the last straw and I would've turned around and gone home. Even *I* have a breaking point.

Settled in the nice, air conditioned, huge SUV, he said, "So, how was your flight?"

I wanted to say "Good, until I landed," but I didn't. I bet Vivi would have had no problem saying that. Oh well, I wasn't Viv. But sometimes I wish I could channel her.

Bryan pointed out things as we drove along, and I asked questions. I was starting to get over my irritability. The radio was playing golden oldies and that was cheering me up. My feet were tapping to the music.

About forty minutes later we pulled into his condo complex. My first impression was "Motel Six." The outside was made of gray cinderblocks. No pool, just covered parking with big numbers in front of the spaces. He told me everyone was allotted two spaces, so he'd have one for himself and one for guests.

For now, his Harley was parked in the extra space.

"Wow," I said. That's some bike, it's much bigger than I expected."

He had told me what to bring for motorcycle riding. I had to have long, tight fitting jeans so I wouldn't flap in the wind and a form fitting shirt and maybe a light jacket. I had the jeans and brought an adorable pink tee that said, in rhinestones, *Harley Davidson*. Viv bought it for me as a going away gift.

I also had to bring substantial footwear. I couldn't ride in flip flops. Damn. I bought pink sneakers to match my shirt. If nothing else, I would look adorably put together. Unless I fell off the bike. And then I probably wouldn't care because I'd be DEAD.

I couldn't even imagine putting on all those clothes in this heat. Oh well, when we did stop it would be to go into an air-conditioned restaurant and Sedona was, hopefully, a bit cooler.

"C'mon, let's get you inside before you melt." There were three levels to the condo and Bryan's unit was on the second floor. There was an elevator, and given he had my luggage, we took that up to his place.

We entered a tiny foyer. To the left was a small coat closet and to the right was a nondescript, tiny kitchen which left a whole lot to be desired. Straight ahead was the living room with double sliding doors that led to the covered deck which overlooked the golf course. The living room was a nice size but the camel-colored carpeting had to go. It was depressing but no more so than the dark brown accordion doors against one wall. I couldn't imagine what they were for.

Pointing at them I asked, "Where do they lead to?"

"That's the guest room. I plan on getting rid of those ugly things and walling that space up. In the hall you can access that room through a door. I guess leaving them open might make for a bigger living room but that's already a good size."

There were two bathrooms, one off the small hallway that led to the guest room and straight ahead was the master suite complete with its own bathroom. The bedroom was large and had a king size bed and a desk by the big window that also overlooked the golf course. Everything seemed to be old, not good antique old but 80s's and 90's old. The bathrooms were functional but certainly didn't make a fashion statement unless "Ugly" was it. The master bathroom was small, but it did have a tiny space with a mirror and shelf where one could sit and do hair and makeup. I would say the overall color scheme was beige and brown throughout.

We were in the master bedroom when he pointed to the dresser and said, "I cleaned out two drawers for you and part of the closet too." My bags sat there, ready for me to unpack.

He was quickly redeeming himself. I was feeling a little better about being here. Then he turned around and gently kissed me. Ooo-la-la. Very nice kiss that made me tingle right down to my toes. Now I really felt better.

That first night we went out to a Mexican restaurant for dinner where we ordered way too much food. We took half of it home. I can eat, but not that much. I was starting to get nervous again, bedtime was looming. It had been a long time since I had slept with a man. My sleeping partners were dogs. Literally.

We'd also had a pitcher of margaritas with dinner, which helped lessen my anxiety. Bryan seemed oblivious to it all. Men! Not a clue.

When we got back to the condo he asked if I wanted a little after dinner drink and though I'm usually not a big drinker, I said yes. Worst case scenario, I passed out and then I would no longer have to think about having sex for the first time in forever.

I took my shower and put on my sexy little nightie. Black, lacy, and hopefully alluring. I took a breath and walked into the bedroom. Bryan was reading. He looked up at me admiringly.

"Sweetie, you look beautiful. Come on in here." He picked

up the blanket, and patted the bed.

I scooted into bed and into the crook of his arm. He pulled me close and then, continued reading. READING??? Was there something wrong? Did he not like what I had on? Was he not drawn to me? I was supposed to be alluring. My self-esteem took a nose dive.

At that point, I got out of bed, retrieved my iPad and opened it to my book. I also threw on a light robe. This was absolutely not what I had envisioned for the first night. Hmmm, maybe after reading hour was over? I would rather die a sexless old maid than make the first move.

Bryan turned to me and said, "I think we're probably both tired. And, I shouldn't have had that nightcap. Let's just go to sleep tonight, okay?"

"That's fine, Bryan." He thought we were *both* tired? I was not tired. I was so disappointed I wanted to cry. I told him I wanted to read a little longer and if my light disturbed him, I could sit in the living room. He said to stay, rolled over, and within minutes, was sound asleep.

I awoke to a sun-drenched bedroom. Ugh. Too much light, way too early. I looked at the clock. Six A.M.? And no Bryan? Ah, I could hear him clunking away in the tiny kitchen. A few minutes later he came in, carrying a tray with coffee, cream, sugar and pancakes. Oh boy, I don't eat breakfast that early, I like to have my coffee and wake up a bit first.

"I thought I'd make you breakfast in bed, Sweetie. Do you want ice cream on your pancakes?"

Oh my God, maybe I was still sleeping and having a nightmare. At least I hoped that's what it was. Ice cream? On pancakes? For breakfast? Where's the meat I asked myself. You know, sausage, bacon?

"Oh Bryan, what a lovely breakfast. I'm so sorry but I can't eat this early. At home I usually have coffee and skip breakfast. If the pancakes will last in the fridge, I can eat them later."

And ice cream? How disgusting. Of course, I kept my thoughts to myself. The gesture was very nice, even if it was only 6 A.M.

I could tell he was a little disappointed and I started to talk myself into eating them because he went to all that trouble. My inner voice kicked in and said, "Don't you dare cave. Be yourself. You're the new Venice, and you're NOT GOING TO EAT THOSE PANCAKES." After all, I was more than a little discouraged about last night, and let's not forget the airport fiasco. That was much worse than turning down pancakes. I wanted to go home.

"Why are we up at the crack of dawn? I'm surprised the sun isn't still sleeping."

"I thought we'd get an early start for Sedona."

"Wait, wait, wait, I need to learn how to ride on that thing first. You can't just plunk me down behind you and take off."

"I never thought of that. Get dressed and we'll have a quick lesson. You'll pick it up, after all, you'll be the passenger, not the driver."

Did I mention I wanted to go home? I do believe he just gave me orders. There was no question in that sentence.

I dressed in my motorcycle clothes which, given the oppressive heat, were going to dehydrate me before I made it downstairs. I was hoping, once on the bike, it would be breezy, even a hot breeze would be better than this.

He showed me how to get on and off the beast and took me for a short ride around town. The passenger seat was comfortable and I was ecstatic that it had a backrest. It gave me a little boost of confidence that I wouldn't tumble backwards into oncoming traffic, although if I did, Bryan probably wouldn't even notice I was no longer there.

I'd bought a small pouch for my money, credit cards and lipstick. I also had my lip balm which I was sure I'd need. I had a choice of a small helmet, leaving my face naked to the elements, or a larger one with a face guard. I chose the bigger one that might keep my face intact and the bugs out of my mouth. I wouldn't be able to wear my killer sunglasses with rhinestones. They were last year's Christmas gift from Nellie. Viv's love of anything bling was starting to rub off on me. I'd bring them with me because, sooner or later I'd have the damned heavy helmet off my head. You don't go outside in Arizona without sunglasses.

We went back to the condo parking space and I practiced getting on and off. It wasn't easy given I was so much shorter than Bryan. Finally, we were ready to go. At least as ready as I was ever going to be. And now I had sweat stains on my beautiful pink shirt. I had pulled my hair back into a pony tail, no use styling it, I was just going to have the windblown look.

Off we went. I was apprehensive at first but after about an hour, when I was no longer terrified I'd fall off, I settled down and started to enjoy the ride. In the beginning I had a killer grip around his waist and now, here I was, hands on my thighs. Weee Hooo.

Every now and then he'd reach around and squeeze my hand and yell, "Are you okay?"

I'd yell back, "Yes, I'm fine." Any conversation would be

gobbled up by the wind.

We stopped a few times to stretch our legs, mine especially. He'd help me off and I'd walk around a bit and do stretches to limber up. Five minutes later we were back on the road.

Going up the mountain road to Sedona was both scary and thrilling. Up, up, up, we went. I could look out at the vista below and see for miles. After a while the terror gave up and was replaced by excitement. I was really getting into this. I didn't know if I'd ever be able to use my legs again, they felt welded to the bike, but for now it was exhilarating.

Being on the back of a Harley, arms around my good-looking man, wind whistling, I felt free and full of adventure. My eyes were on the vista spread out before me, which was absolutely intoxicating.

When the Harley made turns, my body responded as if it was part of the bike. Even though I was okay not clinging to Bryan, it was lovely to just put my arms around him. It had been a long time since I'd hugged a man. It was good to feel an arm around my shoulder, a hand in mine, a fleeting kiss here and there. I was starting to believe I was infatuated with him. Even if this feeling only lasted for today, I was happy to have it. This was one of the best days I'd had in a while. All red flags were forgotten.

It was cooler in Sedona, still hot, but more bearable. We stopped for lunch at a little mountainside bistro with seating outside. The food was okay, the best thing being the small lizards flitting across our path. Wildlife. Lizards count, they're both alive and wild, I think.

After lunch we went up the mountain to the Chapel of the Holy Cross. Once parked you had to walk up a long, curved ramp. On the southwestern wall was a 90-foot-tall iron cross.

Inside it was very cool and the lighting was dim. It felt like a holy place in its simplicity and quiet beauty. I found it calming. We stayed for about fifteen minutes and then it was back on the motorcycle. He sure didn't like to linger.

We drove all over the place, stopping to see Cathedral Rock, Tlaquepaque Arts & Crafts Village, where there were galleries, shops, and more galleries. I wanted to buy some things but there was little room on the bike for purchases. Damn.

On the road again, after about twenty minutes, I realized we were leaving Sedona. I yelled at Bryan to stop. He yelled back he'd stop in a little while at a bar he'd been in. A bar? I hope he wasn't thinking of drinking. I may not speak up much but I would not accept drinking and driving. Especially on a motor-cycle. If you got in an accident, I'm pretty sure you could kiss your butt goodbye.

We pulled up to a dumpy looking place. A whole host of bikes were parked outside. Ah, he was taking me to a biker bar.

We got a table outside and he excused himself to go to the bath-room. While he was gone a tough looking "Biker Chick" came over to my table. Bryan wasn't back yet. A lot of her teeth were missing and she had tattoos over every inch of her body, and they weren't the pretty kind. She leered at me. Yes, leered. Oh my God, was she trying to pick me up? Where the hell was Bryan? I was getting scared. At that moment I saw him walking toward me and felt a wave of relief.

He looked at the woman and said, "Sorry, she's mine." She got up and walked away. Once back in the parking lot, we had a good laugh over that experience. "I guess I have to protect you from men *and* women. That's how cute you are." He didn't drink so I was relieved about that.

I did not want to get back on the motorcycle and asked Bryan to get me a coke. Why did I have to ask for everything? Could he not take the initiative? I finished my soda and suggested we spend the night in Sedona and go home the next day. I was tired and getting cranky.

"I'd like to get home," he said. "Can you make it? I promise we'll be there in about two hours and I'll stop frequently so you can stretch. Deal?"

"Okay but I'm not going to be able to walk when I get off this thing. You're going to have to carry me up the stairs to the condo."

"My pleasure," he said.

He made good on his promise. The only glitch came when we were almost home. The person in the car in front of us threw an empty can out the window that bounced off the bike's wind shield. It pissed him off and frightened me half to death. It made me realize just how vulnerable we were.

Bryan was willing to carry me up the stairs but I declined. I think I had bow legs, like a cowboy. Once there, I threw myself on the couch and told him I was never moving again. There was no intimacy that night either but this time it was my doing. My poor legs would never be the same, especially my thighs. My knees felt a bit wobbly also.

"If we're going anywhere tomorrow, I would prefer the car," I said.

"No problem. You were a real trooper today."

I thought, whoopee doo. I didn't ever want to be a trooper again.

The next day, Bryan said we were going to Dead Man's Mall. "What's that" I asked.

He said, "If you haven't noticed, we have an abundance of old people here. They die. Frequently. All the stuff in their condos that their heirs don't want, goes to the consignment shops in the mall, thus the name."

"That's awful," I said laughing.

We rummaged through all the shops and I came out with a few things. One was a very small leather bag that I could use if I ever got back on the Harley again. And it was on sale. I paid a whopping .75 for it. Oh boy.

On the way home we stopped at Costco. He had to pick up a prescription and Mr. Big Spender bought me a hotdog for lunch.

We were eating in tonight, Bryan was cooking. With my help. He informed me he made delicious tomato sauce so we'd have that and some hot and sweet Italian sausage. Simple enough. When it was almost time to eat, I snuck a taste. Yuck, he had added sugar. It was sweet. While he was in the bathroom, I scoured his kitchen and found basil, and oregano which I quickly threw into the sauce. Then I threw some grated parmesan in and tasted it again. Better but it wouldn't hold a candle to mine or Viv's cooking.

Bryan took a spoonful of sauce to taste and said, "This is really good. I think I'm a better cook than I gave myself credit for. Here, you taste."

"Oh yes, you're amazing." A little ego stroking never hurt. I was hoping that's not all I'd be stroking. Ahhggghhh. I was becoming a sex maniac without the sex.

We watched a movie after dinner then Bryan pulled me up off the couch and held me tight and kissed me.

"Why don't we head into the bedroom," he roared, thumping his chest like Tarzan. No, he didn't roar or thump but just picturing it made me smile.

"An excellent idea." Wow, the tingles were back.

Suffice it to say it was a pretty good evening. Fireworks didn't go off but he did. It wasn't as good as I imagined it would be but at least we did it. Now I knew what prescription he'd picked up at Costco.

The next day, my last, he asked if it would be okay for him to play a round of golf with the oldsters in the morning.

"Yes, of course. Go have fun. How long will you be gone?"

"A couple of hours, tops."

"Why don't you leave the keys to the bike and I'll take a ride."

The look on his face was priceless. "Only kidding Bryan, but you could leave me the keys to the car."

And he did. I drove around the neighborhood looking at houses and cacti, and at that point, I ran out of things to see. Then I went to the supermarket and bought my favorite brand of cold-cuts, Boar's Head. I got turkey, ham and swiss and picked up some potato salad and rolls. When Bryan came home it was lunchtime and he was delighted with my little meal.

"Are you up to taking a short trip on the motorcycle?" I

thought we might go over to Scottsdale. It's a fun place, lots of galleries."

"Yes, I would like that," I said. And off we went. I was fully recovered and he was right, it wasn't a long drive at all. This I could handle.

We went into a very expensive gallery where we pretended to be wealthy and the salesman bent over backwards to accommodate us. He even brought us glasses of champagne, which Bryan declined but I drank mine. I told salesman there were several paintings I was interested in but wanted to think about it.

Scottsdale was fun. On the way back to his condo we passed an "Open House" sign so this time we pretended to be married and very interested in the place. Being a realtor, I felt bad for lying but it was an open house. It's not like we made an appointment.

That night was even better in bed. It was a good end to my trip. We'd be up early the next morning and I'd be on my way home. I would miss him but I was missing the dogs, Viv and Rainbow Realty. This was fun but I really was ready to go home. I clicked my heels and *voila*, I was standing in my living room. I wish.

CHAPTER FIFTEEN

Venice was coming home today and I was deliriously happy. I really missed the hell out of her. And I could hardly wait to hear all about her trip.

I put the dogs in the SUV telling them they'd be seeing their Mom soon. I swear, they understood what I said because their tails started wagging with much enthusiasm.

When they saw Venice, they went insane, jumping and slobbering all over her. Ven was laughing and hugging them back. I think I saw a tear or two. She totally ignored me. Then she hugged me and licked my face. No, no, that was Sassy who did that. Licked my face that is, Sassy doesn't do hugging.

I dropped Ven and her dog children off and invited her for dinner later.

"Is dinner going to be Domino's pizza?" she asked.

"No Ven, it's going to be a real home cooked meal. I promise. And Sassy has invited Mr. Snigglebottom and Betty. I have a little something special for them too. I'm so glad you're back, I've missed you terribly."

"And I've missed you too, more than I thought I would," said Venice, smiling.

I had honored Ven's wishes and hadn't called her once. I wanted to, but I knew she needed this time with Bryan. Dinner was at 6 P.M. She didn't know it, but I had a surprise for her as well.

Venice opened the door saying, "Knock, knock." Everyone yelled "Welcome Home." There was a giant welcome home banner across the sliding doors and Annie, Gloria, and Erika were there. They had parked around the corner so she didn't see their cars. She was so surprised she started to cry.

"Oh, you guys. This is so nice but really, I've only been gone five days. It does seem like a month though."

"It seems like a year to me," I said.

I'd have to wait to hear the intimate details, and there had better be intimate details. Meantime she told us all about her trip, the motorcycle, Sedona, everything. It sounded like she had a wonderful time and I was genuinely happy for her. While she was gone, I gave a lot of thought as to how badly I had behaved toward the relationship thing with Ven and Bryan. Well, there would be no more of that. I was a brand-new leaf.

I had made pot roast with roasted carrots, potatoes and a green bean casserole of which I would not partake. I hate green veggies, I know they're going to find that they cause, acne, or personality disorder. I had a big salad for Vegan Annie.

I even made a cake. Yesterday my kitchen looked like a disaster. I had every cake decorating tool out, plus the ingredients for it all. I made a lemon cake with lemon/blueberry frosting and blueberries set around the edge of the top and bottom. It was truly a work of art. I was very proud given I don't bake that much. I'm certainly not Ven's caliber and I hoped it tasted as good as it looked.

The dogs were in the backyard with marrow bones. Erica had

asked if she could bring Sheba and all four of them seemed to get along just fine. They had a new friend. The dogs would most likely write me a glowing "Thank you" on their personalized, monogramed, stationary when they got home tonight.

We ate, drank, and were merry. I wanted to ask Gloria about the bridal murder but she wasn't Det. Traynor tonight so I dared not. I wanted to know about Bryan, stuff Venice wouldn't tell anyone else but me. I was hoping that would be soon.

Annie left first. Then Gloria and Erika were saying their goodbyes when Gloria handed both Venice and I both, gift-wrapped box. "Do not open these until I'm gone and don't make a big deal out of it. You can call me in the morning. At the station."

Erika said, "Excuse Gloria, she can't do anything nice without getting all gruff and grumpy. Might mess with her 'Tough cop' façade. Thank you for a lovely dinner Viv, and *Welcome Home,* Venice. Goodnight."

"Wait," I said. I went into the kitchen and wrapped up a huge piece of cake for them. "Here, enjoy, if it's here I'll just eat it all and then I'll have to go for a run which I hate. Take it, you're doing me a favor. I'm sure Sheba would love it." Sheba was already in their car.

Air kisses for Erika, a verbal goodbye for Gloria and they were all gone. Whew. I looked at the kitchen. Oh my God, what a disastrous mess. When you have a small space, it fills up quickly.

Venice offered to help me but I said, "No, I absolutely must hear the juicy stuff. There *is* more, isn't there? Please tell me there's more."

"Okay, I'll tell but we can talk while we clean. I'm not leaving you with this mess."

"Why don't we get the dogs in here, they'll lick it all clean. Spotless. Okay, not too sanitary, but I won't tell if you won't."

"Viv, get in here now if you want me to talk."

I ran the two steps into the kitchen. Okay, see, I'm cleaning, now out with it."

"You won't believe this and before I say anything you have to promise not to pass judgement. Just let me finish and then you can...say nothing. Okay, I realize what I just said would be an impossibility for you. Just try not to be unkind."

Uh oh, was there something for me to be unkind about?

"We didn't have relations until the *third* night. And I think I know why, because we went to Costco that afternoon and he picked up a prescription."

"I don't get it. What are you saying?"

"A prescription? Like in little blue pills?"

"Holy shit, Viagra? Isn't he a bit young for that? Who cares, did it work? Obviously, it did because you had *relations*. God Ven, you're such a prude. You had sex. Good, old fashioned sex. Or maybe kinky sex?"

"Viv, stop it right now or I won't tell you anymore. Not that there's much to tell. I'm not giving you a detailed description of my time in bed. Frankly, it would only take a few minutes and then bore you to death.

"Well, that doesn't sound good," I said. "I'll just watch the video. You did record it, didn't you?"

"VIVIANNE! No video. The sex was okay. I mean, not spectacular but...okay."

"And why wasn't it spectacular? Did he not know how to do it?"

A big sigh from Venice as her face turned the color of fresh blood. "I don't know how to say this but it was... small. Really small."

"His penis? His penis was that small? Maybe the Viagra wasn't working."

"No, it was small. He's a big guy, tall, muscular, I expected *it* to match the rest of him."

"Shit Ven, that must have been a big disappointment, or should I say 'small' disappointment?"

"I'm done discussing this now. That's all I'm going to say on that matter."

"But you had a good time overall, right? I mean your trip to Sedona and the Harley?"

"Yes, maybe, well, some of the time. A tiny red flag, I think he's a bit on the cheap side. That's not good. He also didn't seem to care that I was sore from all that riding and he pushed to go home instead of staying at a motel and continuing the next morning. He did say I was a trooper. I think we could have gone on a shorter trip for my first motorcycle ride."

"Ah, the bloom is off the rose?" I queried. "I'm sorry, Venice. I really am. What now? Is it over? Maybe you should talk to him first."

"Hey, what have you done with Vivi? VIVI, where are you?"

"Are you some kind of idiot or what?" I asked.

"Oh, there you are. It's just that I thought you said I should talk to him before I made any kind of decision. I guess I misheard you."

"Don't be a smartass. I did some thinking while you were gone for those six months and decided I was wrong. You deserve to be happy."

"Vivi, where's the smelling salts? And that six months was only five days. What am I to do with you? I know you want me to be happy, and I am. I'm just not sure Bryan will bring me more happiness than I already have."

"I'm simply saying you shouldn't do anything rash. This was the first time you two were together for any length of time. He may not be happy either. And if he's not, he's brain dead so get rid of him."

"I guess you're right. I don't have to think about it now, he's in another state so it will give me time to ponder. Yes, I'll ponder."

"Ven, you're weird. Who says 'ponder'? Speaking of pondering, I'm going to continue to see John. I meant to speak to you about this. He's invited us out for an evening on his yacht. ON THE FOURTH OF JULY!" I said, doing s little twirly dance. "You have to go; there won't be a better vantage point to see the fireworks, unless you're in a plane. And maybe you might want to invite Bryan. If you do, that means he'll be staying at your house. Maybe that will give you better perspective, better insight. Your house, your rules."

"I'm in. However, I was just with Bryan and it may be too soon to invite him up here. The fourth is next week. What about my pondering time? I wouldn't want him here for long either, how do I tell him there's a time limit? You're so much better at this than I am. They don't call you 'Mouth' for nothing."

"Wait, who calls me that? Ahh, who cares, it fits me doesn't it? If you're afraid you'll offend him, have a lie ready. You can say we're going for a spa week and Annie is going to watch the dogs so you can only invite him for five days. If he doesn't like it, he can decline the invitation."

"Yeah, but that would be dishonest."

Rolling my eyes, I said, "Your point? You're not married to him and the lie is necessary to save his ego. What do you want to say, 'I'm inviting you for the fourth of July but I won't be able to stand you if you stay too long so five days is my limit?' You think that's better than my lie? If so, be my guest. But don't be surprised if you never hear from him again. God, the man has a nonexistent penis, you need to be very careful of his ego."

Laughing, Venice said, "I'm going to do it. Invite him that is. And you're right, I'll lie. I can do that over the phone, he won't see my lying eyes."

"Why don't I ask John if we can invite Annie. She can bring whomever. She's been through a lot lately what with finding the body and now having to learn the alarm system and, I love the kid. Hey, speaking of kid maybe my sister and Nellie would like to join us. Mom and Wes too."

"Vivi, you're getting carried away. Do you even know how big the boat is?"

"Yacht Dahling, it's called a yacht," I said in my upper snooty accent. A boat would have oars. A yacht does not. Wait, maybe he does have oars for the emergency lifeboats. It's still a yacht. I guess I am getting a bit ahead of myself. It's only for one night, nobody is going to fly in for that. But I will ask about Annie. The more the merrier."

I called John and he was 'On Board' with inviting Annie. He knew Annie from when he came into the office. He told me to invite as many people as I wanted. He had rented a huge yacht for the party; he'd included some of his friends also. His regular yacht could sleep seven, and while it was beautiful, it was too small for this event. Also, the rental came with staff so he could enjoy the party with his guests.

Venice was just about to call it a night when she noticed the two gift wrapped boxes Gloria had left for us.

"Hey Viv, we forgot to open these. Let's do it now."

They had been sitting there unnoticed. I picked mine up and ripped off the wrapping in a second. "Oh my God, I can't believe this. Do you see what this is?"

Venice didn't look too pleased. "Yes, I see that we now have our very own cards that say we're consultants to the police. Did Gloria forget your snooping, getting into trouble, and screwing everything up? Has she lost her mind?"

"I have news for you, Venice. She gave these to us because she values my input, my detecting skills and my wisdom. The only reason you also have them is because she knew I'd want you as my assistant consultant. Now we can consult for real."

"I think she gave these to us in hopes that now you'll keep her in the loop. Whatever, it was nice of her. But I hope you realize this is *consulting.* You're not a real cop."

"Don't be a killjoy. I think I may start taking online classes about police work. Just so I'm knowledgeable. She won't be sorry she gave these cards to me and this also means we won't have to sneak around behind her back anymore. At least not as much. I'm very moved by this."

"Oh boy," said Venice.

The next morning when I got to work, I asked Annie to come into my office. "Uh oh," she said. "I just want to say, I didn't do it."

"Ah HA, what didn't you do Annie? Oh, here's Venice." I waved for her to come in. Now Annie was really nervous.

"Now that we're all here I have something to say. You know we love you but I'm sorry to say…"

"Oh my God, you're firing me. Oh my God." And she started to cry.

"Annie, no, I was just screwing with you. I didn't mean to make you cry. We've decided to give you a raise. Now, it will have to be a larger one because I'm an idiot. And, we'd love for you to join us on John Berkman's yacht for the fourth of July. You can bring someone if you'd like."

Annie wiped her eyes. "You know I never cry but the thought of not working here…it would be awful. I feel like this is my home away from home. Don't ever do that again. Now let's talk about this yacht. And how much of a raise am I getting?"

Annie's sense of humor was back. There was nobody special in her life at the moment so she'd be going alone. Bryan jumped at the opportunity to leave the heat and see Venice again so he too would be attending He'd be flying in the day before the party, and leaving five days later. Venice being Venice, had told him the truth. She didn't say it was only five days because of him, she said she had to work. Which was partly true. He understood completely.

The week went by, we were both busy with work. The brokerage was doing very well. Our agents were all productive but that wasn't surprising given it was summer. We had to reap what we could because winter would be much leaner.

I called Venice and asked her, "What time are you picking up Bryan?" He was taking the Airporter so she would be picking him up in Port Hollow.

"I'm getting him in a few hours, why?"

"I thought I'd have you both over for dinner if you'd like."

"I was going to ask you to dinner at my house. I'm not going crazy though. I thought I'd do the cooking outside. I've got Chilean sea bass, corn on the cob, and baked potatoes. No green veggies so it's right up your alley. Want to join?"

"That sounds delicious. Let's invite John and Annie."

"You do know it's my invitation to you, not your invitation to everybody else?"

"Sorry, you're right. It's your dinner, you get to pick the

guests."

"Call John and invite him and I already invited Annie. I thought this would be a good venue for her to socialize with everyone so she'll feel more at ease at the party. I'm making a salad so she can have that. It will be a fun evening. And I won't have to be alone with Bryan."

"You do realize we're not staying the night. You could always put him outside in a tent."

"Very funny, I don't even own a tent. Goodbye, Viv."

At least she said goodbye.

It would be nice to have dinner with a bunch of people, who I liked. Well, I was still reserving my opinion of Bryan until he earned more points.

Before Venice flew into my life, I tended to be a lot more solitary. Now I socialized with people who weren't clients, people I actually enjoyed being with. I could still be isolated in my house when I felt like it, but the thing was, I didn't feel like it anymore. I had metamorphosed into a social butterfly thing.

John declined dinner at Venice's since the yacht party was tomorrow and he would be busy making sure everything was in place. He did say he was looking forward to seeing me.

A fun evening was had by all. Dinner was superb, Annie got to meet Bryan, and I found him a lot more personable. Maybe it was the sex that made him more confident. I noticed he called Ven 'Sweetie' and they seemed to be good with each other. I'd better keep my eye on this.

The next morning, I got up, and the first thought was, yay, the fourth of July is here and it's going to be fabulous. What to wear? I decided on a colorful cotton sundress with criss cross straps in the back. I better not stay in the sun too long or tomorrow I'd have a big X on my back. I'd bring a light summer jacket because it usually got a little chilly in the evening, especially on the water. My red hair, kissed by the sun, was now more of a strawberry blonde. It had natural waves so I only needed to blow dry and fluff.

Venice looked delicious in a hot pink halter dress with adorable sandals to match. Bryan had on light khaki pants with a white shirt, opened at the neck. He looked very dashing.

There was a small motor boat that could handle four people and that's what took us out to where the yacht was waiting. John told me the boat was called a *Tender*. The ship was out on Hood Canal. I'm guessing it wasn't deep enough for it to make it all the way in to the dock. It was gargantuan.

John looked like a captain, dressed in white pants and a dark navy blazer with gold buttons. There were already about ten people on board, drinks and canapes were being passed around by waiters in white pants with white, short jacket, and even white gloves. Very elegant as Wes would say.

"There you are," said John. He gave me a big hug and a small kiss. "You look good enough to eat. Let me introduce you to my guests, bring Venice and Bryan along,"

At that moment Annie appeared. Now *she* looked the part. Hair the color of a fire engine with a blue and white short sleeveless dress. This all came together with her red vintage heels that matched the color of her hair.

"Annie! You look adorable. I love the patriotic look going on. Come on over, John is going to introduce us to his other guests."

We met Martha and George, Harry and Kate, Harold and Maude, and of course, Thelma and Louise, and Laverne and Shirley too. Okay, this wasn't the real guest list. Everyone was pleasant and the mood was festive. The dress code ranged from casual to fancy. I'm guessing we fell in between those two categories.

"Wow, this is some shindig," said Venice.

"You think? And it's only the cocktail hour. Dinner will be at 8 P.M. and it will be a buffet. I'm sure the food will be scrumptious. Remember his last party? When he was with Tiffy?"

"How could I not? What a disaster, but we won't talk about that now, we're having a great time, aren't we Bryan?"

Bryan looked at her adoringly and said, "That's because I have you by my side."

I vomited over the side. Not really, but I wanted to. Instead, I plastered a big smile on my face.

"Annie," said Venice, "You are the epitome of patriotism. How are you always so put together? And why are you wasting your fashion talents working at Rainbow Realty?"

"You've got a point there, Venice. Vivianne, I quit."

"Oh no you don't, we just gave you a ridiculously large raise."

"Yeah, you did. Okay, I'll stay. What time do the fireworks start?"

"John figured the Seattle fireworks would start around 10, when it was dark. I'm sure this will be quite the show, being in the middle of the water. Oh, we're moving."

John came over and put his arm around me. It felt very good. I might have to admit, I was very fond of him. But I'd keep that to myself, for now.

"Why are we moving John? Are you whisking us away to a deserted island?"

"If it were only you and I that would be a very good idea but there's all of them," he said as he waved his arm toward the guests.

"I'm planning a little surprise. I'm not going to tell you because if I did, it would no longer be a surprise now, would it?"

"So, you would rather torture me?" I said.

"You don't have to wait that long, I promise, now how about we get some food before the big display?"

As predicted, the buffet consisted of everything you could possibly want. It was impossible to pick so I just took a taste of it all, except anything green and I did forgo dessert.

Our immediate party went to the upper deck, the perfect vantage point from which to watch the fireworks. It seemed everyone else thought this the ideal spot too. I sat down, ouch, what was that? I picked up a small round something and at that moment the sky exploded with "Will you marry me Viv?" It didn't really, but John's surprise was his very own firework display, along with the City of Seattle's show. It was the most spectacular fourth I had ever seen.

He stood next to me and said, "You like it?"

"YES, I love it. What a wonderful surprise. I'll never forget this fourth. It's been the very best."

There we all stood, John and I, Venice and Bryan and Annie and someone who seemed to like her very much. He had his arm around her. What a perfect night.

CHAPTER SIXTEEN

I hadn't seen much of Venice after the fourth, and I understood. Bryan was visiting and he'd be leaving tomorrow so I not only pretty much left her alone, I even took over some of her realtor work so she could be with him. I didn't just turn over a new leaf, the whole tree got flipped. I was very proud of myself.

I did have John to occupy my mind. This coming weekend he invited me to his new house for a home cooked dinner, made by him. I hadn't known he could cook, but I'd better reserve that thought until I tasted the food. This seemed to be the year of the date. Annie had met Jerome on the yacht and now she was dating too.

It was Saturday and Bryan was leaving later today but, hearing all about her dalliance with lover boy would have to wait because I was on my way to John's house. Venice knew where I was going so she would go over and take Sassy for the evening.

I was really looking forward to my dinner date. I arrived a few minutes late and John opened the door before I could knock. "Hi, Viv, you look lovely. Come in to my humble abode."

Humble my ass. However, he got one thing right, I did look pretty good. I was wearing a new outfit. Since we were on the beach, I had on yellow capris and a multicolored blouse decorated with Hummingbirds. I even had on tiny hummingbird earrings. Maybe the real ones would flock around me thinking I was a big flower.

"Something smells good enough to eat. Is that our dinner?"

"Yes, and don't ask, you'll see what it is when it's on the table. I know you by now so put your impatience away. I have a wonderfully relaxing evening planned."

"I can't tell you how good that sounds. And I am *not* impatient. So, what's cooking?"

We both laughed and then I said, "The place looks terrific. Did you pick all this out yourself?"

"I did. I could have hired a decorator but I'm more of a hands-on guy. I really enjoy trying it all out first. I went to Seattle and spent an entire day sitting on sofas, testing dining room chairs and picking out the most luxurious bed. It comes with a remote and does more things than I thought possible. Hell, I don't even need a woman anymore."

Smiling lasciviously, I said, "Oh, is that so? Then I guess I'll be going now, given my obsolescence. I never thought I'd be replaced by a remote."

"You were planning on staying the night?" asked John, "I'll throw the remote out the window right now."

"Let's not get ahead of ourselves. I think I'll take that drink now. Bourbon on the rocks please."

And the flirting was off and running. I hadn't flirted since...I can't remember. I believe it was sometime during the Triassic age of the earth. Maybe not quite that long. After all, that age ended in mass extinction, and I'm still here.

He brought out my drink in a crystal glass that was so heavy I needed a forklift to get it to my lips. And the hor d'oeuvres were surprisingly good. He served prosciutto wrapped shrimp, little cheese puffs and tiny pastry shells with ham and swiss melted in them.

"John, you've outdone yourself. Did you really make all this for me?"

"I confess," said John. "I cheated on the hor d'oeuvres, I only made the shrimp and prosciutto. The rest were compliments of Costco."

"I hope dinner will wait because I'm going to partake of everything."

And I did, with a refill of the best bourbon I'd ever had. I asked what it was and he told me it was Blanton's Single Barrel Bourbon Whiskey. Probably nothing I could afford. Did I say the super-rich lifestyle wasn't for me? I think I may have been a bit too hasty. I could really get used to this.

The main course was stuffed lobster. Okay, now I knew he didn't cook this. Who cooks stuffed lobster other than a chef?

"Did you have this catered? C'mon, tell me the truth. You didn't make this. *I* can't even make this. I don't think Venice can make this."

"Ye of little faith," he said. "I did make dinner, from scratch. I'll let you in on a little secret that not many people know about me. A few years back I went to culinary school. I appreciate good food and I wanted to know how it all came together. After all, when you think about it, cooking is just like following directions, the directions being a recipe."

"Yes, you do have to follow the recipe but you also have to learn techniques. And there are many secrets in cooking, like old family recipes. And if you're an accomplished chef you have to know enough to improvise. Maybe even make up a recipe or two."

He put his arm around me, gave me a quick kiss and said, "Wait here just one minute." He departed and returned wearing a waiter's jacket complete with a very tall, white chef's hat. He filled up a huge tray of food which he served. Once on the table and ready to eat, he went back into the kitchen and changed his jacket, took off the hat and was transformed back into my dinner partner.

He sure made me laugh.

The stuffed lobster took center stage but the filet mignon was a close second. It was medium rare and the most tender filet I'd ever eaten. The lobster was stuffed with crabmeat, real crabmeat, not that fake stuff. I think he had his techniques down very well. I wondered what other techniques he had.

Meal finished I realized I was as stuffed as that lobster. I hope he hadn't made dessert; I couldn't fit even a lettuce leaf in my now bulging stomach.

"You'll have to give me your recipes. All of this was heavenly," I said as I pushed my gargantuan body away from the table.

We had after dinner drinks in his library, no shit, leather chairs and all, with floor to ceiling bookshelves. And there were even good cigars to go with the brandy. He also had an exhaust fan that was quietly running, my guess was, to suck the smoke out of the room.

He opened a humidor and presented one to me. I took it. It seems there's a whole routine with the lighting of a cigar. First you cut the tip off, then you run a flame along the outside to warm it up. When lighting you take several pulls to get it going and you don't inhale. Seems like an awful lot of pomp and circumstance.

The first puff I accidentally inhaled which caused paroxysms of choking and coughing. I found the taste rather disgusting. I'm guessing this was an acquired thing, and passed on the cigar.

John did enjoy his though and, it smelled better than it tasted. I concentrated on the brandy which I found excellent. And it warmed me all the way down to my toes.

"Viv, why don't we take our drinks and sit by the water. The moon is almost full."

I sat down on his outdoor loveseat, and we snuggled up together which led to kissing which led to that brand-new decadent bed. That led to a very good time had by both. I know it was great for me. And by the smile on his face, I'm thinking it was for him as well. I didn't think I could or would ever get out of that bed. I texted Venice and asked if she could keep Sassy for the evening.

"Sure Viv, and now isn't the time but I definitely want to hear about this tomorrow. YOU! Spending the night. Never thought I'd see the day, or night."

"Thank you, goodnight Ven."

The next morning, I awoke in the luxurious bed next to John. Wow, what a night. Perfect dinner, perfect man and...need I say more? I didn't think he'd be needing that remote anytime soon.

As if last night wasn't enough, he made the best coffee, probably a blend flown in from Columbia and delivered on a donkey with a man wearing a huge sombrero. This was followed by a delicious breakfast which we had outside while listening to the waves gently caressing the shoreline. Did I say I could get used to this?

"I was hoping we could spend the day together and maybe I could coerce you into another night here?"

"I'd love to stay but we'll have to make it another time. I have work to attend to."

"You certainly outdid yourself, in every aspect of the evening. Maybe next week you could dine at my place?"

"I'm glad you enjoyed it. As far as dinner at your house, name the day and time and I'll be there. Should I bring a date?"

"Why don't you do that and see what happens."

After a leisurely stroll down the beach, we said our goodbyes and I headed home.

That evening Venice came over. We had a ton of stuff to talk about and none of it, even remotely about work.

I ordered a pizza and, after sharing it with the children, we settled down to business. Medication first. I poured a bourbon, a much inferior brand to what I had last night, and had made Ven a potent margarita. Alcohol makes you tell all.

"Here, drink this and don't be shy. I have a whole pitcher of Margaritas with your name on it."

Half our drinks were already gone and it was time to pry. "How was your five days with Bryan visiting here, compared with your five days in Arizona? Do you think it was better since you were on familiar territory?"

"It was much better here. I can't put my finger on it but he was more present. When I went to Arizona he had just moved there and was still unfamiliar with the place. But up here he seemed more at ease."

"That's great but and I'm sure it was your stellar personality, your delectable cooking, and your stunning good looks."

"Oh boy, you saved yourself there. Sex still was sparse but maybe he's working on that. He's seems to be trying and that says something. At least I'm worth trying for, right?

"You most definitely are."

"He was probably distracted in Arizona, getting familiar with it all, and then entertaining you. I bet the next time you visit him he'll be more relaxed."

"I think you're right, said Venice. "And I do hope to visit him again. Enough about me, tell me about your night with John."

"Dinner at John's was delicious and what made it more enticing was the fact that he cooked it all himself. Don't tell, but when he went to the bathroom, I looked in his garbage for take-out containers, which just goes to show how yummy the food was."

Venice said, "And how little you trust him. Shame on you."

"Oh, Venice, it would only be a shame if he'd caught me, which he didn't. And I would think that would be a compliment that the food was so good I thought professionals prepared it. You know I'm a pro at sneaky. Det. Traynor didn't make me a consultant for nothing, did she?"

"We're going off subject, stop stalling and get on with it."

"John was charming, interesting, and the perfect host. I can't believe I thought him old and stodgy. Well, I never did think of him as stodgy and he's not all that much older than I am. I love his sense of humor too." I told her about the chef's gear and the change back to host.

"After dinner, we sat outside and it was a clear evening with the moon shimmering on the water. It was almost as if he'd ordered the ultimate night. And then came a spectacular kiss. Need I say more?"

"Oh yes, you most certainly do. You're not getting off that easy."

"Speaking of getting off…"

Venice clapped her hands over her ears yelling, "LA LA LA LA LA, I don't need the specifics thank you, I would like only the Disney version."

Laughing, I said, "In keeping with animation, his penis was very animated. Okay, okay, I'll stop. Let's just say I enjoyed myself immensely, and I believe it was unanimous.

CHAPTER SEVENTEEN

T he next day Venice dropped by bearing deliveries.

"Hi Ven, come in. Oh, is that my dry cleaning? You're such a doll."

"It was nothing; I was dropping off my clothes anyway. I saved you a trip. Oh, I almost forgot. She pulled an envelope out of her bag. The dry cleaner gave me this."

She held up a very small sealed manila envelope. "He found something in one of your jacket pockets and is returning it."

I ripped it open and when I turned it upside down a tiny button fell into my hand. Frowning I took it over to my desk and looked at it through my magnifying glass.

Venice, leaning over my shoulder, said, "What is that? Did you lose a button?"

After peering through the magnifier for a few seconds I let out a gasp.

"What? What? What is it?"

"I believe you're looking at the missing button from the bridal dress," I said. See here, the thread used to sew it on is frayed. This wasn't cut, this was yanked off, either by accident or on purpose. I went and got the button I clipped off the dress, and it was a perfect match.

"Where did you find this Viv?"

"It's coming back to me now. It was on John's yacht or whatever you call it, steamship, cruise line? Remember we went up to watch the fireworks? I sat down and felt something and I picked this up. Then the fireworks started and I dropped it in my pocket and completely forgot about it. Holy shit."

"Does that mean the killer was on the boat? Had to be. Unless the killer is John or one of the crew."

"I'm sure it wasn't John," I said defensively. "Maybe it was Bryan who dropped it. He was up there with us too."

Venice said, "I'm sorry, I shouldn't have said that. I don't think it was either one of them. But it dropped out of someone's pocket. Maybe it wasn't even from that night. Maybe it was there when the boat was last used."

"No, I definitely think it was someone who was present that evening. But maybe it wasn't dropped, maybe it was placed there on purpose.

"It had to be from that evening, those ships are cleaned from top to bottom before any event. You know what? I'm going to give it to Det. Traynor. They have the means to check out the guests. I just hope she tells us if there's a suspect or two. My ulterior motive, you know I always have one, is that she may trust me enough to fill me in when or if she has more information."

Venice laughed. "You do understand she'll probably faint when you give this to her. You, who never tells her anything until it's too late. I think it's an excellent idea."

"I'm still going to ask John for a guest list. Maybe someone or something will stand out. It's definitely a long shot but nothing ventured, nothing lost."

I called Det. Traynor and told her about the button and Venice was right. She fainted. Not really but I could tell she was... shocked? Disbelieving? Yes, but also pleased although she would never let on. I was proving my consultancy.

"For once you did the right thing by telling me about the button, although it's odd that it was found on the yacht. I'll get a list of all the people on board. I'm sure you all took pictures. I'd like you to get everyone's photos from that night and email them to me. Give me Mr. Berkman's number, I need to speak to him too."

Again, with the orders? You'd think I'd get some respect given I was such a good consultant.

Det. Traynor, I can only get the pictures taken from the people I know. There were many guests and I have no idea who most of them were."

"Get them from the people you know, leave the rest to me."

I called John and filled him in and told him Det. Traynor would be in touch so it would be helpful if he could start on that list and to please make a copy for me.

"All my friends were told they could invite up to two guests. I had to put a limit on it so we wouldn't have hundreds of people milling about, but I didn't know all of them. However, I'll start on that list of those I know were there."

"How come you didn't give me a limit of two?"

"Because you're my special lady."

I could feel myself beaming. I couldn't believe he said that. I was *special*, at least to him. I felt very honored. Maybe *I* should propose to *him*. Not happening. But I was really liking him more and more.

"John, you make me feel special. And you're my special man and if I had a yacht, I would extend the same courtesy to you. I know this is going to be a pain in the ass for both you and the detective but that's her job. And she has plenty of help at the station. As her consultant I'll do what I can." I really loved saying that. Consultant, that is.

"Consultant?"

"Yes, didn't I tell you that? Must've slipped my mind. She had cards made up identifying both myself and Venice as consultants. I wouldn't put too much stock in it. I don't think I have any authorization to do anything. This was simply a ploy to stop me from withholding information. Which I do. Sometimes."

"The Detective is calling now; I'll talk to you later, Honey."

I was now John's "Honey" and Venice was Bryan's "Sweetie."

I called Venice. "Hi, Sweetie, it's Honey calling."

"Viv, are you off your meds again?"

I explained the endearments and the talk with Detective. I also called Annie and asked her to send any photos of that evening to the station. This was going to be a long week

Over the next few weeks, the guests were identified and eliminated as suspects. The staff traveled with the ship and had alibis. They weren't even in Washington when the murder happened, they were moored in New York.

That left me, Venice, Annie, John, and Bryan. Of course, there were guests of guests and someone could have slipped by. It was determined that Lauren was abducted just before 5 P.M. in Oregon, so that was probably about fourteen hours from the time he took her to when he left her at our brokerage. All of us were here in Washington and were seen within that window except John and he was on a plane headed back to Seatac from New York.

Now what? I didn't have a clue. Literally.

After John had gone over the guest list with Det. Traynor he had to fly to his house just outside of London to take care of something or another and he was now home, at least home in Washington. Surprisingly, I missed him. On the other hand, I didn't understand why one person needed so many houses. He had access to a private jet, couldn't he just go and visit and stay at a bed and breakfast? Okay, maybe a posh hotel?

It was late July and the weather tended to be in the eighties now. Still mild compared to other parts of the country, and never humid. I wouldn't want to be Bryan; Arizona was 113 degrees this morning.

I called John. "Hey, how was your London trip?"

"It was good. I met with my solicitor because I've decided to sell the London house. I hardly get there anymore. This house here in Havenville is now my favorite, because this is where you are. I feel relaxed and calm sitting by the water in the morning and enjoying the sunsets. Would you like to come over or go out to dinner tonight?"

"That's why I was calling. I thought I'd invite you over for dinner. Remember, I said when I was at your house, next time it would be my turn. No water views but maybe we'll see the bear. And the tree view is unparalleled," I said laughing. "How about tomorrow night at 7 P.M, or do you need a few days to catch up with the time zone?"

"And miss seeing you? I'll be there. Can I bring anything?"

"How about that small Monet? Kidding, just bring your lovely self."

Next call out was to Venice. "Hey, what're you doing?"

"It all depends on what you want."

"Now you've hurt my feelings. What could I possibly want other than to hear your melodious voice?"

"Scones, that's what."

"Now that you mention it..."

"I'll be right over. Do you want blueberry or raspberry?"

"It's too early to make choices, why don't you just bring both."

Scones were devoured in the backyard with coffee and the children. I had a little black wrought iron table and chairs set up under the cedar trees to give us shade. Even though it would be in the mid-eighties today it would barely reach that here in Havenville. We were on the northern most tip of the peninsula and our weather conditions had something to do with the water surrounding us on three sides. Don't ask me what, but I was very happy with our cooler climate here. Just fifteen miles into Silverhill it was at least 10 to 15 degrees warmer.

"So, how is Bryan these days? Has he melted yet?"

"He's good but yes, he's dying of the heat. He now realizes he made a mistake moving in the summer. I felt sorry for him so I invited him up here. He'll be here for a week; I didn't want to extend the invitation for more than that because I don't want him to get the idea that this will be his summer retreat. Can you imagine if he were here for months?"

"I can't," I said. I didn't say that I couldn't imagine him up here for a whole week either.

"What about you?" I asked Ven. "Can you see this becoming something like that? You go down to his condo in the winter and he comes up here for the summer? Don't get any ideas, I don't mean the WHOLE winter."

"I've given that some thought and even though I'm enjoying being with him, I don't think I want to live with him. I love our time together because I don't see him for long stretches. It makes for a more exciting reunion. I don't know if I ever want to make things permanent but then he hasn't asked. What about you and John?"

"My situation with John is different than yours in that he lives minutes from me. So far, we haven't gotten to the point where we see each other that frequently. I suppose that might happen if things continue as they are. I'm very fond of John and I always have a good time with him. He's interesting and intelligent and most importantly of all, he has a sense of humor. But living with him? I'm with you. While you may change *your* mind, I won't."

"Why wouldn't you Viv, if you fell in love with him?"

"For me it would be stultifying to have to live with someone 24/7. The magic, the anticipation, the excitement, would be nonexistent. We would fall into a dull and boring routine. I don't want to see or be with someone all the time. Frankly, I don't even think it's the natural order of things. I guess it's different if you have a family but it can also be hard work. And, I'm nicer when I don't live with anyone."

"Okay then. I guess you won't be living with John. You do make an abundance of sense. Maybe that's why Bryan and I get along so well, we have that space. I suppose there are people that don't like to be alone and my parents seemed to have a good marriage, but they probably had their ups and downs too."

"Enough of this," said Venice, "Let's go into the office. I have tons of paperwork to look over and possibly a new client."

"Who's the new client?" I asked, "Anyone I know?"

"No, her name is Louise, and she seems to be a bit difficult. She's looking at houses in the $600K range so it's worth it to put up with her. I have a few homes to show her, the last being in Silverhill. Maybe you'd like to meet up for lunch?

"I have a listing appointment in Silverhill," I said, with Sid. He's an old guy, probably around 80 and he wants to sell his house and move. How about I call you when I'm done and we'll see about lunch."

Life seemed to be on an even keel for a change and I was happy, Venice was happy, and shit, I had to call Mom and ruin my happy bubble. It had been a few days. She was back to her old self. I was hoping for a new and improved self but at least I didn't have to call her every day now.

"Hi Mom, what's going on at the Tess and Wes house?"

"Nothing much, it's too damned hot and humid to do anything but go from the car to the store. I'm thinking of having a surprise birthday party for your Dad in September, could you make it then? It would be good to have all you girls present."

"I'll put it on my calendar and unless something huge happens, I think that's doable. How old is he going to be?"

"Only 65, don't forget he's 8 years my junior. Women should always marry younger men, they have more energy, if you get my drift."

Christ, LA LA LA LA LA. Yes, I got her drift and I wish it would drift right out of my mind.

"Did you hear anything new about the murder? I hope they'd solve it so I don't have to worry."

"Mom, there's nothing to worry about. I doubt it had anything to do with me, I think it was the fact that the brokerage used to be a bridal salon. Who knows, the murderer might have thought it was still there and when it wasn't, he had to improvise."

"I'd still feel better knowing whoever did that heinous thing was dead or in jail. Preferably dead."

"Me too," I said. "I'm sorry to cut this short but my client just came in and I have to go. I'll call soon."

"You make sure you do that, Vivianne. Now that I'm back to my perfect self, you don't call as often, and I haven't even gotten the latest on John."

"Okey dokey, bye, Mom."

I lied; I was going to Sid's house, he wasn't coming here, to the brokerage, but I wanted to go over my presentation. I was hoping he'd be reasonable and not want more for his house than it was worth as most sellers did.

I drove down to Silverhill and knocked on Sid's door. I was expecting a little old man but he seemed to be in excellent condition and he had a sparkle to his eye. I liked him already.

We went over everything and Sid asked that we increase the price by $10K just to have some negotiating room. I agreed, he signed the contract, and I called my sign man, and made a date for him to put everything up. It would be a few days before it went live as I had to have flyers made and make sure the house was show ready. I would be out there in a few days, right before I pushed the active button. Given his age and how long he'd lived there I was surprised it went so smoothly. Venice wasn't as lucky with her client.

"What happened with Louise?" I asked Venice. I was calling her to see if she'd be free for lunch. She wasn't.

"What didn't happen. First of all, she was horrible. Mean as can be. You know me Viv, I can put up with a lot. After all, if I can put up with you, I can put up with anybody," she said chuckling.

"There were three houses to see. She had issues with them all and not reasonable ones either. She complained about the décor, the paint colors, the neighboring houses. It was a litany of grievances. After showing her the third house she turned to me and called me a 'Stupid bitch.' That did it for me. I told her she was a mean and nasty person and I wouldn't work with her for one more minute. I locked up the house, got in my car, and left her standing there with her mouth gaping open."

"I hope she didn't drive with you," I said trying not to laugh.

"And thank God for that because I think I would have thrown her out on the highway, while going 60 mph. I really have to be pushed to the limit and beyond for me to do something like that, so you know she was incorrigible, and that's too mild an adjective but I'm trying not to stoop to her level. Let's just forget it. I'm not in a good mood now."

I told Annie if Louise called, I'd take it. And Louise did call. She started by badmouthing Venice and that's where I stopped her. I wasn't as nice as Venice and I wasn't taking her shit.

"Listen Louise, and listen good. This brokerage will not represent you. Go somewhere else, your business is not wanted here. And you may want to take a course in how to be a decent person." With that said, I hung up. I told Annie if she called back, to tell her nobody was available to take her call. Ever.

After work, I dragged Venice to the *Copper Bottom* for dinner, my treat. I told her about the phone call and by the end of the evening, she was her old, cheerful self. I was proud of her. She stood up for herself. There was no excuse for Louise's behavior, and she lost a damned good agent.

My cell chirped just as I opened the door to my house. Sassy was dancing maniacally while Lola was purring and weaving around my legs. There's nothing like a pet's exuberance when you walk in. It made me feel loved, and missed.

It was Det. Traynor. That didn't make me feel loved.

CHAPTER EIGHTEEN

I held my breath as I said hello.

"Vivianne, we have a little more information in our murder case. Do you have a minute?"

Was she kidding, even if I was near death, I would find a minute.

"Need you ask, Detective?"

"Probably not," she said

"There's a staff member of the yacht, Sam, who was working at John's Fourth of July party. Well before anyone boarded, a man was on the upper deck, where you found the button.

Sam is in Oregon, waiting while the boat goes through a routine inspection and that will take a few days so he said he'd drive up to speak to us and possibly help us do a composite sketch of the guy he saw. If you want to meet him, he'll be here tomorrow at noon. He'll tell you all about it."

"Really? You're not messing with me, are you?"

"No, Vivianne, even *I* wouldn't be that mean. You can bring Venice too if she's free."

"We're leaving now," I said.

"Didn't you just hear me? TOMORROW AT NOON."

"Okay, okay, no need to yell. We'll be there. Bye and thanks." This time I ended the call before she could. Ha ha ha ha. I'm such an adult. I was thrilled, not only to be a part of this, but that the Detective actually included me. Not surprising since I was now, a *CONSULTANT.*

"Venice, Venice, are you in there?" I asked as I knocked repeatedly on her door. It was around 7 P.M. and, since I had just had dinner with her, I knew she was home."

I saw her hurrying toward the sliders. Even if she didn't hear the knocking, okay, maybe it was more like pounding, the dogs were barking their fool heads off and Mr. Snigglebottom was almost apoplectic.

"Hang on Viv, I'm almost there," she said as the reached the door and slid it open. "What's going on? Is your house on fire?"

Petting the dogs as I entered, sat down, and told her everything. "Aren't you excited? You *are* going, aren't you? You have to."

"Now that you put that so succinctly, I guess I must. Honestly Viv, one of these days you're going to give me a heart attack. Didn't you invite John for dinner tomorrow night?"

"Oh yeah, in all this hullabaloo, I forgot. It's okay, I'll still have plenty of time to make the pheasant under glass."

"What are you really making? If you need help getting it

ready, I'm available."

"Thanks, and yes, the help and the company would be welcome but you have to leave before John arrives."

"Oh gee, I thought I could be your server. Again, what are you making? And of course, I'll be long gone by the time he gets there."

"I was thinking I'd do a shrimp fest since I picked up two pounds of them, fresh, right off the boat from Jimmy." Jimmy was a local who had a license to catch and sell shrimp and I was on his call list.

"I told him to put aside two pounds for me. Do you want any? I can call him back."

"Yes," said Venice. "Put me down for two pounds also. I love shrimp. Now tell me about this dinner."

"First, I'll have cold shrimp with my homemade cocktail sauce, then we'll have a nice crisp salad and for dinner, it's shrimp scampi. Dessert will be shrimp ice cream."

"Very funny, there's no such thing as shrimp ice cream. What are you really making for dessert?"

"How about my meringue cookies but with chocolate drizzled over the top? They're so airy and light, they melt in your mouth. I've never tried them with chocolate so John can be my guinea pig. If they don't turn out well, he can have me for dessert."

"Ugh, too much information. Besides, I'm thinking he'll have you no matter what. I'll be over tomorrow at 11 A.M. or do you need me earlier for kitchen duty? We have to be at the station at noon."

"No need to come early, we should be home in plenty of time to get things done before John arrives. He's not coming until 7 P.M. so we can discuss what we learn from the Detective while we work. I hope this guy, Sam, has some concrete information. We sure could use a break in this case."

"We?" asked Venice. "Viv, I hate to burst your bubble but this isn't *your* case, it's Det. Traynor's case. She never should have given you those consultant cards.

"By the way, who is this Sam guy and what did he see? You said he saw a man but what else?"

"I have no idea. I was so enthralled that she invited me to the station, my mind went blank from the shock. She said he'll fill us in tomorrow."

We got to the station the next morning with time to spare. Det. Traynor signaled us into her office and closed the door. Not a good sign.

"I'm sure I don't have to tell *you* this Venice but Vivianne, you're not to speak or ask questions while I'm taking Sam's statement. When I'm done, you can ask away. That's it. Not a word out of you two until I say so and questions only. Do not, I repeat, do not, reveal anything about the case. If he asks anything, I'll be the one to respond. Do I make myself clear?"

We both nodded yes.

"And one more thing. If you fuck this up in any way your consultant cards will be confiscated and you will no longer be asked to help."

Again, we both nodded, this time, vehemently. We got the message loud and clear.

Venice turned to me and said, "This is for you, use it if necessary." It was duct tape. Bitch!

"Where are you going to interrogate him? In one of those rooms with the two-way mirrors?" I asked.

"Vivianne, this isn't an interrogation, he's not a suspect. We're simply taking his statement."

Sam arrived and looking at him I determined he was quite the hunk. Way too young for me but I do have an appreciation for the finer things in life, even if they are out of reach.

Introductions made, we went into a room, NOT an interrogation room, a statement room. They looked the same to me.

Det. Traynor started off by telling him his statement would be taped. She then asked him to give his full name, social security number, date of birth and credit card numbers with passwords. At least it seemed like she asked him all of that.

"My name is Samuel Aaron Waters."

I stifled a snort. His name was Waters and he worked on the water. I think I needed the duct tape.

Det. Traynor gave me a warning glance and continued. She asked him to tell her what happened on the fourth of July, on the yacht, which was named "Lucky Lady."

Sam said, "As you know, I'm employed by the corporation that owns the Lucky Lady. The day of the Berkman party, about an hour before guests were boarding, I was doing a final inspection to make sure it was shipshape. When I got up to the superstructure at the bow of the ship, I saw a man lurking around. I couldn't see much of his face because he had on a baseball cap, sunglasses and the rest of his face was covered by a mustache and full beard. He was tall, well over six feet, dark hair, including his beard and mustache. He had a muscular build. He seemed in good shape. I remember his shirt because it was decorated with little blue anchors. He had on white shorts and flip flops.

"I told him he wasn't supposed to be on the ship and asked if I could help him. He apologized and said he was just looking around because he was thinking of chartering it for next year. I suggested he make an appointment, gave him my card, escorted him off, and didn't give it another thought.

"A short time after that I got news that my Dad had passed away. It was sudden, a massive heart attack and they said he was probably dead before he hit the ground. We were all in shock. I immediately made arrangements to fly back to Pennsylvania, that's where my family is, and forgot all about this guy. I'm so sorry."

Det. Traynor said, "My condolences and you have nothing to apologize for. What made you remember this now?"

"Oh, this is the important part. We're moored in Portland, Oregon for an inspection and a few minor repairs. That night, it was two days ago, we all went out to the local bar. There were a bunch of us and some were at the bar but I was at a table with a some of my crewmates when the door opened and in walked a man. I thought he looked familiar but I couldn't place where I'd seen him. As he walked up to the bar, I saw that he had on a shirt with blue anchors, the same shirt the man on the yacht had on. I noticed his height and when I heard him ordering a beer, I recognized his voice. He had a deep voice that was unmistakable. He was minus the baseball cap and sunglasses, and even though it was dark in the bar, I got a good look at his eyes, they were blue.

"He noticed me looking and I quickly turned away. When I glanced his way again, he was at the door, leaving. I don't know why, but I went after him. I got outside just in time to see a white SUV turn the corner. There was an eight in the license plate number, sorry but that's all I got. I would've gotten outside quicker but the place was hopping and it took me a few minutes to get through the crowd."

"I appreciate you coming in for this. You seem to have a good eye for details."

Sam smiled and said, "It comes from many years of people watching on board the different vessels I've worked on. It's keeps me entertained and staves off the boredom."

I'd like to keep him entertained, I thought.

"Vivianne, Venice, do you have anything you'd like to ask him?"

"Yes," I said, "I'd like to know if you're free for dinner tonight?" No, I didn't really ask that, John was coming for dinner and I don't think he'd be too pleased to see Sam.

Venice picked up her cell and hit a recording of a message from Bryan asking Sam if the *Mystery Man*, which is what we now thought of him as, had a similar voice.

"Yes," said Sam. "He sounds exactly like that guy."

"Okay, now we know what he sounds like, but it certainly wasn't Bryan, he was with me the entire day, including when you saw the man on the yacht. And, Bryan doesn't fit that description." said Venice.

"For once I can't seem to think of anything to ask. I'm sure things will come to me later. Why don't you give me your cell number?"

"Wait, what bar were you in and where was it?" I asked.

Sam said, "I wrote that all down and gave it to the Detective. It's the Portland Pub. I don't know the address but I'm sure you can Google it."

Sarah knocked and entered. She was the artist and Sam was going to help her do a composite sketch but none of us were too optimistic given most of his face was hidden and when he was in the pub it was dark. Damn.

We were told we could leave which meant we should leave. We did. But first, I asked Det. Traynor if she could send us a picture of the sketch which she said she'd do.

Outside Venice said, "Good thing Bryan has an alibi."

"Ven, I'm sure there are lots of guys with deep voices. Who's the actor who has a very distinguishable voice? He has a full mustache...Sam Elliot. Now there's a unique, and *very* sexy, voice."

Det. Traynor was going to call the Portland Police and explain what was going on. She would send them the sketch and a transcript of Sam's statement. They'd question the pub owner and surrounding neighborhood and keep Det. Traynor in the loop.

It was 2 P.M. We were at my house and I had just taken the

shrimp out of the refrigerator. I had cooked enough for the appetizers; the rest would be cooked with dinner. Venice was helping me wrap them in prosciutto, which I decided we'd do since that's one of the things John had made for me.

"What do you make of all of this?" I asked, referring to what we'd learned today.

"I think it's better than nothing and maybe we're a speck closer but only if someone can add to what Sam just told us. Maybe the *Mystery Man* was a local and frequented that bar and the barkeep can identify him."

"Maybe, but it doesn't fill me with optimism. I think it's a longshot."

Venice left and John arrived. He not only looked good, he smelled good too.

Dinner was delicious and the encore even more so. Afterward, as we were drifting off to sleep, his arms encircling me, he whispered in my ear, "I'm falling in love with you, Vivi." I made believe I was asleep. Did I love him? I think I might just be falling too but something held me back. I just needed more time. There was no need to rush into things. Then I really did fall asleep.

Over the next few weeks, the guests were identified and eliminated as suspects. The staff traveled with the ship and had alibis. They weren't even in Washington when the murder happened, they were moored in New York.

That left me, Venice, Annie, John, and Bryan. Of course, there were guests of guests and someone could have slipped by. It was determined that Lauren was abducted just before 5 P.M. in Oregon, so that was probably about fourteen hours from the time he took her to when he left her at our brokerage. All of us were here in Washington and were seen within that window except John and he was on a plane headed back to Seatac from New York.

Now what? I didn't have a clue. Literally.

After John had gone over the guest list with Det. Traynor he had to fly to his house just outside of London to take care of something or another and he was now home, at least home in Washington. Surprisingly, I missed him. On the other hand, I didn't understand why one person needed so many houses. He had access to a private jet, couldn't he just go and visit and stay at a bed and breakfast? Okay, maybe a posh hotel?

It was late July and the weather tended to be in the eighties now. Still mild compared to other parts of the country, and never humid. I wouldn't want to be Bryan; Arizona was 113 degrees this morning.

I called John. "Hey, how was your London trip?"

"It was good. I met with my solicitor because I've decided to sell the London house. I hardly get there anymore. This house here in Havenville is now my favorite, because this is where you are. I feel relaxed and calm sitting by the water in the morning and enjoying the sunsets. Would you like to come over or go out to dinner tonight?"

"That's why I was calling. I thought I'd invite you over for dinner. Remember, I said when I was at your house, next time it would be my turn. No water views but maybe we'll see the bear. And the tree view is unparalleled," I said laughing. "How about tomorrow night at 7 P.M, or do you need a few days to catch up with the time zone?"

"And miss seeing you? I'll be there. Can I bring anything?"

"How about that small Monet? Kidding, just bring your lovely self."

Next call out was to Venice. "Hey, what're you doing?"

"It all depends on what you want."

"Now you've hurt my feelings. What could I possibly want other than to hear your melodious voice?"

"Scones, that's what."

"Now that you mention it…"

"I'll be right over. Do you want blueberry or raspberry?"

"It's too early to make choices, why don't you just bring both."

Scones were devoured in the backyard with coffee and the children. I had a little black wrought iron table and chairs set up under the cedar trees to give us shade. Even though it would be in the mid-eighties today it would barely reach that here in Havenville. We were on the northern most tip of the peninsula and our weather conditions had something to do with the water surrounding us on three sides. Don't ask me what, but I was very happy with our cooler climate here. Just fifteen miles into Silverhill it was at least 10 to 15 degrees warmer.

"So, how is Bryan these days? Has he melted yet?"

"He's good but yes, he's dying of the heat. He now realizes he made a mistake moving in the summer. I felt sorry for him so I invited him up here. He'll be here for a week; I didn't want to extend the invitation for more than that because I don't want him to get the idea that this will be his summer retreat. Can you imagine if he were here for months?"

"I can't," I said. I didn't say that I couldn't imagine him up here for a whole week either.

"What about you?" I asked Ven. "Can you see this becoming something like that? You go down to his condo in the winter and he comes up here for the summer? Don't get any ideas, I don't mean the WHOLE winter."

"I've given that some thought and even though I'm enjoying being with him, I don't think I want to live with him. I love our time together because I don't see him for long stretches. It makes for a more exciting reunion. I don't know if I ever want to make things permanent but then he hasn't asked. What about you and John?"

"My situation with John is different than yours in that he lives minutes from me. So far, we haven't gotten to the point where we see each other that frequently. I suppose that might happen if things continue as they are. I'm very fond of John and I always have a good time with him. He's interesting and intelligent and most importantly of all, he has a sense of humor. But living with him? I'm with you. While you may change *your* mind, I won't."

"Why wouldn't you Viv, if you fell in love with him?"

"For me it would be stultifying to have to live with someone 24/7. The magic, the anticipation, the excitement, would be nonexistent. We would fall into a dull and boring routine. I don't want to see or be with someone all the time. Frankly, I don't even think it's the natural order of things. I guess it's different if you have a family but it can also be hard work. And, I'm nicer when I don't live with anyone."

"Okay then. I guess you won't be living with John. You do make an abundance of sense. Maybe that's why Bryan and I get along so well, we have that space. I suppose there are people that don't like to be alone and my parents seemed to have a good marriage, but they probably had their ups and downs too."

"Enough of this," said Venice, "Let's go into the office. I have tons of paperwork to look over and possibly a new client."

"Who's the new client?" I asked, "Anyone I know?"

"No, her name is Louise, and she seems to be a bit difficult. She's looking at houses in the $600K range so it's worth it to put up with her. I have a few homes to show her, the last being in Silverhill. Maybe you'd like to meet up for lunch?

"I have a listing appointment in Silverhill," I said, with Sid. He's an old guy, probably around 80 and he wants to sell his house and move. How about I call you when I'm done and we'll see about lunch."

Life seemed to be on an even keel for a change and I was happy, Venice was happy, and shit, I had to call Mom and ruin my happy bubble. It had been a few days. She was back to her old self. I was hoping for a new and improved self but at least I didn't have to call her every day now.

"Hi Mom, what's going on at the Tess and Wes house?"

"Nothing much, it's too damned hot and humid to do anything but go from the car to the store. I'm thinking of having a surprise birthday party for your Dad in September, could you make it then? It would be good to have all you girls present."

"I'll put it on my calendar and unless something huge happens, I think that's doable. How old is he going to be?"

"Only 65, don't forget he's 8 years my junior. Women should always marry younger men, they have more energy, if you get my drift."

Christ, LA LA LA LA LA. Yes, I got her drift and I wish it would drift right out of my mind.

"Did you hear anything new about the murder? I hope they'd solve it so I don't have to worry."

"Mom, there's nothing to worry about. I doubt it had anything to do with me, I think it was the fact that the brokerage used to be a bridal salon. Who knows, the murderer might have thought it was still there and when it wasn't, he had to improvise."

"I'd still feel better knowing whoever did that heinous thing was dead or in jail. Preferably dead."

"Me too," I said. "I'm sorry to cut this short but my client just came in and I have to go. I'll call soon."

"You make sure you do that, Vivianne. Now that I'm back to my perfect self, you don't call as often, and I haven't even gotten the latest on John."

"Okey dokey, bye, Mom."

I lied; I was going to Sid's house, he wasn't coming here, to the brokerage, but I wanted to go over my presentation. I was hoping he'd be reasonable and not want more for his house than it was worth as most sellers did.

I drove down to Silverhill and knocked on Sid's door. I was expecting a little old man but he seemed to be in excellent condition and he had a sparkle to his eye. I liked him already.

We went over everything and Sid asked that we increase the price by $10K just to have some negotiating room. I agreed, he signed the contract, and I called my sign man, and made a date for him to put everything up. It would be a few days before it went live as I had to have flyers made and make sure the house was show ready. I would be out there in a few days, right before I pushed the active button. Given his age and how long he'd lived there I was surprised it went so smoothly. Venice wasn't as lucky with her client.

"What happened with Louise?" I asked Venice. I was calling her to see if she'd be free for lunch. She wasn't.

"What didn't happen. First of all, she was horrible. Mean as can be. You know me Viv, I can put up with a lot. After all, if I can put up with you, I can put up with anybody," she said chuckling.

"There were three houses to see. She had issues with them all and not reasonable ones either. She complained about the décor, the paint colors, the neighboring houses. It was a litany of grievances. After showing her the third house she turned to me and called me a 'Stupid bitch.' That did it for me. I told her she was a mean and nasty person and I wouldn't work with her for one more minute. I locked up the house, got in my car, and left her standing there with her mouth gaping open."

"I hope she didn't drive with you," I said trying not to laugh.

"And thank God for that because I think I would have thrown her out on the highway, while going 60 mph. I really have to be pushed to the limit and beyond for me to do something like that, so you know she was incorrigible, and that's too mild an adjective but I'm trying not to stoop to her level. Let's just forget it. I'm not in a good mood now."

I told Annie if Louise called, I'd take it. And Louise did call. She started by badmouthing Venice and that's where I stopped her. I wasn't as nice as Venice and I wasn't taking her shit.

"Listen Louise, and listen good. This brokerage will not represent you. Go somewhere else, your business is not wanted here. And you may want to take a course in how to be a decent person." With that said, I hung up. I told Annie if she called back, to tell her nobody was available to take her call. Ever.

After work, I dragged Venice to the *Copper Bottom* for dinner, my treat. I told her about the phone call and by the end of the evening, she was her old, cheerful self. I was proud of her. She stood up for herself. There was no excuse for Louise's behavior, and she lost a damned good agent.

My cell chirped just as I opened the door to my house. Sassy was dancing maniacally while Lola was purring and weaving around my legs. There's nothing like a pet's exuberance when you walk in. It made me feel loved, and missed.

It was Det. Traynor. That didn't make me feel loved.

CHAPTER NINETEEN

It was now the end of August. Gloria and Erika would be getting married in a few days. The ceremony was private, just family but they were having a reception upstairs at Goldens, which was reserved for large events, and parties. It was the perfect place to have a reception, the food was good and it was lively. We were invited, naturally.

John was out of town, this time he was in New Zealand. It was the beginning of their winter season now. Venice was my date; Bryan was back in the blast furnace.

I had asked Gloria if Erika had a stand mixer. She didn't so that was one of our wedding gifts. We then asked Erika what to get Gloria. We ended up with top-of-the-line garden tools with a black tote, with her name embroidered on it, so she could carry her tools while planting. We also included gardening gloves and a Northwest Pacific gardening book.

The party was a lot of fun but no bullshit bride stuff. Gloria would not have it. Erika wore an off-white dress; no gown and Gloria wore a lovely pantsuit the color matching Erika's dress. All in all, it was a total success and they both looked radiantly happy.

In less than a week it would be September and we'd be headed for winter. The bartender in Oregon was questioned and he'd seen *Mystery Man* in there a few times, but again, given the diffused lighting and the facial hair, he couldn't add much to the composite drawing, and he hadn't seen him since that night when Sam spotted him.

No posters were put up because *Mystery Man* wasn't a suspect, not yet. The authorities had very little to go on, but they did want to question him. Canvassing the neighborhood didn't result in anything either. This was one difficult case and I was losing hope it would ever be solved. At least there were no more murders.

It was time to call my loving mother. I needed bourbon.

"Hi Mom, how's it going?"

"Vivianne, would you like to be more specific? How is what going? If you're talking about my health, it couldn't be better."

"Just things in general, but I'm glad to hear you're healthy and happy."

"Who said I was happy? I have so many preparations to do and I'm up to my head in it all."

"What are you talking about Mom? Oh, Wes's party?"

"I'm not planning anything but your father (he is NOT my father) is planning on taking me to England for my birthday in October. I have clothes to buy, hair appointments to set up, itineraries to be made, it's so much work. Given Wes's surprise party was a surprise, he won't know it's no longer going to happen. I'm only one person, I can't be expected to do everything."

Only my mother could turn an exciting trip into an arduous task. I would love to go to England. I could just wear the clothes I already had on, no appointments necessary and who cares about itineraries, sometimes spontaneity is the best way to go. I knew she was pleased with this gift from Wes and I think he knew it too.

"How is your John doing?"

"Which John, Mom? In my profession there are a lot of Johns if you're lucky."

"Don't be vulgar Vivianne, you know damned well what I mean. I take it you're not engaged yet as I'm sure when that happens, I'll be the very first you call. I can make the wedding dress and Kat can be your maid of honor and Nellie the flower girl. Wes and I will give you away."

Oh, I yearned for them to give me away. As long as they made it clear, I was not to be given back.

"Mom, you're getting carried away. I'm not engaged but the relationship does seem to be moving along very well. And Nellie is too old to be a flower girl. She'll be a bridesmaid."

"Vivianne, what are you waiting for? You're not getting any younger."

"Mom, maybe I'm waiting for John to propose, I'm certainly not doing it, and if I'm not getting any younger neither are you."

"Goodbye, Vivianne, call me with good news the next time."

That was excellent. I managed to make her hang up on me I thought, chuckling.

Next call was to Kat.

"Hi Sister, I'm calling to find out if you want to be my maid of honor and Nellie a bridesmaid. Mom suggested Nellie be the flower girl but I pointed out she's a bit too old for that."

"Really? Oh Sister, I'm so happy for you. What fun this will be."

"No, no, no. I'm not engaged, I'm not getting married. This was all our lovely mother's idea. She's got me mired in matrimony, barefoot in the kitchen but thankfully, I'm too old for babies. Can you picture that?"

"The marrying part I can picture but the rest, I cannot. You, barefoot? No bunny slippers?"

I spoke to Nellie too and that was it for my family duty calls although my sister and Nells was a happy fun call. We talked almost every day. Ssshhh, Mom must not know that or she'll want me to call her every day and then I'd have to kill myself.

"Hey, before I go Kat, since Mom seems to be so busy with England did you know she's no longer throwing a surprise party for Wes?"

"Surprise party? She never mentioned that to me. Maybe it was a ploy to get you back here. It does seem perfectly plausible that she would put herself and England ahead of Wes and his birthday. As usual, he can't be disappointed because he never expects anything."

Tomorrow I had a showing at 7 A.M. Shit, that was super early. The lockbox was usually set so you couldn't get in before or after a certain time. I had to call the listing agent to ask her if I could get in that early. Since the house was vacant and the time could be changed via her iPhone, it was no problem. Except for the fact that it was before the crack of dawn and I'd have to drive in the dark. It wasn't that far; I'd just have to manage.

The agent had changed the lockbox setting for 6:30 A.M. so I could arrive early and turn on lights. I was tired and bleary eyed when I unlocked the door. I walked in, and wait; were those voices I heard? Taking out my taser and clicking on the flashlight on my phone I tiptoed down the hallway, peering in all the rooms as I went. Nothing. Until I came to the last bedroom.

There, on the floor, were three people, two in sleeping bags and a woman just getting up. When she saw me, she gave a little cry of surprise.

"What are you doing here?" I asked.

The two other people were now sitting up, staring at me. They were just kids.

The woman looked so frightened, I said, "It's okay. Don't be scared, I'm not going to hurt you. I'm the real estate agent and I'm supposed to show the house in about twenty minutes. How did you even get here? I didn't see a car."

She started to cry and then the kids started to cry. "I'm so sorry, we just wanted showers and a warm place to sleep. We would have been gone by 7 A.M. Nobody ever shows up this early. Are you going to turn us in?"

"No, I take it you're homeless. Where do you usually stay at night?"

"We have an old car we parked a block away and we've been sleeping in that. I'm afraid if I go to a shelter, they'll take my children away because I have no home for them."

217

"How did you even get in? Never mind that, my clients will be here shortly. You can fill me in later. It's okay, we'll figure this out. I want you all to get in my car, it's safe, and when I'm done here, I'm taking you out to have a nice breakfast. We'll make a plan."

"I don't have too many choices, do I? I guess I'll have to trust you, we're all very hungry. I've been begging on the street corners while I leave the kids in the car. I get enough money for MacDonald burgers and every now and then someone gives me a twenty-dollar bill and we get better food."

The family rolled up the sleeping bags and waited in my SUV. My clients showed up and it turned out they didn't like the house, but this wasn't all for nothing. I had found a family in need.

I was afraid the mother had bolted but they were all in my car, waiting for me. As promised, I took them to the Sugar Shack which was well known for their hefty breakfast menu.

The mother introduced herself as Emily and her kids were Jenny, nine years old, and David who was 7. They were so sweet. Emily didn't want to order much but I made them all get the Lumberjack breakfast. It came with everything, pancakes, eggs, bacon, sausage and biscuits. I ordered a big pitcher of orange juice. This would be filling and healthy for them.

While waiting for our order to arrive I asked Emily how she came to be homeless. There was a table for the little ones with crayons and coloring books to keep them busy and we sent them over to play. Now Emily could talk without the kids hearing us.

"First of all, thank you for all of this. It's very kind. I didn't want the kids to hear even though they probably know more than I give them credit for. We've only been in this situation for about a month now. My husband was a horrible person. I wanted to leave but I had no place to go. He threatened me all the time that if I left, he'd come after me and hurt the children.

"Then, about a month ago he put us all in the car and said we were going for a ride. We live, or I should say lived, in Oregon. A town called Aurora. We drove for hours. We stopped at a fast-food place to eat and when the kids went to the bathroom to wash up, he told me he met someone and didn't want us anymore. Just like that. He was throwing us away, like garbage. He slid an envelope over to me and walked out. When I looked in it there was $2,000. Ten years and two beautiful children were only worth a lousy $2,000 to him. And, we were stranded, I didn't even know where we were."

"Do you have any family you could go to?"

"No, my father is a drunk and my mother left years ago. My kids and I, we're family."

"Why didn't he just ask for a divorce?"

"Because that would mean he'd have to pay spousal and child support. He'd never agree to that but then they'd garnish his wages or throw him in jail. They've gotten quite strict about deadbeat dads. This was his easiest way out and he knows I won't report him, I'm afraid of him, not just for me, but for the kids too."

The children came back to sit with us when the food arrived, and they ate every morsel. I excused myself and called Venice. I told her the story and without any hesitation she said to bring them to her.

"Hey kids, how would you like to stay at a nice house

with two very friendly dogs?"

Jenny and Davey started jumping in their seats, eyes glowing with excitement. "Can we Mom, can we go there? We want to see the dogs, please, please?"

Emily had tears in her eyes. "What about my car? I left it about a block from the house you were showing."

"Don't worry, why don't we get you settled in and to-morrow I'll take you to your car. If you need anything that's in there, we can get it now."

"Well, there are our toothbrushes and clothes but really, nothing much."

I called Venice again and told her we'd be there in a few hours. I was taking them shopping first. We went to Walmart and I bought them toiletries, new clothes, pajamas, slippers and sneakers. They were like kids on Christmas day. It gave me a warm feeling in my heart to see them happy. Emily said she didn't need anything, but I insisted she get jeans and a few tees and, sneakers too. She was crying again when she hugged me and thanked me for saving their lives. It felt wonderful.

It was now nearing noon so I took them to lunch at a fun burger joint and then on to Venice and the dogs.

Venice threw open the door saying, "Hi and welcome, come in, come in."

The little boy asked shyly, "Where are your doggies?"

"They're outside, would you like to meet them? They're very friendly and I'm sure they would love to meet you."

"Me too, me too," said Jenny.

"Oh my, I don't want them to be any bother," said Emily. "You two are the nicest people we've met and what you've done for us...it's just so generous. You don't even know us."

The kids were introduced to Betty and Mr. Snigglebottom and I ran over and got Sassy to join in the frolicking. They were all playing in the backyard, rolling and laughing, even the dogs.

Emily said, "I haven't heard that laughter in a very long time. I can tell you the rest of the story now if you'd like."

It's a nice day, why don't we sit outside with our drinks, and we can watch the kids while we talk," I said.

Emily continued the story she started in the restaurant. "There was a motel a few blocks down from where Ryan, my husband, dropped us off or I should say, left us. It didn't look fancy so we went and got a room. I asked the clerk if there was any place I could get a cheap car. I didn't care what it looked like as long as it ran.

"The motel guy got in touch with a friend who had a used car he was selling and asked him to bring it to the motel. He wanted $1,000 for it but I said no, it was more money than I had. We finally settled on $700. It's an eyesore, but it runs, and there was a half tank of gas too. We were in Bellingham and we got on I-5 and drove until we hit Blainton. We didn't much like Blainton, we wanted someplace small and safe, so we ended up in Port Hollow. It isn't small enough so people would notice us but it also doesn't seem to have any bad neighborhoods. Nothing was permanent given our situation. I just didn't want to be close to where he dropped us off in case he changed his mind and came looking for us. Even though we're homeless, it's better than living with Ryan.

"Since I'm a real estate agent, well, my license has lapsed now, but I was a realtor, I knew the routine when an agent was showing a house. I knew the house where you found us was vacant and yesterday another agent showed it. When she said goodbye to her clients and went in to lock up, I was watching through a window and while she was upstairs, I slipped in and hid in the closet until she was gone. I left the back door unlocked and we waited in the car until I was pretty sure there wouldn't be any more showings. At 9 P.M. we went in, rolled out our sleeping bags, took showers and settled down for the night. I had a bag of burgers and fries that we ate. We went to sleep and the next thing I knew, you were there.

"We had planned to be out by 7 A.M., as I told you, usually the lockbox isn't set until around 8 A.M. When you found us I was so frightened. I thought you were going to call the police. And then they'd arrest me and take my kids away."

"You've got your miracle," I said. I had no idea what we were going to do with them. They couldn't live with Venice, but they definitely weren't going back to living in a car either.

I was supposed to see John tonight and I called and told him everything and said I needed to stay with Venice until we figured it all out. I didn't want to leave her alone with a stranger even though Emily was a sweetheart. She was also desperate and desperation makes people do strange things.

A few hours later John called back. "Hey Viv, I've solved the problem. I just rented them a small house, fully furnished and I've paid for the first year. There's two bedrooms and a bath and it will give Emily time to get on her feet and figure out her life. The utilities are in my name and I'll pay those too. Why don't I pick you up and we can go shopping for food and fill their pantry.

I was overwhelmed at his generosity. We were still outside when I told Emily and she started to cry again.

"I've got another idea." I said to Emily. "I'll get you started on renewing your license and you can work for us. I guess with all this going on I didn't mention that Venice and I own Rainbow Realty and we'd love you to be our newest agent. What do you think?"

"I think that would be the most wonderful thing ever. I loved being a realtor but my husband forbid it shortly after we were married. He didn't want me out and about meeting people."

"What's this bastard's name and where does he live, Emily?"

"Oh please, I don't want any trouble."

"Listen to me, and listen good," I said. "You cannot start this new life until the old one is over and all those loose ends are tied up tightly. We'll make sure he doesn't know where you are and he'll sign the divorce papers and state that he's giving up his parental rights."

"He'll never do that, not that he wants them, he's just plain mean." said Emily.

"You leave that to us. It's all going to be okay, I promise."

Thanks to John, the next day we moved the family to the house in Kingsville. Since it was already furnished and John and I took care of everything else, all they had to do was put their new clothes away. Venice drove John and I over to pick up Emily's car.

Instead of driving it over to Emily's new place we went to a car dealership where John traded it in for a used SUV. Perfect for a family and, soon to be realtor.

"I don't know what to say John, this is incredibly generous of you."

"I had an ulterior motive, now you're free and I can see you tonight," he said. "See how selfish I really am?"

Over the next few weeks, John had divorce papers drawn up as well as the affidavit saying Emily's husband, his name was Ryan Smith, would give up all parental rights. He'd sign it because John would offer a payout that he couldn't resist. If he was dense enough not to sign the papers there were other ways. He would never bother Emily and the kids again.

Emily had given us Ryan's phone number but when we called, it was disconnected. They owned a small house in Aurora and we drove down there only to find it had been sold and the new owners had no idea where the seller had gone. They never even met him. They gave us the number of their agent though and we called him. He gave us the number of Ryan's agent and we then spoke to him and he said he listed the house, it sold quickly, and he had no idea where Ryan went, or what he looked like. He never met him either. Ah, the digital days, when nobody has to know anybody.

Bad things happen to good people and then, sometimes they get a second chance. Emily renewed her real estate license, Jenny and Davey were enrolled in school, and they were all flourishing. Emily was determined to take full advantage of this second chance and be the best agent she could be. If Ryan showed up, we'd handle it, but as far as we knew he didn't know where she was. As a precaution, we had an alarm system installed, in her house. I don't know about Emily, but it made me feel better.

CHAPTER TWENTY

V enice would be leaving soon for her trip down to visit Bryan. She'd be gone a week.

Funny how things work out. Now that I was seeing John steadily, I didn't freak out over Venice and Bryan. I was pretty sure she'd never leave her life here to live with him in Arizona and I sure wasn't going anywhere. My Mom and Wes were headed for England shortly, and I asked Kat if she and Nellie would like to visit while Mom was gone.

They both agreed it would be the perfect time for a clandestine trip. They would stay for eight days and get back before Mom and she'd never know they were here. That's the beauty of cell phones, you could be on the moon and nobody would know it. Hooray, Sister and Nells were coming. I was so excited.

We got the schedule all figured out. Kat and Nellie would arrive three days before Venice left for Arizona so they'd get to visit with her. She already had her ticket to visit Bryan, otherwise she would've postponed it for a week. Mom and Wes would be in England by then.

Venice and I spent the week preparing for incoming guests and her outgoing trip. She asked if Kat and Nellie would like to stay at her house so they could take care of the dogs. I asked them and they were thrilled at the idea. Maybe I should stay there too. No, then I'd have to leave Lola, she loved sleeping with me on the bed.

Two days before Kat and Nells arrival, Bryan surprised Venice with a quick visit. He was picking up the last of the things in Seattle from his storage and would be taking the final load down to Arizona. He suggested Venice drive down with him instead of flying but, she already had her tickets and she wanted to visit with Kat and Nells. She sent Bryan back alone, promising he'd see her in a few days.

Sister and Nells had taken the Airporter and we picked them up. Nellie had on her rubies and she looked slightly more grownup, which was not good. I wanted her to be a little girl forever. I felt old. Which is fine as long as I didn't look old. When I saw them, we had a group hug and then I kissed and hugged Nellie until she begged me to stop.

"Getting too old for kisses and hugs, are we?"

"No Auntie V, I'm trying not to get suffocated to death," she said laughing.

We stopped for lunch on the way back, we'd be having a scrumptious meal at my house tonight. Nellie's favorite, and mine, homemade pizza. Venice would make the dough; I'd do everything else. I don't do well with dough; I tend to beat it to death.

Everyone went over to Venice's house while I stopped to pick up Sassy and some felt sticky pads so I could quickly fix her wobbly hall table, it was driving me nuts.

Walking in, I could hear everyone on the patio. I put Sassy down and, being a party girl, she headed straight for the festivity.

The only thing on the hallway table was a handblown glass bowl that Venice always dropped her keys in. Removing that, I turned the table over and that's when I saw something black, the size of a dime, stuck to the underside surface. Was that a bug, the kind that listens to your conversations? I took a picture, stuck the felt on the leg and turned it back over. Okay, at least the table was now stable. But shit, a bug? Could that be?

"Hey Viv, where are you, do you need help?"

"No, I'll be out in a minute." I quickly sent the photo to John and in less than a minute he texted back confirming what I suspected. He also texted he was on his way over.

Just as I picked up my drink to head out to the patio I heard Kat ask, "So, what's with the bridal murder case? Anything new?"

"Nope, not a damned thing," I said. "Come with me, I have something to show you. I hope it's still there."

I led them to the front of the house. We were outside and I felt it was safe. I mean, really, were the bushes bugged too? I told them the house was bugged and showed them the picture I took of it.

"What the hell?" said Kat. "Are you sure about this?"

"Yes, I am. I sent a picture of it to John and he's so concerned, he's on his way over. Let's go back to the patio, I'll make up some plausible reason I had you all follow me."

Nellie said, "Why don't you say how amazing it was to see the Yellow-Bellied Sapsucker? We can all agree how rare a sighting it was."

"Oh Nellie, you're so funny," said Kat. "But, before we leave our non-bugged spot, I *would* like to know how the murder case is going. Especially now that you're bugged. And Viv, maybe your house is also bugged."

"I'll mention that to John. He always has solutions. And I meant what I said, the murder case really isn't going anywhere."

Venice chimed in, "Who in the hell is this *Mystery Man*? He's looking mighty good for the murder, but why was he on the yacht, and did he leave the button? What's his agenda? Is he the bugger?"

"Let's brainstorm. "I'm a teenager now so I know it all," Nellie said, giggling. "Maybe *Mystery Man* was trying to implicate someone but he was interrupted by Sam, the boat guy."

"Wait," said Kat. "The bug, that's how he knew about the yacht in the first place."

Nellie said, "I think you should keep the where it is and maybe we can think of something to lure him out of his deep, dark, lair."

"And if we manage that Ms. Drama Queen, what do we do with him when he's lured out?" I asked.

"Shoot him," said Nells.

Thankfully I didn't have to address shooting someone, John had arrived and got out of the car followed by a short man, a little chubby, balding, with glasses. He looked cherubic. He wasn't. He was Greg, John's security man, head honcho, whatever.

They told us to stay out front and Greg went around to the patio. He came back shortly telling us the patio was clear. Good thing too because that's where our drinks were.

Greg was in the house now, checking everything. John walked back to where we were, in our noninvasive area.

He signaled us to the kitchen, "Lucky me, I seem to have a dropped in on a very attractive harem." he said, winking to let us know we should follow his lead.

"Hey, no harem. You have me; these other females are my minions, except Nellie, she's too young to be in a harem, she's my foot massager," I said.

They all glared at me. Nellie said "Yuck, I don't want to rub anyone's feet."

We were all watching Greg. After just a minute or two of pointing the device that was checking for bugs, it started blinking red. We all stared at him. He continued checking the house, as we waited impatiently for the findings.

Greg was done and we went on the patio. He told us that all the rooms were bugged except the bedrooms and bathrooms. He was now headed over to my house to check that too.

John got up and said, "Let's go inside and follow my lead. If someone is listening right now, I want them to hear what I'm about to say. I'll explain later."

Once inside, John said, "I'm sorry I dropped in un- announced but I was in the area and thought I'd invite you all to dinner tonight to celebrate Kat and Nellie's arrival. What do you say girls?"

He silently indicated we should say yes. We did. To hell with the homemade pizza, I could make that tomorrow.

"Okay then, it's a date, I'll be going now, but I'm looking forward dining with four lovely ladies this evening."

He signaled for me to follow him out to where Greg was. "More bad news," he said. Vivianne, your house is bugged too but only the living room/kitchen area."

"So, what you're saying is I can run around naked but I can't talk?"

"That's right," said John, "but if you choose to run naked it's mandatory that you call me first, so I can join you."

"Voyeur."

Once he stopped laughing, he switched to his serious face and said, "Tell everyone to be careful about what they say. We don't want whoever did this to know we know so; we're leaving the listening devices in place for now.

Greg had us all bring our cell phones out and they were checked and cleared.

I wasn't happy with any of this and then John suggested Greg also sweep the brokerage. Christ, I hope that wasn't bugged too.

"Viv, you're going to have to be on the alert until we get to the bottom of this. I want you to promise me you'll lock your doors from now on, even if you're just at Venice's house. Don't worry Viv, even with the bugs, nobody is listening 24/7. We'll talk more later, I'll pick you all up at 6 P.M., okay?"

I promised I'd lock up and be careful.

John and Greg left and I went to report to everyone out on the patio.

I told them about my house and that the brokerage would be

checked on Sunday when there was usually nobody there, and that our phones weren't compromised, although I don't know how they could've accomplished that, given we were never without them.

We wanted the next part to be heard if anyone was listening, so we went into the kitchen again, making believe we were helping clean up.

Venice said, "So when is John picking us up? And where are we going?"

"He'll be here at 6 P.M. and he said it's a surprise, and his surprises are really good so I'm looking forward to whatever it is."

"I'm thinking of getting another dog," I said, winking to let them all know I wasn't serious. They picked up on it and we had some fun making up stories.

Nellie asked, "What kind of dog do you want Auntie V?"

"Hmmm, maybe an Irish wolfhound. Something that could rip someone's throat out if need be. You know, like a guard dog, but family friendly."

"I know just the breeder," said Venice. "Why don't we take a ride up to Vancouver when I get back. Jeanine has a pristine reputation when it comes to dog breeding and Irish Wolfhounds are her favorites. I think we could find you a puppy or at least get your name on the waiting list."

Kat joined in; "I think you should get a killer cat instead. My friend has a cat who's very strange. It sits up in its tree house by the front door and when anyone enters, it bops them on the top of the head with its paw. His name is Henry. The weird thing

ASHLEY ADDISON

is, he knows when someone is coming, even before they enter the building. He's like a guard cat."

We kept this charade up, telling crazy stories. I was thinking we'd just invented a great game. Maybe I could sell it on that Shark program.

Even though lying was lots of fun, we were all very happy when 6 P.M. rolled around and John pulled up with a carriage and six white horses. Okay, he had a blue SUV, but I could envision the horses. All of us, including John, sat in the back with plenty of room. John's driver was at the wheel.

"I take it we can talk freely now?" I asked.

"Yes," said John. "Greg makes sure all is as it should be and he does it remotely so he doesn't have to be with me every minute. Ah, don't you love technology? Now, we have to get Det. Traynor in on this and maybe set a trap for *Mystery Man*."

"What kind of a trap?" asked Nellie. "This is exciting. It's never boring visiting you Auntie V. Can we be part of the sting?"

"Sting? Nells, you're watching too many cop shows."

"I was thinking, it would be exciting to have a career in law enforcement. Maybe I could even join the FBI," said Nellie."

"That is absolutely not happening, Nellie." I said. Kat agreed. "Unless you want to go into something like forensics. Dead bodies can't shoot you."

"Kill joy," said Nellie.

About a half hour later we pulled up to Apex, a very upscale restaurant in the neighboring county. Leave it to John to find the best.

Once we were all seated in a very private corner of the room, and cocktails ordered, mocktail for Nellie, we all started talking at once.

"Why did I ever think dining with this many females would be easy," said John. "Fun, yes. Viv, why don't you start first. You look like you're about to burst."

"I am," I said. "I was wondering if Detective thought to question the staff at the bridal salon. Not the one Lauren went to in Oregon, the one that used to be where our brokerage is.'

Venice said, "Do you think he thought it was still there? He must have surveilled the place beforehand. He had to know the comings and goings...oh no, if the brokerage is bugged too, he certainly would know the comings and goings."

"In answer to your question, he had to know it was no longer there," I said. "I'm sure Detective has a theory but I'm betting he was watching Rainbow Realty for a while. He seems to have planned everything else perfectly so I'm sure, if that was the case, he knew Sally's schedule. There was no evidence that he broke in, so he must have gone in while Sally was there and hid until she left. Then he drove to the back and, we know the rest. Why don't we find out who owned and operated the bridal shop and talk to them and the staff? Maybe he was a customer. Maybe he was there with Lauren. Yes, yes, let's do that. I'll ask Detective. I don't want to keep anything from her."

Kat looked stricken. She said, "Are you feeling well, Sister?"

"Do I look sick? Of course, I'm feeling well. What's the matter with you?"

"Oh, I'm sorry, I thought I heard you say you didn't want to withhold anything from Det. Traynor. I guess I must have perceived that incorrectly."

"She's got a point," said Venice. "I too thought I heard erroneously."

"Alright everyone, cut it out. Now that I'm a consultant I have to act like one and a consultant doesn't keep important information from her superior."

"She's gone completely insane," said Kat. Everyone concurred, even John. I was out-numbered.

Nellie came to my defense, saying, "Auntie V isn't insane, she's simply becoming a mature and responsible adult, and she's doing the right thing."

"Oh God, not that," I said. "I refuse to become mature and all that crap you just said. I'd rather you all think of me as insane. I'm sure it's just temporary. And there is a method to my madness. Det. Traynor can find out who owned the salon and question the bridal people easier than I could. It would take forever. I'll also get lots of points for making her think I'm mature and that other nasty word you said. Responsible? How absurd. And, last but not least, maybe she'll share what she finds out. It was my idea after all."

We all finished the first round of drinks and almost all the appetizers. We ordered more imbibements and put in our dinner order but told them to take their time. We had a lot to discuss.

John was next. "I realize it's going to be very difficult carrying on conversations in your homes and business, if the brokerage is bugged, but for now, you're going to have to be conscious of what you say. You can always sit outside and talk.

"He already knows everything you've been saying for God knows how long. I'm sure he knows Venice is leaving for Arizona. Think, what else does he know?"

Venice said, "He knows that Viv, Kat and Nellie are going to stay at my house while I'm gone. There's more room for both the humans and the dogs. Sassy would love to hang out with Betty and Mr. Snigglebottom."

"Ven, I decided to stay at my house because of Lola. So, he knows that too."

Venice continued, "I don't think where you sleep is relevant. If we knew why we're bugged it would be a good start. And when and how were these things installed?"

Nellie spoke up, "Maybe *Mystery Man* is bugging you to see how the investigation is going. I'm sure you talk about it."

"We do, but just today we commented on how little we know and that we can't figure this out. Maybe, and I hope I'm very wrong about this, but maybe one of us is his next victim."

"Vivianne, don't say that. Especially with Nellie here. You'll scare her to death," said Kat.

I looked at Nellie and smiled. "After what happened in New York, I think Nells might scare *Mystery Man* to death. You're one tough cookie. If he's after one of us, it's either Venice or me."

"No," Venice said. "You forgot someone. Annie. She's the one who found the dead girl."

Venice said, "We should call Annie right now and tell her to meet us here so we can fill her in. We should also check out her house too."

"Good idea," I said. Annie answered right away. "Hi, it's Vivianne. I'm going to tell you something and if you're at home, don't react. Your house may be bugged with listening devices. We're all at Apex restaurant, do you know it? Just say yes or no, don't repeat the name."

"Yes, that would be fine," said Annie.

She was letting us know she knew where we were and would join us. None of our cars had trackers so we assumed it would be safe for Annie to drive here.

"She's on her way. And, Mystery Man doesn't know where we are now, unless there's a bug up my ass." I said

"Viv," said Venice, "There's always a bug up your ass."

"Is not," I said.

John asked Venice, "When are you leaving for Arizona?"

"The day after tomorrow?"

"If it's okay with all of you, I'd like to have a little going away party at my house and I'd invite the detective and Erika. We can fill them in on all of this."

"Oh John, that's so sweet," I said. "Yes, I'm in. You'll be sick of me by the time this is all over. I'll call Det. Traynor and Erika when I get home. Oh, no, I forgot about the ears in the house. I'll call her now, excuse me for a minute."

"Vivianne?" John said, "Before you make that call, let me say, I would never get sick of you."

Wow, and he said it in front of everyone. I was impressed and very pleased.

I was done talking to Det. Traynor and her and Erika would be at John's house tomorrow evening. She was very moved that I filled her in on everything. She didn't actually say that, but I could tell, and I'm sure she was pleasantly surprised. Everyone else agreed and the party was on.

Annie arrived and we spent the next half hour bringing her up to speed.

"Wow, this is getting very interesting. Do you think I'm in any danger? I mean, I do live alone," said Annie.

John said, "No, I think you're okay for now. I would like to have Greg's team put in security systems on your homes, your home too Annie. They'll install them so they're not noticeable from outside or inside. If someone is trying to get in, they won't try to disarm a security system if they're not aware it's even there. Just one more precaution. After all, I don't want anything happening to any of you, but most of all, my girl."

I actually think I blushed. I then asked, "Who are you John, a former CIA/FBI man, or perhaps some secret organization that we know nothing about?"

"Sorry, that's classified," he said laughing. "If I tell you, I'll have to kill you."

Walking into Venice's house we were greeted by a multitude of excited canines. Annie was staying the night with Venice, while Kat, Nellie, and I would be in my house. Greg would take this time to investigate Annie's place and, install the alarm systems over the next few days. Ven would be gone when he did her house so I'd have to explain how it all worked when she returned.

Back at my house I said to Kat and Nellie, "Tomorrow night will be fun. Venice has no idea this is a surprise going away party. Make sure you don't slip and tell her. She won't know that Gloria, Erika, and Annie will be there too."

Good, I just made sure *Mystery Man* knew about tomorrow night. If he was listening. We never did talk about baiting him, we'd wait for Gloria and see what she came up with. Or would she be Det. Traynor? Hmmm, since this was at a party, I would think Gloria would be in order but then we'd be discussing police work so maybe Det. Traynor would be best. Or, Det. Gloria. She'd kill me if I called her that.

CHAPTER TWENTY-ONE

T he faux surprise party was a success. At least we could talk freely.

"Gloria, I hope I can call you that this evening?" I asked, not waiting for an answer. "What about the former owners of the bridal salon? I thought maybe you could talk to them and show Lauren's picture and the composite drawing of the man on the boat."

"That's an excellent idea Vivianne, but I followed up on that quite a while ago. My team spoke to them all and showed the photo and drawing but nobody recognized them, except one of the former sales clerks, and she was vague, saying she thought they looked familiar but wasn't sure."

I was now feeling a bit left out and disappointed that she hadn't told me this, however, she *did* say it was and excellent idea.

She also told us that baiting *Mystery Man* was a good idea but none of us had the slightest inkling as to what he intended to do next so we didn't know how to lure him or where to lure him to. It was frustrating. She said she'd give it more thought and let us know if she came up with a plan. I hope she meant the part about "Letting us know."

Annie's house was bug free. That was a relief. John gave us what looked like a remote control with buttons. If we wanted to interrupt the listening abilities of the bugs, we could jam them but he cautioned us not to do it too often or too long or the bugger would get suspicious. I promptly named the remote the Bugbasher. I really wanted to call it the bugbugger but it was way too hard to say. Try saying that three times quickly. See? It's a bitch.

The next day Kat, Nellie, and I drove Venice to the Airporter and a bunch of hugs and kisses later, she was on her way. She had mentioned she hoped this time he at least would be there, in the airport, to meet her. She told us flowers would be great but she wasn't expecting them knowing Bryan's cheapness.

"Hey Kat, how about I make my pizza tonight. I never got a chance with all the bugging shit going on."

"That would be..." Kat's phone rang. She looked at it and said, "It's Mom so don't speak."

"Hi Mom, how's England?"

"Oh, wow, I hope he's going to be okay. Yes, yes, I'll tell Vivianne. Tomorrow? Uh, call me when you get home."

A few minutes later she was off the phone. "What did Mom have to say?"

Kat looked at me, then at Nellie. "Our asses are fried," she said. "Wes got sick and they're at the airport about to board to come home. She wants me to come over tomorrow. What are we going to do now? Help."

"Tell her I asked you to come out after she left. It was a sudden decision."

"Nope," said Kat. "That won't work. She'll know we were

hiding it because I didn't tell her just now."

"Okay, don't panic. I'll call the airlines and see if we can't get you home before she wants to see you," I said.

Nellie spoke up. "Listen you two, this is getting to be ridiculous. Just tell her Auntie V invited us after she left for England. You didn't say anything just now because she was about to board. Or, here's a novel idea. You could tell her the truth. Auntie V invited us after we were all sure you were in England because we didn't want you to come."

Kat looked at her daughter and screamed, "ARE YOU IN-SANE!!??"

"I agree, ARE YOU INSANE?"

"I never thought I'd see the day when my mother AND my aunt turned on me," said Nellie. "Okay, maybe the truth would be a little harsh. Auntie V, when's the next flight out?"

We all started laughing and then I called the airlines when we got home from dropping Venice off.

"I can get you on the redeye but we have to call the Air-porter and make sure they can pick you up because I absolutely cannot drive you all the way to the airport. I'd have to get on I-5 which is the worst highway in the world and it would be dark. Not happening. I'd rather face the wrath of Mom than do that."

"Call the Airporter first then call the airport and see if we can get on that flight," said Kat.

The Airporter was all set and the redeye had seats but nothing in first class. This was so crazy. Then I remembered the house had ears. If someone *was* listening, they would now know we were all insane. And, Kat and Nellie were supposed to be staying at Venice's house. Shit, shit, and shit again. Wes never got sick, why now?

I got them to the bus and was bitterly disappointed they had to leave. This wasn't fair. Now I had no sister, no niece and no Venice. Maybe I'd go home and say, very loudly, "Hey you, you who's listening. You with the bugs. Want to come over and keep me company?"

At least all the dogs would be with me. I now had to go to Ven's house and get them since Sister and Nel wouldn't be there. The dogs would be my security system, and they would probably be better than a real one.

Then the phone chirped. It was Emily, what a pleasant surprise. She wanted to invite John and I to her house tomorrow night for dinner.

Emily had renewed her license and was doing well at Rainbow Realty. She had one small sale under her belt already... I was betting she'd be one of our best agents in the near future.

I remembered to go outside where I explained to Emily that John was out of town, as was everyone else, so it would only be me. Okay, my sister and Nellie were in town, theirs, not mine.

The next night, the kids were watching for me and before I even had a chance to knock, the door was flung open and I was embraced by two little pairs of arms.

Emily said, "Kids, let Vivianne get in the house at least. Sorry about that, they were so excited when I told them you were coming. Let me take your jacket. What would you like to drink? I have both red and white wine."

"First, here's a little something for you, Davy," I said as I handed him the gift with the car in it. "And this one's for you Jenny." I had gotten her a lego set. Both kids could play with that.

I then went back to the car and hefted a big heavy box. I put it on the counter for Emily. "It's a little house warming gift for you," I said.

I went a little overboard and bought her a Kitchen Aid stand mixer. In red.

"Oh, my goodness, this is too much. How did you know I've always wanted a stand mixer. I love to bake and cook; I'll certainly get a lot of use out of this. Thank you so much. I promise, the first thing I bake will be shared with you.

The kids both thanked me too, and we all settled down in the living room. Emily and I with wine and the kids playing with their new gifts. I could see the difference in all of them. They were now a very happy family, which made me feel warm and fuzzy.

"So, how is everything going?" I asked Emily. "The house looks great; you've made it warmer and more inviting. I'm so proud of you."

"We love it here. And this has been such a turnaround for the kids. I hated that they were worried all the time. Kids shouldn't ever have to be worried. Now the worry is gone and they've been enrolled in school. They're settling in very well."

"Emily, I meant to ask you, do you have a picture of your husband? I think it's a good idea for us to know what he looks like, not that I think there's a concern, this is just a precaution. As you know, we inquired about the house and he sold it and his phone was disconnected. Hopefully he's moved somewhere far away, but we'd still like to get you that divorce."

"Oh, John already asked me that. Ryan wouldn't allow me to have a cell phone and there are no pictures. The alarm system and the cameras outside add to my feeling of security. Just last night I heard noises in the backyard. I pulled up the camera on my iPhone and there was a little bandit trying to get into the garbage."

Laughing, I said, "I found an easy fix for that. I feed those raccoon bandits, so it's no longer necessary for them to scavenge through my trash. Why don't you and the kids plan on coming over to my house for dinner in a few days. I think they'd enjoy the wildlife and the dogs will all be there. They can run around with them in the backyard."

"Why, thank you. That would be nice. We never had much wildlife when we lived with Ryan, he would always try and shoot them but thankfully he was a lousy shot and missed. After a while the animals stopped coming around."

Emily had made Chateaubriand, actually we had a delicious pork roast with apple stuffing. It was cooked to perfection.

For dessert Emily appeared with the most decadent chocolate cake and she did it all from scratch. Me? I would've bought a cake mix and called it a day. I could definitely see she'd benefit from her new mixer.

I was at the front door, about to leave when I remembered to tell Emily about the bugs in mine and Venice's houses. I wanted to warn her not to say anything important while in my house. Emily said she'd talk to the kids. It was still mild outside, maybe I'd just have a barbecue which would keep us all out of earshot. The bugs were definitely bugging me.

I had such a great time; I really enjoyed her kids. I didn't even have to drive home in the dark. It now stayed light until well after 9 P.M.

I still missed Venice and John but at least I had people to entertain and cook for. Tomorrow, the day before Venice was due home, Emily and the kids would be over for dinner and I invited Annie too. I had planned on making my lemon parmesan pasta with shrimp. It was one of my favorite meals to cook and it was easy. I had all the ingredients so I didn't have to shop.

I would make a separate pot of pasta and lemon minus the shrimp, for Annie, since she was a Vegan. Oh wait, the parmesan cheese. I don't think that's on the Vegan list.

I called Annie. "Can you eat parmesan cheese?" I asked. "I know not to put shrimp in but wasn't sure about the cheese."

"Actually, you can put both the shrimp and cheese in. I've decided Vegan is just too restrictive and Jerome isn't Vegan so I've compromised. I'm now a Pescatarian."

"What in the hell is a Pesca...whatever you just said," I asked. "It sounds like a religion."

"You're funny Viv, a Pescatarian is one who eats fish but no meat," said Annie.

Jerome was the guy she met on the yacht on the fourth of July. They were still going strong. I wouldn't be surprised if they ended up married.

"Hey, speaking of Jerome why don't you bring him tomorrow, we've got plenty. And, you just made my life easier. Now I no longer have to rack my brain trying to come up with fake food."

"Oh Vivianne, it's not fake food. But since it's no longer an issue, why argue? I'll ask Jerome to come with me. He's such a Sweetie."

Ah HA, they *were* going to get married. I felt it. Ooohhh, a wedding. How much fun would that be? Then I remembered the bridal murder and felt sad for Lauren all over again. Would I never be able to think of a wedding without thinking of her? Maybe if we caught *Mystery Man*, I could rest easier.

I had an idea. I'd still make the lemon pasta but would throw some hotdogs on the grill for the kids. Don't all young children love hotdogs? They could have the lemon pasta too if they wanted. I could still serve in the backyard, out of earshot of the bugs.

Kat and Nellie made it home in plenty of time to go to Mom's house the next day. She never knew they were here. Whew, that was close.

I called Mom. "Hi Mom, how is Wes feeling? I sure hope he's okay."

"Vivianne. It's his gall bladder, he'll be going in for surgery tomorrow and be home the next day. They certainly don't keep you in the hospital for any length of time anymore. And, they want you dancing and jumping through hoops the minute you get off the operating table."

Mom added, "You should come for a visit, he'd like that."

"Yes, so would I," I lied. "Unfortunately, Venice is in Arizona and I'm dog sitting. I'll call him every day though and maybe we can even Facetime." Venice would be home by then but no need to tell Mom. I wasn't going back to New York since I had been there not too long ago for her surgery. There's only so much familial bliss I can stand.

"Facetime? You mean that thing that allows you to see the person you're talking to? Kat and Nellie will be here, of course, so they'll set the face thing up for Wes. That would be nice, given you won't be here in person."

Ah, I was wondering when the dig would gouge its way under my thick skin.

I managed to get through the next few minutes. I told her I'd call Kat and we could set up Facetime. Wes would be home in a few days, and I doubt he'd be running to fetch my Mom's wine anytime soon. Oh well, Kat could take over. Do not tell her I said that.

CHAPTER TWENTY-TWO

My phone chirped. It was Venice.

"Hi, and to what do I owe this pleasure? I miss you."

"Bryan is running errands and I didn't feel like going so I decided to play hooky and call you. I must say he's being so much better than he was on my first visit. He not only came into the airport to get me but he actually brought me flowers. It's like he read my mind. I think he knew from the last time how annoyed I was.

"What's going on with you? How are my dogs doing? They do miss me, don't they?"

"Yes," I fibbed. "They go to sleep crying every night. Oh, the raccoons are here, I'm going outside."

"I gather you just made that up so you could talk freely," said Venice.

"Of course, I did. Tomorrow Annie, Jerome, Emily, and the kids are coming over for dinner. I thought we could have it in the backyard to stay away from prying ears. If you get on a plane now, you could make it home in time to join the party. Emily invited me to her house the other night so I'm reciprocating and adding Annie to the mix. And guess what?" I didn't wait for Ven to guess, I blurted out, "She's no longer a Vegan. We can thank Jerome for that, but she still won't eat meat. However, she will eat fish so she'll get shrimp while everyone else will have their pick of good old-fashioned meat. Although I'm not sure what's in hotdogs, they may not be considered meat at all."

"Oh, yum and damn. We'll have to do it again once I'm home. I take it you're not missing me that much with all this socialness."

"Don't be an ass. I miss you terribly. Who's going to make dessert?"

"Viv, you're so shallow. You only love me for my baking."

Smiling, I said, "I'll see you soon at the Airporter. I'm glad to know you're having a good time. You are, aren't you?"

"I am, but there's a few things I want to run by you. Nothing serious, at least I don't think so."

"I hate when you do that Venice. The suspense will kill me. Why can't you just tell me now?"

"Because I love to torture you. Bryan will be back soon. Kiss, kiss."

And with that she disconnected. I was happy to hear her voice and could hardly wait for her to get home.

The party was in full swing, barbecue going, drinks in hand and nibbles on the table for all. I thought I was brilliant for having it outside until one of the kids had to go to the bathroom. Emily went in with Davey and Sassy snuck in after them. Jenny ran in to get Sassy and when Emily and Davey came out, he yelled, "Mom, Jenny has Sassy."

Jenny answered back, "Davey, Sassy was looking for you. I think you're her favorite." It put a big grin on Davey's face. It also told the listening devices just who they were, not that I thought there was any correlation. It would just be one more bit of information Bugass would know, *if* he was listening.

At that moment Jerome poked his head in and asked after Sassy.

Jenny said, "It's okay Jerome, Davey has it all under control."

Davey looked at Jerome and asked, "Are you and Annie getting married?" Leave it to kids to blurt out the most awkward things.

"Maybe," he said. Then he noticed the look on my face and realized they were talking in the house. Annie had filled him in on the bug situation.

He signaled for them all to go back outside, closed the door and said, "Gee Vivianne, I'm really sorry. I forgot."

"That's okay Jerome, I sometimes forget too. I'm getting so tired of this. If we don't come up with a plan by next week, I'm going to take my hammer to every one of those things. We'll have a bug smashing party."

Everyone left at around 8 P.M. The kids were exhausted as well as the dogs. Annie and Emily offered to stay and help clean up but I knew Emily wanted to put the kids to bed and Annie wanted to go home with Jerome. I shooed them all out.

I too was tired but someone had to clean up this mess. I turned around and gave the finger to the room knowing whoever was listening couldn't see me but it gave me satisfaction nonetheless. I was getting very cranky.

The dogs were all passed out and snoring. Not one of them offered to help me. Ingrates.

The next day I was thrilled that I would be taking the dogs and picking up Venice at the Airporter. Betty was driving, Sassy and Mr. Snigglebottom were too short to reach the pedals.

When she disembarked, get it, barked? Okay, the dogs slobbered all over her. They were so happy to see their Mommy. But why was Sassy slobbering? Her Mommy was right here. Traitor!

"Oh Viv, Mr. Snigglebottom, Betty, and look, even Sassy is welcoming me home. I'm so happy to be here. Not that my mini vacation wasn't spectacular, I was just ready to be home."

Venice was a shade darker from the sun. She looked contented, carefree, and glowing. I, on the other hand, looked pale in comparison. Sickly even. Sigh. And, without a dog, since Sassy went over to her side.

On the ride home I educated her on the workings of her new security system. She installed the app on her phone and now she could pull it all up at any time and turn it on or off.

"Your password it 'Bettysniggles' which you might want to change," I said.

"So, how was Bryan? It seems he did a complete turn-around since you were last there. Were you satisfied with him? Wait, wait, bad choice of words. Were you okay with the way he treated you?"

"Yes, I was captivated by his charm. Let's wait until we get home and we can sit outside and have a drink. I need a drink to tell you about the next part."

"Really??? And with that I put the pedal to the metal and we were home in record time.

Once at Venice's house she went in without saying a word, rummaged around for about ten minutes, still quiet, and came out to where I was happily ensconced in her most comfortable deck chair.

"I'll need you to help me bring out the goods. I'm being totally quiet so no talking. I will no longer say anything as to why I'm doing something, like sitting outside. Whoever is listening can just deal with it. And I'm telling you now, these things have to go and soon so Gloria better have an end in sight."

"Look who grew a set of balls while in Arizona. Did anyone else grow anything?"

In we went and came out bearing trays of drinks and munchies. The dogs were happily chewing on marrow bones and having martinis, with olives.

Back in my deck chair, drink in hand, I said, "I'm listening."

Venice started, "First of all, he was so much better this time around. I already told you about the airport and flowers. He was funny and attentive. You know, if this trip didn't go well, I was ready to pull the plug on the whole thing."

"If this trip didn't go well, *I* would have pulled the plug. I'm happy for you Ven, I'm glad it's working out. You really do deserve it."

"Come on, Viv, you still don't like him, do you?"

"That's not true. Okay, in the beginning I was jealous and then scared you'd run off with him and I'd never see you again. Then, the way he treated you on your first trip to Arizona made me want to slap his face off. But everyone deserves a second chance and he's really stepped up the game so, no, I don't dislike him. As long as he keeps being good to my best friend, he's okay in my book. But I'm keeping a close eye on him," I said, laughing.

"Thanks Viv, that means a lot to me. It really does. Are you ready for the juicy stuff now?"

"Juicy??? By all mean, bring it on. The juicier the better."

"The sex was amazing. His thing, I know, I know, his *penis,* ugh, I don't like that word. What can we call it that doesn't make me cringe?"

Rolling my eyes out of my head I thought for a moment. "How about Dick, wanger, member, oh, here's a good one, his phallus? Or his hot molten rod?"

With that we both cracked up and fell off our chairs. Well, almost.

"I give. I'll call it his Mickey. You know...he slipped me a mickey."

More hysterics. Mickey? Really?

"Look, give it a name and let's get on with it. I'm dying here."

"You won't believe this but his mickey has grown since the last time I saw it. And not just excited big, I mean flaccid big too. How can that be?"

"Oh, it can be. Not that I know from experience. I've had small, medium and large. Then there was huge and believe me, I ran. I've never had teeny tiny but sometimes it can be too big. Maybe there's a pill for growing it. Maybe he was so excited it just grew and grew. Maybe, every time he lied it grew. Who cares? You seem to have enjoyed the new and improved model, so stop questioning, and go with the flow."

"You're right. Let's just say it was a definite upgrade. Both the sex and his attitude. Maybe I should move to Arizona."

"Over my dead body."

"Don't worry, I'm not planning on killing you anytime soon. I don't particularly like arid desert so it wouldn't be for me. It's a respite from the winters here. It's warm whereas here it's rainy, dark, and just plain nasty. The dogs hate the rain. Maybe I'll take them with me next time."

"You're not leaving me with no dogs, it's bad enough *you're* gone. So that would be a no, you're not allowed to take them to Arizona."

"Silly, I wouldn't subject them to air travel. Betty is too big to stay with me in the cabin and I'd die not knowing if she were okay. Besides, Bryan isn't allowed to have any animals in that ugly condo. Not even a hummingbird feeder. What do they think, it's going to spoil the Motel Six décor?

"All in all, I had a very nice time. We went to Prescott and did the wildlife center which was terrific, and one day we went to a lake with a lovely restaurant. I forgot the name but it was perfect, and seeing a body of water in the desert was amazing. We cooked too and then went for local rides. Don't forget, the bike was in for repairs, and I have to admit, I liked the air-conditioned car a lot better."

"You look happy and relaxed," I commented. "Now that you're back, are you going into the brokerage tomorrow? There isn't too much happening right now."

"No," said Venice. "I think I'll just spend the day kissing my dogs and relaxing. I need a vacation from my vacation. Say hi to Annie and give Rainbow Realty a big hug."

I was at Rainbow the next morning by 9 A.M. Early for me. I had a client to take out for showings and wouldn't be back until late afternoon. Sassy was with me, she always added charm to my already charming self.

When I got back to the brokerage it was almost closing time and I was surprised to see Emily and the kids there. They had come in just before Annie was going to lock up the place. As I opened the door, I got a text from Venice. It said, "Annie, Emily, and the kids are at the brokerage, so I want you all to go in the back room. I have a big surprise for you. I'll be there in a few minutes."

CHAPTER TWENTY-THREE

T his was certainly puzzling. I told everyone what Venice had texted.

Annie asked, "What's going on? It seems we all got a similar text."

"I have no idea, let's go back and wait, she said she'd be here in a matter of minutes."

We all gathered in the back room, which made me think of where the dead bride was found. I didn't say anything but I'm sure Annie was thinking the same thing. Why would Venice want to meet us back here?

There were two ways to get to the back. You could enter via the brokerage offices and the other door led outside, to the back of the building, it was a mandatory fire exit.

I got some metal chair that were folded against the wall so we could sit.

The door from the offices opened, and in stepped Bryan.

My brow, furrowed in confusion, I asked, "Bryan, where's Venice?"

Emily said, "Ryan?"

I turned to Emily as her children sat wide eyed and said, "Ryan? No, Emily, that's Venice's Bryan."

Emily got up so suddenly, her chair tipped back and fell with a clatter. "No, no, that's Ryan. What are you doing here? How did you find us?"

Ryan/Bryan said, "Sit down Emily, and shut up." He had a gun. It was in his hand which was hanging by his side, so I hadn't noticed it. It was now pointed at Emily.

"I want you all to shut up and put your phones on the floor and slide them over to me. Turn them off first. I don't want to hear one phone ringing. Do it. NOW."

I jumped a foot but did as he said.

"Who are you?" I asked. "Bryan or Ryan or are you one in the same?"

"I'm Ryan. And before anyone moves, the doors are locked and the front door can't be opened because there's a crowbar though the handles. Nobody is going anywhere, and if you try, I'll shoot you on the spot."

Jenny and Davey started to cry. "Shut those brats up or I'll shut them up for you," he snarled.

Emily kneeled down in front of them and hugged them to her. She made soothing sounds, telling them not to cry or Daddy would be mad. Everything was going to be all right. They still sniffled but the crying had stopped.

Icy tentacles of fear trickled down my spine. "What have

you done to Venice? If you've hurt her..."

"Venice is fine. We're going to get married and nobody is going to stop me this time." He started laughing maniacally.

I was hoping to stall him. Maybe Venice could see us on the cameras. There were cameras in this room, I had them installed as an afterthought and nobody knew they were in here but if Venice looked, this room would come up on her cell phone. Wait, her cell phone.

"Tell me Ryan, how did you get Venice's phone if she's okay? It was you that texted us, wasn't it?"

"Get me a chair," he demanded from Annie. "I'm going to sit down and tell you a story before I blow this place and everyone in it to smithereens. Minus myself, of course." He started with that laugh again, it was like nails on a blackboard.

He sat down, facing us as would a teacher to a classroom.

"Let's start at the beginning, shall we? It all began, well, at the *very* beginning. In the womb."

That's certainly the beginning, I thought. If he's going back that far maybe by the time he's done talking help will be here. But how? We needed a miracle.

Bryan/Ryan started his story, "My lovely mother was a druggie. It was all there in the hospital records which I read when I hacked into the system. I'm quite good at hacking. You didn't know that, did you Emily? Oh, Emily, Emily, you were so innocent and malleable. Maybe even a bit stupid. You never knew anything, not even what I did for a living.

"The records revealed that my mother was an addict and

was pregnant with twins. She was giving us up for adoption. A couple wanted both of us. She was living with them the last three months before we were born so she wasn't doing drugs but it was too late. The damage had already been done. The couple, Sharon and Roger Davidson, had agreed to pay her handsomely for us. They even signed a contract and in it they promised to name us Ryan and Bryan. She was giving us up, I don't know why the names were important to her, nothing else was.

"She went into labor a month early and died giving birth to us. No loss there. If she'd lived, she would have taken all the money from selling us and gone back to her drugs. They would have killed her eventually anyway."

"When we were born, I was the twin who was the frailest and sickest. We were both in NICU but Bryan thrived, I didn't. When Bryan was strong enough to go home with his adoptive parents, I remained in NICU. Sharon and Roger Davidson adopted Bryan and decided it would be too much work to take me too. TOO MUCH WORK?

"I'll tell you why I was so sick. Because that fucker twin took everything in the womb. He tried to kill me even then, to take it all for himself. Why was I the one to be left behind, sick and struggling for my life?

"It took months and they all thought I would die but I didn't. I finally started to get stronger. I was still weak and underweight but I wasn't in danger of dying anymore. I was now a ward of the State of Oregon. When I was able to leave NICU, I went into the foster care system. Until I was eighteen, I was sent from one foster home to another. I hated them all.

"When I was sixteen and still living with my last foster family, I worked three jobs to save enough money to go to community college. That's where I learned everything I could about computers. As they progressed, so did I.

"I met Emily about ten years ago. She was crazy about me. And she was a pretty little thing. I'm partial to small women.

"It was good in the beginning. She worked too, and then she got pregnant. I started to feel stifled, saddled down with a kid, and then she got pregnant again. I wanted her to get an abortion but she wouldn't do it. That was probably the only time she went against my wishes. The second kid was born and I never touched her again. I wasn't going to fuck up my manhood by getting a vasectomy and she wouldn't get her tubes tied, so that was that. No sex, no shitty little kids.

"Emily had her brood, I had nothing. I would go to work and, on the drive home, would fantasize that I'd get there and see the house had burned to the ground. In my imagination, Emily and the kids would have perished in the fire and I would finally be free. But that didn't happen, did it?

"It was Lauren who changed everything. Until Lauren, I just had meaningless flings. After all, a man needs some release. They were all brainless whores. They meant nothing to me.

"I remember the night I met Lauren. I was driving home; it was dark and the rain was coming down in torrents. I barely saw her, almost drove right by. She was on the side of the road and she had a flat tire. I pulled over and changed the tire for her. She was so thankful, she said I was an angel.

"She gave me her phone number and the rest is history. I didn't tell her I was married at first. When I knew she was in love with me I told her Emily, who I renamed Mona, was my wife, and that I was about to file for a divorce when we found out she had terminal cancer. Lauren thought I was a saint for staying with Mona until the end. I never mentioned the kids."

"What were you going to do with Emily, Jenny, and Davey? Lauren was bound to find out sooner or later," I said.

"You're wrong. Lauren never found out about anything. I even made up a story about driving Mona to see her ailing mother. I told her Mona wanted the chance to say goodbye to her Mom and I had dropped her off for the weekend. Lauren and I took the opportunity to drive up the coast to Washington. We decided to take the ferry into Kingsville. Lauren had visited the place a few years back and had fallen in love with the town.

"We pretended we were married. I even bought cheap rings for us. I also had my disguise on. She laughed and said I looked good in dark hair. I had even brought a disguise for her, a blonde wig. I have to say, I prefer dark hair. But it served the purpose, we were both unrecognizable.

I told her the disguise was so Mona wouldn't find out before she died. Again, Lauren thought I was a saint and a martyr.

"Driving off the ferry we saw the bridal salon." I said to Lauren, 'Let's go in, we'll tell everyone we're getting married and you want to try on gowns. I told her this would be practice for when we really did get married. We went in and the next few hours were spent pretending. She must have tried on a dozen dresses. She would make a beautiful bride for me.

"I would think of a way to get rid of Emily and the kids. Then Lauren and I really would get married. Lauren would just think 'Mona' had died.

"I told her we could buy a house and live in Kingsville after we were married. She liked that. And, I would have her all to myself. No in-laws, all her friends back in Oregon, it was perfect."

Annie spoke up then, she had caught on to what I was doing, which was trying to keep him talking. She asked him, "What if Lauren wanted children? That would be a game changer, wouldn't it?"

"Oh, that wasn't happening. She was on birth control pills when I met her. No, I was not having any more kids. Lauren wouldn't care, as long as she had me, why would she need kids? It ruins everything."

"What if Venice wants children? Have you thought of that?" I asked?

"Don't' be a fool. Venice is a little old for that."

Ah, but she wasn't. She was 41 and as far as I knew, it was still possible. Venice and I never discussed it. Why would we? We were satisfied with our dog children. And Bryan, no, Ryan, had a point. Why would she want kids this late in the game? God, I wanted her to be okay. I wanted to live to see her again. What a mess this was.

"What happened to Lauren? I take it you killed her, right here, in this very room. Or was she already dead when you brought her here?"

"I met Lauren on our regular night. I had figured out what to do with the bitch and her snotty kids. I'd drive them far away and leave them with money and threaten Emily. I'd make sure she knew, if she ever told anyone about me, I would hunt her down and kill the kids. She loves those bloodsuckers more than anything, she would obey me.

"Lauren was waiting for me in our room that night. I brought her flowers to celebrate, but before I could tell her the good news, that I was free, she told me she couldn't go on any-more, she was ending it.

"I was speechless. This had to be some weird joke. Leav-ing me? No way. But it wasn't a joke. She started to cry and told me it hurt her to tell me but she had met someone else. She really was ending it. All my planning, for nothing. What about Kingsville and our life there?

"I was incredulous. My Lauren? With someone else? I told her she needed to think about this. Do you know what she did then? She said it was too late and ran out of the room, got in her car and drove away.

"I sat there, for hours. I was numb. Then I was angry. How dare she do this to me. Me, who was her perfect man. Me who made all those sacrifices. How could she do this when I just lost my wife to cancer? What kind of person does that?"

"Ryan," I said gently. "She was wrong to leave you, but your wife wasn't really dying of cancer."

"No shit, but Lauren *believed* she had cancer and was dying so to Lauren that was true. Again, what kind of person does that? Then I realized she didn't mean it. She would come back to me, I was sure.

"I started following her in the evening. I wanted to see if she really had someone else. I thought, if she did, it would run its course and then she'd come to her senses and we'd get mar-ried. I followed her for months. I saw her with that guy. What could he possibly offer her that I hadn't?

"It was easy to bug her apartment. The locks were infer-ior and I knew when she'd be gone. I wore my disguise and easily picked my way in and planted a listening device in her closet. It's probably still there.

"Then she got engaged. I was livid. I watched, waited, and listened. I was patient. It made me sick to listen to their fornicating, but it would all be worth it.

"I heard all her conversations. I knew when she was going to the bridal salon for alterations, I knew her every move. I was just waiting for an opportunity. And that opportunity came when she made an appointment to pick up her dress just before closing. She'd be the last one in and her car couldn't be seen from the shop or road, the parking was in the back. The time had come. I had to act quickly or she'd be married and that wouldn't do. If she wasn't married to me, she wasn't going to be married to anyone. She promised herself to *me*.

"I was waiting behind a tree when she came out. I got her with the Isoflurane from behind, and quickly threw her and the box in the trunk of her car. I had parked my car a few blocks away where there were plenty of apartments and nobody would notice it. You see, I thought of everything. I also had on my disguise just in case I was spotted. They would never be able to point the finger at me.

"First, I drove her car with her in the trunk to a vacant lot, that was not easily seen, not far from where my car was. I then walked to my car and drove it back to the lot where Lauren's car was. I then transferred her from her trunk to my car, putting the boxed dress on the back seat. I'd need that for later. She was almost lucid so I dosed her with more Isoflurane, and gave her a shot of the benzo, that would keep her out for hours. I sat her in the passenger seat. She looked like she was peacefully sleeping. I even put a pillow under her head.

"We were on our way to Kingsville. Once we were there and in the bridal salon, she'd see she was making a mistake with that other asshole. She'd see it was me she wanted to marry. Of course, the bridal salon was no longer there. I had spent many days in Kingsville watching your brokerage. Once, when your girl," and he pointed at Annie, "was out to lunch, I went in to use the bathroom. I quickly looked in the back so I knew the dais was still there and I knew that space wasn't used for anything.

"You," he said pointing at me. "Give me that bottle of water, I'm just about to wrap this up."

"Wait, this is quite a story. It's evident that you're very intelligent. You've gotten away with it all. That took brains. I can see how you're better than Bryan. That was you who brought Venice flowers at the airport, wasn't it?"

"You know Vivianne, I like you. It's a shame I have to kill you but it's necessary. As you said, I'm smart. And yes, that was me at the airport. That moron of a brother didn't know how to treat a woman right. I listened and I knew. I knew it all. How do you think I stepped into Bryan's persona so quickly without any suspicions? I had planted listening devices there too, it was easy, I did it before my idiot brother moved into the condo."

He tapped his head grinning.

"It's all up here. Venice will never guess I'm not Bryan."

"Please Ryan, at least tell us the rest of the story. What happened to Lauren? Why did you kill her? Was it because she was too blind to see what she had with you?"

"I didn't mean to kill her. When I got her here, it took me a while to get the gown on her. The veil was there too and it was all flawless. An exquisite bride. But then, she didn't wake up. When I felt for her pulse, there wasn't any. That's when I realized I must have overdosed her. You see, I didn't mean for her to die.

"I felt sad but at least I knew that she would've picked me. I had no doubt. I bent down and kissed her lightly and she was still warm. I told her I loved her. I would always be with her. It was a beautiful moment, and then I replaced the engagement ring with the one I bought her. She would no longer be engaged to *him*, and now, in death she'd be eternally engaged to me. She was mine forever."

I doubt very much it was a beautiful moment for poor Lauren. Shit, this guy was an psycho egomaniac. And a killer. If he killed us all, it would only be a matter of time before he killed Venice. I didn't think she was dead, he still thought she loved him. Sooner or later, something would happen to make him murder her too. Maybe she'd find out the truth before that happened. SASSY. Shit, I forgot she was out in the car. I was hoping the car was far enough away so that if, or when he blew the place up, she'd be okay. I had no idea what time it was but he'd been talking for what seemed like forever and he was now winding down.

"Why did you leave the button from her gown on the yacht?" I asked. "Why did you even take it? Was Venice with Bryan while you did this? And, most of all why Venice, why did you pick her, how did you even know her?"

"These are the last questions I'll answer. I took the button as a good luck charm. I carried it everywhere with me. That's why I was never caught. I was curious about that yacht; I knew all about it from the listening devices I planted. I wondered if I could blow it up with all of you on it. It didn't matter because that man caught me and threw me off. And, I had to replace Bryan before I killed everyone.

"Later, when I felt for the button in my pocket, it was gone. I must have dropped it. Then I laughed because if you found it, which I doubted you would, it would be another piece of a puzzle you'd never solve. Even though my lucky button is gone, the luck has stayed with me.

"I had found Bryan you see. Quite a while ago. I kept tabs on him, I knew his day would come, I'd make sure of that. After I lost my Lauren, I decided to stay here, until some time had passed and I could feel safe back in Oregon. I did go back to get my stuff and that's when the boat guy saw me in the bar. But it was my disguise he saw, not the real me.

"I rented an apartment in Blainton, far enough away so I wouldn't run into Bryan but near enough to keep tabs on him. I never went out without my disguise on and I was very careful.

"Then my brother met Venice, and she was perfect. If Bryan was good enough for her, I would be even better. Now I had a plan. His day had come. Bryan got everything, now it was my turn to take it back, and that included Venice, and we love each other.

"I knew Bryan had bought the condo in Arizona and I went down there before he moved and, in the middle of the night, I picked his pathetic lock and planted my listening devices in there. That's how I knew everything he did and said to my Venice. It was easy taking his place.

"Enough, it's almost time. Nobody will ever know I'm even here, in Washington, but when Venice calls me crying, it will be me who will come running to take care of her, to love her. She won't have you Vivianne and she won't have Rainbow Realty either. You do see, don't you? I'm all she'll have and all she'll ever need."

CHAPTER TWENTY-FOUR

Venice

I opened my eyes. I was lying on the floor. Why was I on the floor? Was I hurt? I gingerly moved my feet, legs and arms. I wiggled my toes and fingers. So far so good. I was very groggy and disoriented. It was a struggle to get to a sitting position.

As the seconds ticked by, I felt a little less dizzy. The dogs, where are the dogs? I tried to get up quickly and broke out in a cold sweat. Breathe I told myself. I was no good if I was going to pass out again.

I didn't trust myself to walk just yet so I crawled over to the sliders and there, in the yard, were my babies. Jumping up and down now that they saw me. I reached up and slid the door open before I sank back down to the floor.

Mr. Snigglebottom was crazed thinking I was on the floor to play. But Betty, in her infinite wisdom, knew something was wrong. She dialed 911. I wish. Speaking of dialing, where was my phone?

I sat on the floor for about fifteen minutes before I felt strong enough to stand. I crawled over to the kitchen chair and used it to pull myself up. I sat down and took some deep breaths.

That's when my memory came flooding back. I remembered a hand over my mouth with something foul smelling and then, nothing. Was he still here? I didn't even know the time.

The kitchen stove said it was 6:30 P.M. I needed a phone. I'd been out for a while, but I knew Viv had a landline in case of emergencies. Could I make it over there? Where was Viv anyway? Was she home? I didn't know, no phone.

I stood back up and though a bit wobbly, I could walk slowly. I got the keys and drove over to Viv's house. I wasn't going to crash the car driving across the street, and it was much faster than walking, easier too.

I saw that Viv's car was gone. I drove into the carport and let myself in. I got to the landline and called Viv. It rang and rang and the voicemail kicked in. I didn't leave a message. Something was very wrong. Next, I called Det. Traynor. I explained that someone drugged me and I needed her immediately, and I was at Viv's house. She didn't ask questions and said she'd be here in ten minutes.

That was the longest ten minutes of my life. I saw Det. Traynor's car come down the driveway and I flung open the door for her.

"What the hell is going on? Where is Vivianne?" she asked. "Are you okay Venice?"

"Yes, I think I'm okay. I couldn't find my phone; I think someone took it. I came over here to use Viv's landline."

"You think whoever did this took your phone?"

"Yes, I always have it nearby when I'm in the house and I couldn't see it anywhere."

"Hang on Venice, I'm calling the station and I'll have them track the GPS signal. Hopefully the phone is still on and intact."

"She stayed on the phone for only a few minutes and said, "No signal, give me your phone number."

Det. Traynor's phone rang and she picked it up immediately. "Yes, I got it. Thanks." Turning to me she said, "We know where your phone is, it's at Rainbow Realty."

"Look Gloria, something bad is going on and I'm afraid Viv's in trouble. I called her and she didn't answer, and she has Sassy and its past Sass's dinnertime. Can you take me to Rainbow Realty? No, wait. I'm not thinking clearly. I can pull up the security cameras on my phone. Crap, I don't have my phone." I was rambling.

"If you can pull up the security on your phone you can also do it from your iPad or computer. Let's get you back to your house."

With Gloria breathing down my neck I pulled the cameras up on my computer. I scrolled through and then came to the back room.

"Oh my God, look. I didn't even know we had a camera back there but here it is. That's Bryan. And there's Vivianne, Emily, and the kids, and Annie too. Is that a gun he has?"

"You stay here, I'm going to the brokerage and I'm calling for backup on the way."

"I'm going with you," I said. "And don't argue. If you won't take me, I'll go in my own car, but I *am* going. That's Viv in trouble and she would go if it were me."

Gloria let out a sigh and said, "Are you sure you're not Vivianne? This is something she'd pull. C'mon, let's get going," she said as she called the station.

On the phone to the station, she said it was a code 2. I asked her what that was.

"That means it's urgent and no siren or lights when approaching the brokerage".

I had my iPad on my lap and wasn't taking my eyes off the screen. Maybe I could discover what was going on. Bryan seemed to be talking. There was no sound but I could see his lips moving and expressions on his face. Every now and then he'd laugh. Nobody else was laughing which wasn't a good sign.

"My team will park across the street from Rainbow Realty. They won't do anything until I get there. I'm sure Bryan has locked all the doors and I don't want to tip him off. The bomb squad will be there too, just as a precaution."

"BOMB SQUAD? Oh no. Oh no. Please hurry."

"Venice, if he intends to blow up the place it won't be with him in it. He's the one who probably knocked you out. There was a reason he did that. If everyone is dead and you didn't see him, he's in the clear. It makes sense. Trust me, this isn't my first rodeo; I know what I'm doing."

"Maybe you'd like to fill me in. Then I'll think about trusting you. Don't let anything happen to them and I'll trust you for life. Is that a bargain?

"Why do you think we need a bomb squad?" I asked.

"If he shoots everyone, someone might hear the shots, said Detective, "there would be evidence too. But, if he blows the place up, the crime scene and everyone in it will be reduced to ashes, and he walks away free and clear. He's rid of everyone and everything in one big explosion.

"This is pure speculation but maybe Bryan is jealous of Vivianne and your business. He knew you'd never leave either one. I think maybe the others just got caught in the crosshairs."

"Maybe you're right," I said "But he never gave any indication of jealousy. Also, I can't see him doing something like this. It doesn't matter why, it only matters that we save everyone, then we can figure it all out."

We arrived across the street from the brokerage where everyone was waiting for us. Gloria barked out orders and eight men ran, hunched over, and surrounded Rainbow Realty. Two men for each side of the building. The bomb squad had a sniffer dog. Was this really happening? Please, please, let them all be okay. If even one person was hurt, I would tear Bryan's eyes out myself and shove them down his throat until he choked to death.

The guy with the dog came back and told Gloria there were homemade bombs on the outside of each corner of the building. They were well camouflaged and could be detonated by Bryan's cell phone. Bomb guy said they were rudimentary and could be neutralized quickly. He signaled for his men and they soundlessly went to work.

"Gloria," I whispered, "He's getting up. He's walking to the door. I think he's coming out. Now he's out of the room and he's locked the door behind him so nobody can leave. Son of a bitch. Are the bombs still active? Please tell me they're not."

Gloria didn't answer me for a few seconds. My heart was pounding in my chest. Then I saw a flashlight flicker on and off twice.

"That's it. The bombs are all defused."

I didn't even realize I was holding my breath until it came out in a whoosh. Relief flooded over me.

The men had their weapons drawn, waiting for him to come out. Would he have the nerve to walk out the front door? Or would he take one of the side doors? I had all the cameras up on my iPad and he was walking toward the front. He had a hoodie on and he pulled it up so you couldn't see his face.

I told Gloria, and the men in the front were ready for him. I saw him take a bar out of the handles of the front door. As soon as he was outside, starting to walk away from the brokerage he was ambushed. He was told to drop his weapon.

The first thing Ryan did was push the button on his cell phone. I can only surmise he intended to blow up everything, including himself since he was now caught. I saw the expression on his face. His brows knitted together in puzzlement and then reality washed over his face. I couldn't believe it when he raised his gun toward the police. They opened fire and he dropped to the ground, blood flowing from him. They took his gun and I ran across the street. I bent down and looked at him. He looked up at me, gasping for breath.

"Why Bryan, why?" I asked.

"All for you, not Bry..." and then he was still.

Nobody could stop me as I ran through the building to the back. The door was locked but I yelled, "It's okay. You're safe now. The bombs are gone." Oh no, I had forgotten my keys.

Gloria gently pulled me back as a battering ram splintered the door. I was now hysterical. They were all okay. The kids were wailing but nobody was hurt. I ran in and gave Viv a crushing hug, so hard I almost knocked her over.

"Take it easy Ven, take it easy. We're all fine, a little rattled, but fine."

I ran to Annie, then Emily. I told the kids it was okay. The bad man was gone and he would never be back.

"We don't like Daddy. He's mean. Promise Daddy isn't coming back to hurt us."

Daddy? Now I was sure the knock out stuff had muddled my mind, maybe for good. Viv saw the bewildered look on my face.

"Ven, I'll explain it all later. For now, we'll probably have to give Det. Traynor our statements."

Detective took one look at me and told Viv to get me home. She didn't think I looked well but now that everyone was safe, I was great. Okay, maybe a little nauseous and still a tiny bit dizzy but nothing to be alarmed about.

I thought, Det. Traynor? Oops, I'd been calling her Gloria this whole time. And she didn't even yell at me. I was thinking I'd better go back to Detective, especially in front of her fellow cops. She was most definitely not in her personal role, and I was thankful for that. She saved them all. There were already reporters at the scene. How do they do that? Are they psychic?

I said, "Thanks Det. Traynor. I'm good for my word. I will trust you forever and that's a promise. They're alive and safe because of you."

"No Venice, this was a team effort and you were the most important part of that team. It doesn't matter, as long as it turned out well. At least for them, not so much for Bryan."

I was really perplexed and said to Viv, "When he was shot, I ran to him and asked, why? His last words were, 'All for you,' and then he started to say 'Not' but that's all I heard before he died. He must have thought I was someone else. Why were the kids calling him Daddy?"

"Det. Traynor, we're going home now. I need Vivianne to explain this all to me. I think I'm having a breakdown."

"Go, I'll take your statement tomorrow Vivianne. Meanwhile I'll talk to the others if they're up to it."

CHAPTER
TWENTY-FIVE

A few weeks had passed since the incident. I had told Venice everything. We now knew for sure the man who held us hostage wasn't Bryan, but Ryan, his twin.

The only thing we didn't know, was what happened to Bryan. I assumed he was dead, killed by Ryan so he could assume his identity, but no body had been found to date.

I closed Rainbow Realty for a few weeks. We all needed a little time to heal.

Emily and the kids were doing great. I think it was a relief to Emily that her husband was dead. She would never have to worry about him coming back to hurt her or the kids. As it turned out, Ryan had quite the nest egg, which went to her, since she was still legally his wife. Now, when the year was up, she could afford to pay her own way. She said she wanted to stay here and continue working at the brokerage which made me happy. Emily and the kids were added to my extended family, which seemed to be growing nicely.

Annie's Jerome proposed to her, and she said yes. I think knowing he could have lost her made him realize how much he loved and cherished her. After congratulating her, my first question was, would she stay on at Rainbow Realty. After what happened, I wouldn't blame her if she wanted to find another job.

"Are you kidding," she said. "I'm practically famous. I can tell this story to my kids and my grandkids. This is dope," which I learned from Nellie meant anything excellent or exciting. I'm so outdated.

As for me, I always pop back, no matter what happens. Ah, except for one thorn that will forever stay in my side. My mother. She was glad I was alive, I think, but she went on and on about how, if it weren't for Venice, I could be dead. Venice was moved up to number three in my mother's good graces. I was last, as usual.

John was delighted I was still amongst the living. When he found out what had happened, he was in Italy and he flew back immediately. I was glad he did. He had his security remove all the bugs. Halleluiah. I found myself still censoring my conversations but I was getting over that too.

My phone sang, "With a Little Bit of Help from Your Friends" by Rod Stuart. I made that my special "Venice" ringtone.

"Hey," I said. "What's up?"

"I'm baking. Want to come over for a taste test?"

"I doubt very much you need a taste tester; you could never bake something awful. I guess I'll sacrifice my taste buds for the better good."

I was at her door three minutes later, followed by Sassy who, I'm sure, knew Ven was baking before we even left our house. The smell was intoxicating.

I sat at the table, laden with all sorts of goodies. "Did you not sleep last night? This is a feast of lavishness. I don't know where to start first." Scones, cookies, banana bread, the list went on. I was practically catatonic.

Venice warned me, "Take it easy. Small portions so you won't get full before you taste it all. I just want to make sure I haven't lost my touch." Now I knew Ven was back to her old self. We were just finishing up and, if possible, her baking was even better. My phone chirped. It was Det. Traynor. I hadn't yet allocated her a special ring.

"Hi Detective. I would usually ask about the case but there is no more case."

"Well, Vivianne, the bridal killer case is now closed, however we still had a missing person file that remained open, Bryan."

"Had?"

"Yes, I'm afraid that hikers found his body yesterday, buried in a shallow grave in the desert. Tests were run and it's conclusive, it's Bryan. I'm calling you before I call Venice. I thought you might want to be the one to break it to her."

"I'm at Venice's house right now, I'll tell her." We hung up.

Venice turned to me and asked, "What was that all about? What did you consent to do now?"

"I'm so sorry, Ven. Bryan's body was found. It's definitely him. Here, sit down."

"Oh my, how, when?"

"Hikers found him yesterday in a grave in the desert. Here, let me get you water."

"No Viv, I'm okay. I kind of figured Ryan killed him. How else would he be able to take over Bryan's life, his condo, his car, even me."

"I'm still sorry, I know you loved him."

"I was extremely fond of Bryan but I'm not sure I was in love with him." She started to quietly cry. No sobbing, no hysterics. Just a sadness.

"Here's a tissue. I thought you were in love with him. What happened? Or do you not want to talk about it right now?"

"I think I knew, when I realized I didn't want more than I had. I couldn't see myself living with him, there or here. Especially not in Arizona. I am, I mean, was, extremely fond of him. He was a nice person and didn't deserve to be killed, that's for sure.

"What does bother me is that I was sharing myself with two men, one a murderer. Remember when I last visited Bryan? I said he was different, even his mickey was bigger?"

That did it. We both started laughing, the tension broken. I'd say we were back to normal, as normal as we got anyway.

"Oh, we are bad people and we're going straight to hell," said Venice. "Laughing just minutes after we found out poor Bryan was murdered. I am so sorry for him and will definitely miss him. This sucks."

Venice caught her breath and said, "I do have one question that will, unfortunately, remain unanswered."

"What's that?" I asked her.

"Ryan, or Bryan, which one fathered the child I'm carrying. I'm pregnant."

THE END

.

RECIPE FOR MERINGUE SHELLS

INGREDIENTS:

4 Egg whites
¾ cup Sugar
4 drops Lemon extract
Jell-O Cook and Serve Lemon Pudding. DO NOT USE INSTANT
Heavy cream, about 3/4 cup or a little more

INSTRUCTIONS:

Heat oven to 300 degrees

½ cup of egg whites or egg whites from 4 eggs

Make sure you save 3 yolks and put the fourth in a separate bowl which you can feed to the raccoons. If you don't have raccoons try the dog. If you don't have a dog eat it yourself or throw it out.

Save 3 egg yolks for the pudding if you're using the 4.3 oz. box

Beat on high until stiff, when you lift your mixer up the egg whites will stand in peaks
Keep beating on high while slowly adding the sugar, one tablespoon a time and the 4 drops of lemon extract.

Line 2 cookie sheets with aluminum foil

Now here comes the tricky part and it will take practice

Take a large spoon, like a soup spoon and scoop up a large dollop of the egg white mixture

It's all in the wrist movement. Plop it down on the foil and gently, with a circular motion make a round shell. The bottom should be fairly thin while the sides will be a little thicker, sort of like a pizza crust edge. They should be about 4" across.

Put the meringue shells in the oven on 300 degrees for about twenty minutes or until they start to turn a little golden

Reduce oven to 250 degrees and cook for 40-60 minutes until they are a dry beige. They may be a little sticky when you take them out but should firm up as they cool. If they don't, put them back in the oven for ten minutes, watching them.

Once thoroughly cooled, it's a bit tricky to get them off the foil without breaking them. I slowly peel the foil from under them, one at a time.

Allow to cool thoroughly and put them in sealed baggies being very careful as they are delicate and can break easily.

Do not despair if they break. Once broken the calories leak out and you can feel free to eat them on the spot. They require no chewing; they will melt in your mouth.

LEMON PUDDING:

I use a large box of pudding, (4.3 oz.) and there is always a lot left over but you can eat it without the meringue shells. It's silkily divine.

Make the pudding according to the instructions on the box but add ½ cup LESS water. Making the pudding is time consuming because you have to stand at the stove whisking it the entire time. It's going to take a good 15 minutes.

Once the pudding comes to a boil and thickens put it in a bowl with a bit of saran wrap touching the top. It prevents a skin from forming.

You can leave it overnight in the fridge, because it is very important that it be cold and set.

Whip heavy cream, about ½ to 1 cup. I never measured it but it's okay. I don't think too much whipped cream can hurt the lemon pudding.

Now, put the whipped cream in the lemon pudding, mixing with hand mixer until totally blended.

Dip your finger in it and lick. Now, you'll be in heaven.

At this point, when you take the shells out to be filled, put them back in the oven if they've gotten a bit soft.

Just before serving take a dollop of the lemon/whipped cream mixture and put it in the middle of the shells. If you made a few too thin on the bottom, the lemon mixture will hide the defects and they will be so delicious nobody will even notice.

If you want to add your own touch you can put some raspberries on top or even make a raspberry sauce. I've never made a sauce so you're on your own with that but raspberries on top are fabulous, if they're in season. Do your own thing. It's hard to ruin this.

If you have any questions about this recipe, you can reach me at: info@ashleyaddisonmysterynovels.com

I would love to hear how they turned out.

ABOUT THE AUTHOR

Ashley Addison

Ashley Addison is a New Yorker, who moved to the Pacific Northwest many years ago, and pursues real estate while writing her Vivianne Murphy Mystery series.

She lives with her terrier mix rescue dog, whose picture graces the back of her books. Her cat declined to be photographed.

Sassy (@Sassy14297865) / Twitter
https://www.facebook.com/Ashleyaddisonauthor/
https://ashleyaddisonmysterynovels.com

PRAISE FOR AUTHOR

Book #1 - Real Estate, Murder, and Mayhem

In this debut mystery, a real estate broker's life and work are a series of ups, downs, and the occasional corpse. Realtor Vivianne Murphy earns both a client and a friend when she helps Venice Martino find a new place to live. Venice settles on a log home in Havenville, Washington, just across the street from Vivianne. The two women are soon co-workers after Venice gets her real estate license. There's a pile of money to be made in this business, even if it's sometimes dangerous. Vivianne buys and carries a gun and Taser for protection and has a frightening encounter with a potential client—though this allows her to put her Taser to good use. But real estate has its glamorous side, and Vivianne and Venice are thrilled by the chance to broker the sale of a multimillion-dollar home. They plan to meet the prospective buyers at the house only to discover a body there. Do they call the police? Or do they move the corpse so they won't lose an epic commission? Their ultimate decision has unexpected and hazardous consequences. Addison's lead female characters are captivating, particularly Vivianne. The author devotes a substantial portion of the lighthearted tale to her. Vivianne fled New York primarily to escape her overbearing mother, with whom she maintains a strained relationship. These familial subplots, including hefty backstories on both of Vivianne's failed marriages, are wholly absorbing, perhaps more so than the novel's mystery element. But that's because the mystery, rather than taking center stage, plays out as another subplot. The narrative is generally high-spirited; finding a body, for ex-

ample, spawns dark humor but no scares or suspense. Still, the tense final act offers undisputed perils. Addison's brisk, conversational prose entails periodic sighs, as if Vivianne's narration constantly reminds her how exasperating her life is. Superb, winsome female characters headline this breezy thriller.

- KIRKUS REVIEWS

For Book #1 Real Estate, Murder, and Mayhem

Original crime fiction with a sublime twist of humour, it doesn't get any better than Ashley Addison's debut novel Real Estate, Murder, and Mayhem. Sitting in the Women Sleuths sub-genre it's fleet of pace and laden with a bevvy of top-notch characters with Addison retaining that often elusive balance between levity and suspense throughout.

A lively imagining with the affability of a familiar soap opera there's enough here to keep the most inquisitive reader guessing, but where Addison ultimately excels is in her characterization, creating personalities that are bold and wholly memorable, with dialogue that is timely and keenly observed.

Despite its popularity, the Women Sleuths sub-genre is oversubscribed with lacklustre offerings and those which do well are invariably the ones with the strongest characters. In Vivianne and Venice, Addison has created two genuine gems and it's in the telling of their backstories that the levity of her prose prevails.

They're both smart and pragmatic with snappy voices, but feminine and resilient at the same time and together they will make a great duo as Addison's Vivianne Murphy Mystery series progresses.

A must-read for fans of the genre Real Estate, Murder, and Mayhem is highly recommended!

- BOOK VIRAL REVIEWS

A VIVIANNE MURPHY MYSTERY

Vivianne Murphy, a long-standing New Yorker, moves clear across the country to escape the grasp of her overbearing mother, and to put her two failed marriages behind her.

She settles in the Pacific Northwest, gets her real estate license, buys The Little House in the Woods, and works for a brokerage in the nearby town.

She rescues a terrier mix dog, Sassy, who becomes the love of her life, second only to the raccoons and the occasional bear.

Venice Martino, a fellow New Yorker, becomes Viv's client when she falls in love with the area while trying to settle her aunt's estate.

When she buys a house across the street from Viv, they soon become the best of friends.

Sassy also gains new friends, Venice's two dogs, Betty, a Border Collie, and Mr. Snigglebottom, a stubborn Jack Russell.

Venice becomes a broker with the help of Vivianne's mentoring, and they soon find themselves embroiled in a murder and some very strange happenings.

As the series progresses, Vivianne and Venice open their own brokerage, Rainbow Realty.

Murder seems to find them, especially Viv, and they're fast becoming amateur sleuths.

Real estate has its own set of problems. While it can be very lucrative, it also has its downside. There are crazy clients, dangerous situations, and surprises, both good and bad.

Viv's familial obligations are still very much alive. Her Mom is a force, not to be reckoned with.

Real Estate, Murder, and Mayhem is the first in the Vivianne Murphy Mystery series, followed by book 2, Real Estate, Dating, and Death.

I'm busy working on the next book in the series.

Real Estate, Murder, And Mayhem

A die-hard New Yorker, Vivianne escaped her mother's clutches and moved clear across the country to find her little bit of heaven in Washington State. She is a savvy, smart — and smart-mouthed — real estate professional working in Havenville when she meets Venice, also from New York, and also looking to re-invent herself. Together they make a killer transaction in more ways than one. Real Estate, Murder, and Mayhem is Book One of the Vivianne Murphy Mystery Novels; you will laugh out loud and be on the edge of your seat as the escapades of Vivianne and Venice unfold.

Real Estate, Dating, And Death

In this, the second novel in the Vivianne Murphy Mystery series, a dead bride is discovered murdered at Vivianne and Venice's brokerage, a homeless family is found sleeping in a vacant house and Viv's mother, who is a force, is having open heart surgery.

On a personal level, Venice becomes romantically involved with Bryan, who is moving out of state and Vivianne becomes concerned Venice will follow him. That is, until Viv starts dating a former client who's handsome, amusing, and insanely rich.

In some of the many subplots, Viv's niece has a run in with a kidnapper, there's a wedding, another murder, and a tense final act.